HOME IN
THE MORNING

HOME IN
THE MORNING

Mary Glickman

OPEN ROAD
INTEGRATED MEDIA
NEW YORK

copyright © 2010 by Mary Glickman

cover design by Ann Weinstock
interior design by Danielle Young

ISBN: 978-1-4532-5815-6

Published in 2010 by Open Road Integrated Media
180 Varick St.
New York, NY 10014
www.openroadmedia.com

For Stephen,
My windy boy and a bit

CONTENTS

‘

Ride on Moses

I've been traveling all this day
Ride on Moses
To hear the good folks sing and pray
Want to go home in the morning
They pray'd so long I couldn't wait
Ride on Moses
I knew the Lord would walk that way
Want to go home in the morning

Then ride on, ride on,
Ride on, Moses
Ride on, King Emmanuel,
Want to go home in the morning

When I got there, Satan was there
Ride on Moses
I'm goin' to take the golden car
Want to go home in the morning
I lay my old sins on the shelf
Ride on Moses
And stand right up and shake myself
Want to go home in the morning

ONE

JACKSON SASSAPORT WAS NAMED FOR both the capital of Mississippi and his uncle Yakov, signifying him instantly as Southern and Jewish and, as such, the perfect husband, a man chivalrous and loquacious at once. He had no ability to mislead his wife and harbored far less the desire to do so, for his sensibilities were especially fine. Stella was a trial of a woman, a virago of passionate pursuits who regularly forgot him. Everyone said she was fortunate to land him. And land him she did. After many years, he remained famously devoted to her. To watch her thrash on her dressing room couch in her party clothes on a night that represented the triumph of her career distressed him almost more than it did her to present him with that unholy spectacle: tendrils of red hair flashing like whips, the pulsing veins of her long pale neck, her lips gone white from clamping together to stifle a ragged moan that escaped as a dull murmur of grief. He watched her tantrum helplessly, afraid to touch her.

When she could speak, Stella said: I am not going if she's there, and that's that. I cannot. I will not. I won't.

She was still for the moment, so he rushed forward and dropped to one knee before the tufted chaise where she sprawled, defiant in mauve taffeta and blue silk.

That's ridiculous, he said, in his dark Mississippi drawl, as soothing a tone as man can muster. This is your night. Everyone will be there. Your family. Your brothers, your mama. Mine.

Precisely! Precisely! Stella bolted upright. Her oval eyes went round with anger and impatience. Dear dotty Mother, who waited how long for this night? Forty-eight years? She gave up on me in '67. Her mind's been gone since '92. She thinks it's our wedding anniversary. The boys. They don't respect me. They're both divorced. I can see them now, sitting with Katherine Marie jolly as clams lettin' her spike them up. Your mama? She's been waiting for me to fall on my face since the day we met. No. I'm not going. I'm not.

She rose from the chaise and glided to the bed, where she fell back against the comforter and a flotilla of pillows. Her gaze fixed on the ceiling as she muttered. Gawd. That heifer. Gawd.

Her legs were spread and uncovered, as were her arms. In love with her more than thirty years, Jackson Sassaport was moved by the sight. He got on the bed too, made to stroke her in consolation. Taking a chance—any false move when Stella was like this could be disastrous—he kissed her, and because he remained in love with her after thirty years, he could not ignore her breasts or her backside when she relaxed a little, and that's why Stella was late for her own party. No matter what Katherine Marie said later on, it had little to do with her, less than a jot.

Always the gentleman, Jackson let his wife doze a few minutes afterward while he washed up and put his pants back on then located her panties and shoes, laying them out on the chaise while she repaired her face. She left the bathroom impeccably groomed and in a clearly improved mood, although her eyes were red. Leaning on her husband's shoulder while she slipped on her heels, she said: Long as I have you, Mr. Sassaport, I'll be ok. They enjoyed a quiet connubial embrace. Why don't you leave Katherine Marie to me? he murmured in her ear. I'd be honored by the opportunity. Stella declined. I can handle her. I was just upset at the thought of seeing her at first. It wasn't pleasant news. She squared her shoulders, filled her chest with air. I'm ok now. I can handle her.

She gave her hair a final brushing. He smiled at her back. This was the Stella Sassaport he knew, loved. He couldn't help himself. Strong, exceptional women of mercurial natures peppered his family tree, they were the sum of the dalliances, flirtations, and romances of his youth. They were the women who fed, clothed, coddled, trained, excited, enchanted, and tortured him from the hour of his birth until the day he escaped into Stella Godwin's arms, or so he thought on his wedding day. On that day, he felt he'd married his anti-mother/auntie/cousin/crush, but before the first decade was out, he became convinced he'd married the same old she-wolf in the clothing of a different sheep. He experienced an epiphany on this point quite literally at the hand of the self-same Katherine Marie whose name on the faxed final guest list had thrown Stella into her fit. Jackson's epiphany, like all epiphanies, had a self-evident truth at its core: It was too late to change. Years too late. Whatever Stella was, and there was much that terrified him, he was hers, every ounce of him. If she was like all the others, well, so be it. At least she'd surpassed her type. Nonetheless, he still recalled Katherine Marie's words exactly. They visited him at the oddest times, when nothing particular was going wrong, when Stella rested between projects, when life was quiet, when life was good.

You've been corrupted! Katherine Marie charged that night, stabbing a bony finger into his chest. It's insane you can't see what she's

3

done to you! Changed you into a lowlife weasel! My dear white Southern gentleman manqué. You are a fraud! No true gentleman would do what you've done! For what? For her!

Her tirade was a startling event to Jackson, especially in its naked display of feminine venom, but Stella laughed, hugging herself when he told her about it. She nearly rolled off the bed. For a time, he was insulted she wasn't insulted on his behalf. In those days, Katherine Marie was Stella's latest enthusiasm, a fact of life Jackson Sassaport could either like or lump. Epiphany underscored.

Jackson Sassaport was of the Savannah Sassaportas, seven generations, three states, and a vowel removed from their patriarch, Baruch Sassaporta, a colonist trader with a fleet of three tall ships that made the family fortune. Baruch's people were from Portugal by way of London, thanks to the Inquisition. Jackson's great-granddaddy, another Yakov, not recognized by Baruch Sassaporta's direct heir when some Slavic blood finagled its way into the Portuguese strain, had wandered through Georgia and Alabama before setting up shop in Hinds County, Mississippi, with his brother, Yosel. Both men married clever, ambitious women who bred like rabbits and ran them like overseers. Bella and Hannah were the architects of the Anglicization of the name Sassaporta, an appellation the locals had trouble with as they were not familiar as Savannah folk were with the venerable names of colonial shipping, making two syllables of the "port" and dropping the "a" altogether, at least it seemed to the brothers and their wives, although the "poh-art" was followed by an exhalation of breath that would have been taken by more musical ears for a delicately aspirated "a." At the insistence of those two balabustas, Sassaporta's Dry Goods became Sassaport Clothiers, Yakov became Jack, and Yosel became Joe. In subsequent generations, Sassaport Clothiers begat Sassaport Furniture which begat Sassaport Lighting which begat Sassaport Plumbing Fixtures which begat Sassaport General Emporium which begat Sassaport

Grocery until even a Sassaport Fish and Tackle was added to the register. By the time Jackson came along, there wasn't a citizen of Hinds County who did not have a Sassaport product in his larder, his living room, his closets, his bath, his garage. Jackson's father was a third son and not obligated to join the family business. He became a physician. Jackson chose the law.

It was not what his father intended. Dr. Howard Sassaport expected to establish a medical dynasty just as his grandfather had sired a retail one. This feat was meant to enshrine his name in the family narrative at a par with Jack and Joe, its heroes, the husbands of Bella and Hannah, they whose names were invoked repeatedly in the rearing of children, the constant discussions at the uncles' roundtable on the expansion of market, and at holiday gatherings. In his grandiose moments, the doctor imagined himself as revered by the progeny as the great Baruch Sassaporta himself. Unfortunately, he chose Missy Fine as his bride, selected for her wide hips and thick bones, which he fancied indicated that a sturdy mother slept within them, awaiting his seed to waken her destiny. The daughter of a man who wholesaled shoes from factories up north, Missy Fine was plump and pretty, black-eyed, chestnut-haired, a bored, fierce-minded creature who dreaded more than anything else winding up like her mother behind a counter in some frigid warehouse figuring sums in a green eyeshade. When Dr. Howard Sassaport came to call, she saw her way out of four generations of shopkeeping. With a desperate energy the smitten doctor failed to notice, she divined his dreams and promoted his cause convincingly. Big families are the Lord's greatest blessing, she avowed to him on moonlit nights until his ring was on her finger, then after popping out a paltry two doctoral candidates in seven years, she declared she was too frail to go through that ordeal again. She abandoned the nursery, leaving her second boy in the care of the hired help and Jackson to flounder on his own, retired to the kitchen, and did not come out until she'd gained forty pounds three months later. Making do with the boys he had, Dr. Sassaport was ripe for colossal failure.

Jackson was the eldest. When he was small, the idea of following in his father's footsteps appealed, largely because the man was rarely home while his son was awake. His person was entirely mysterious to the boy. Of the doctor's activities, Jackson was aware only that they were adorned with his mother's most intense respect. He knew Daddy helped sick people, but Jackson was always in perfect health himself— even childhood diseases passed over him like the Angel of Death in Egypt—so he had only the vaguest notions of what sick meant. By five, he'd had his share of scrapes and bruises, but he had no experience of wounds that gushed or festered. In his imagination, sick people had stomachaches or coughed like Cook.

If he'd bothered to share this perception, others could be excused for thinking the boy a bit slow, especially since he and Mama brought a covered supper to Daddy's office every Thursday night. On Thursdays, Dr. Sassaport kept evening hours at the office, principally for the sake of local laborers too poor to take time from day work so that the goiters choking their throats could be measured or the thick yellow veil masking the whites of their eyes assessed. They tended to wait until thirty minutes before the knife was indicated before limping up to the doctor's front door (or its rear, as custom demanded for some). Charity day, Mama called it, and at first Jackson thought "charity" was the proper name of the day of the week between Wednesday and Friday. Yet the child could not be blamed for these ideas. When they brought Daddy supper, they entered the office through the side door, which led directly into his examining room. If Daddy had a patient with him, he did not allow them over the threshold. On the occasions they were granted entry, Jackson found nothing unusual in the place. It might as well have been an office in the bank or Uncle Tom-Tom's insurance company except for its tart, tangy smell, which the boy found similar enough to what Sukie used to scrub the floors at home to consider it only occasionally.

When Jackson achieved the age of five, his father deemed it high time for the boy to be introduced more intimately to the medical arts. His mother disagreed. He's too young for harsh realities, Mama said. Human beings can't stomach much of it. Daddy countered: I can and I do. So will my son. If I acquaint him with reality during his tender years, he'll take the nasty bits of life a heap more easily later on, Missy. I want him to grow a strong stomach. Hell, I want it crisscrossed with scars. Trust me, sweetheart. It'll help him more later on than it'll harm him now.

Asking for trust in such a situation was a dicey business with Missy Fine Sassaport. She trusted nothing but her own mind and—it should be admitted at the git-go—that curious entity's homegrown conclusions were cast in stone as soon as they sprung from the gray matter and propelled themselves into the dull, waiting world. Studying her husband, gauging his determination, she drew in her chin making two of it. She crossed her arms above her chest using that colossal mass as a shelf on which to deposit her certitude.

You're wrong, she declared emphatically in a tone that brooked no contradiction.

I'm the daddy, woman. I'll do what I see fit.

Missy Fine Sassaport snorted her contempt.

Take the child, then. Ruin him if you need to. But when you return him to me, if that child's in any way damaged, he is mine, ya hear? Mine.

She quit his company in a huff, marching upstairs for a lie-down, as she was tired from shopping all day and had no intention of wasting her precious energies on the losing side of a cockeyed dialectic.

That same night a terrible pounding on the back door roused the household after everyone had gone to bed. It woke Jackson immediately and his father as well. Mama snored on even after Sukie, who slept in the kitchen on a cot near the stove, bounded upstairs and burst into the master bedroom without knocking to relay the news that there was an emergency down by River Road, a matter of life and death, life and death! The doctor raised a hand to quiet her, got out of bed, and put on his pants. Grabbing his black bag and a suit jacket as the times were yet formal about such matters whether at three a.m. or four in the afternoon, he hurried into the hall, nearly taking a header down the staircase after bumping into Jackson, who'd wandered from his bedroom to see what the commotion was about. Daddy righted himself, regarded his son. Get your chinos on, boy, he ordered, and your corduroy shirt. You're coming with me. Don't forget your shoes.

It was a boneheaded move, the move of a man still angry over an afternoon's spat with his wife. The doctor had no idea what he was taking the boy to, only that there was an accident, a wound to be closed. How long it been open?, he asked the one who had been sent to fetch him. Just a short while, Doctor. A short while. Forgetting in his heat the appetite of his patients for falsehood and deception, it seemed to Jackson's daddy that a fresh wound was not a bad introduction to the healing profession for a child. The shame of it was he knew better. For fifteen years, he'd taken histories from patients that were fairy tales from beginning to end. "Mama wasn't feeling well last Thanksgiving" would prove after further investigation to translate: "Mama was riddled with cancer and starved at home for six months before she was dispatched by a merciful Lord."

Hastily attired, off the pair went into the dark, humming night. Daddy's Studebaker followed a rickety red pickup down the three or four roads Jackson knew and then down a tree-lined strip of dirt he did not. After several lefts, a few rights, the road got darker and bumpier, which conditions might ordinarily have frighted the boy but on this occasion caused only exhilaration. He was, after all, out and about in the dead of night in the brilliant company of a personal god. For reasons unknown to him, reasons he suspected were seriously grown-up, Daddy had requested his presence on an important errand. What could be more exciting, more intoxicating? Then there was the way Daddy spoke to him, in tones unheard before: hushed, seductive tones meant to color the experience awaiting him. You are about to have your eyes opened, child of mine, for they have been closed, Daddy said. You are about to be welcomed into a world of miracle and mystery where I will guide you to the foot of the mountain it will be your joy to climb. Mama thinks you're too young, but we know better, don't we, Jackson. Mama is only a woman, and this is the business of men. Are you not a man, if a small one? Are you not a man?

Up until that moment, Jackson felt for certain he was not a man, but if Daddy said so then he must be. His narrow chest puffed up, his neck went straight and long to support a head swollen with pride.

Yes, Daddy, I am a man. I am.

Dr. Howard Sassaport laughed from deep in his proper belly and its sound, full and rich, filled up the cab of the Studebaker wrapping around the boy in a thick, affectionate cloak. Jackson near burst with happiness.

The pickup stopped, the Studebaker also. Before the headlights dimmed, Jackson caught sight of a tar-paper shack set near the banks of the Pearl, then all went black except for the small yellow glow of oil lamps lit within. He got confused for a bit thinking they were fireflies, very large ones, flickering where the shack stood, maybe hovering in front of it. Daddy said: Alright, Jackson. Follow me and keep your eyes open. Look and listen, child. That's all you need to do the first time. Keep a good distance back from the sickbed. But look and listen to everything. Can you do that?

Jackson nodded with all the gravitas a five-year-old can achieve. They got out of the car, Jackson jumping from his high seat. His feet sloshed into mud. He took a deep breath of air that was familiar and yet not: a moist air, noisy with insects, heavy with peculiar scents. Crabapple, he thought, like Mama's favorite tree mixed with the lively stench of gumbo mud and underneath something else that caused his nostrils to pinch. A gaunt black woman stood at the entrance to the shack, holding a lamp aloft so they could wend their way safely through a pile of junk, a tiny vegetable garden. The pinching smell got stronger with his every step until he was nearly suffocated by the time they entered the place. Yet bravely, because Daddy expected such, he crossed the threshold with his eyes open and his senses pricked.

Within seconds, he stood immobile, drop-jawed, a mouth-breathing fool. There was a great putrefaction in that house with its dirt floor covered by overlapping mats of plaited river grass and the sickbed set plunk in the middle of what was kitchen, bedroom, and parlor all together. Through eyes stung by loathsome fumes, Jackson saw a man, perhaps once black, now mostly gray with impending morbidity, lying on a bare mattress ripped at the sides with its straw sticking out. The man groaned nonstop. His left leg was split from mid-thigh to groin. Around the edges of the wound, black blood puddled purple in the oily light, and at its center were bubbles of noxious pus from which flies fed greedily. Horrified, Jackson stared, choked, screamed, and ran from the house to the riverbank where he collapsed, gasping, in the muck.

It's questionable whether a boy so young could logically process what had happened to him or what its ramifications might be. In later years, Jackson recalled only that he was rife with guilt at disappointing his father, humiliated that obviously he was not a man, never would be, and plain damn sick from too much reality. While his father did what he could for the wretched man within, Jackson shivered and trembled without. He quaked on his knees, his head buried in his hands. And then Daddy's promised miracle happened. A soft small hand touched his shoulder, a high sweet voice whispered: You're alright. You're alright. Don't cry, boy. You're alright.

Jackson lifted his head to look into two black eyes, round and luminous, eyes that held a world of knowing his did not. They belonged to a young, dark-skinned girl, a smidgen older than he. They were twin beams of light pulling him out of himself into a universe where he was, indeed, alright, which is where the miracle lay. He wanted to ask her dozens of questions, but they would not form on his tongue nor issue from his mouth, so he put his arms around her and hugged for all he was worth. For her own reasons—it was her granddaddy perishing inside—she hugged back just as fiercely. The two stayed that way, united, united so for an eternity, until a voice called from the shack: Katherine! Katherine Marie! Bring that child back up the house. His daddy's gettin' ready to leave.

It was a toss-up which of the children was more reluctant to move, but move they did, each propelled by the other's necessity. Jackson halted at the passenger door of the Studebaker. I'll wait here, he mumbled. I'll wait with you, Katherine Marie said. She stuck her small pointed chin out and pursed her lips as if in defiance or rather, as Jackson imagined, like an angel of God created especially to protect him, to give him strength to keep standing there upright though his knees knocked mightily in anticipation of his father's displeasure.

The doctor emerged from the shack, followed by the woman who'd granted them entry, her hands weighted with slop buckets the contents of which she tossed to the side of the door. Daddy's suit jacket was off, his shirtsleeves rolled up. Even through the dark, Jackson could see his father's clothes were plastered to his skin. The adults spoke quietly together, then Daddy put his hand on the woman's bony shoulder, squeezed, and quit her company, walking briskly to the car with his head down. Get in, he said, ignoring the presence of Katherine Marie entirely, but the girl was having none of it. She left Jackson's side and ran around the car to pull at the back of the doctor's shirt. Is he dead? she asked. Daddy didn't answer. She pulled harder, shouted as if Daddy were deaf. I said, is he dead! The doctor twisted his torso to regard her fierce mouth, her narrowed eyes. Not yet, he said. Father and son got in the car, Daddy turned the motor, stuck his head out the window. He will be pretty quick, though. You best get in there and say your good-byes. The girl started, her shoulders heaved. Then she turned with a grace, a dignity unnatural in a child so young, to walk slowly back into the house of death.

They rode in silence a long while. Jackson did not dare speak, his father had much on his mind and kept his own counsel. The boy prayed that he would continue to do so until they were home, where he could run upstairs and hide in his room. He put his mind on the toys there and the picture books, on his clean, cool sheets, on the seventy-four cowboys painted on the wallpaper. When the car turned down their street and it was maybe a minute before he was home free, Daddy spoke. Or rather he spat his words as if they'd been stuck in his throat the whole time and it needed clearing or he would not breathe another breath—spat them out in a fan of juice that sprayed against the windshield.

Why is it that a ragamuffin gal, brown as a bug, no bigger than my walking stick has more gumption than my own son, Jackson? I ask you that. Why?

Jackson answered with the only explanation he could think of: Because Katherine Marie is an angel of God, he said.

His father slapped the steering wheel with one hand and laughed. This time, his laughter came to the boy's ears as a cruel, belittling chorus, one that echoed in his ears the rest of his natural life. It followed him like demons after the hopeless when he dashed from the Studebaker into his home, then upstairs and into his room where he slammed the door and wedged his wooden chair against it. He heard

Mama's voice, demanding though covered in sleep: What happened? What did you do to him? What exactly did you do? The doorknob of his bedroom rattled as if she'd tried it. Daddy growled explanation. He was irritated, indistinct. The doorknob rattled again. Then dead silence into which Mama shouted without shouting: Leave him alone. It's what he wants. Maybe from now on you'll listen to me once in a while. Her tone deepened to a bass note Jackson had never heard her employ. It prickled his scalp.

Do not forget our arrangement, Doctor Disaster. Do so at your peril.

In the morning, Jackson stayed in his room until he heard Daddy go to the office. When he emerged, bursting with pee and covered in dried mud, Mama greeted him with great good cheer, covering his dirty face with kisses but asking no questions. She bathed him, made him pancakes, in general fussed over him until he wished nothing more than to be left alone. When he returned home at the end of the day, Daddy barely addressed him, although several times Jackson felt his father's eyes boring into his back. Things stayed pretty much that way between them for the rest of his childhood. As for Katherine Marie, she remained enshrined in a far corner of his mind as an angel of God no matter what Daddy thought. A dark angel in tattered robes, but with the biggest wings God ever made sprouting from between her shoulder blades. He vowed if he ever met her again, he'd return the favor of her comfort in whatever way he could.

He did so in time, but while they were children, this proved more complex a vow to fulfill than a five-year-old could possibly imagine. It wasn't a question of proximity. He ran into Katherine Marie from time to time. She'd come to his daddy's office for medical care all her life on charity night, and he saw her there once in a blue moon. The first time he ran into her was two months after her granddaddy passed, on the steps of Sassaport's News and Gifts where he and Mama had just dropped off a casserole for Uncle Julius since his wife, Junebug, was sick. Katherine Marie! Jackson cried out loud, and embraced her impulsively, hugging as hard as he did that terrible night, and she hugged him back just as hard. Mama smiled to watch this sweet reunion, but after they'd quit Katherine Marie's company, she told him it wasn't proper for him to be demonstrative with a Negro girl. In future, he should restrict himself to common greetings and gestures. You don't want to make that gal feel self-conscious in the town, do you? she cautioned. Young Jackson took his mother's wisdom to heart without question or comprehension, although ever after when they crossed paths on the streets of the town or that summer he traipsed all over her backyard in the company of his first friend, he hoped Katherine Marie remembered him and could see the wealth of tender feeling he tried to convey in his eyes.

Katherine Marie's never going to change, Jackson told Stella as they left for the reception. You won't get an apology out of her. So don't go jabbing a stick in a beehive. Smile and say hello and go about your business.

Stella muttered what was likely an obscenity while arranging her skirts in the car.

I don't feel much like changing to please her either.

Jackson sighed with resignation then dearly wished he hadn't, for his wife visibly bristled at the sound and a heat rose from her. An ameliorating response was required, but he was damned if he knew what it was.

He fared best with Stella when he was prepared. On the average workday, before he quit his office at night, before he quit the world in which he was respected and obeyed to inhabit one where he was respected only as much as the consorts of queens ever are and any obedience he experienced was coincidental, Jackson prepared to shift gears. He telephoned Stella first, to gauge her mood and inform himself as to her concerns of the day. Then he took out a yellow pad just as he would during consultations with his clients and made a list of the things she'd just told him. These he headed under the title Requisites. Next he wrote down Advice dividing that section into two subsets: Opinion and Support. Where she'd asked his Opinion, he recorded his assessments as one, two, and three with one a and b, two a, b, and c. Where she'd solicited only Support of her own view, he found something positive to scribble under that subtitle even if in his heart of hearts he disagreed. The final section was Cautions, and hardest to compose. Under Cautions, he struggled to invent ways in which he could express his true thoughts without setting her off. While the first categories came to him in seconds, the last could take ten or fifteen minutes. Only when he accomplished that task did he shut the lights and head home. This is the way Jackson Sassaport kept the peace. It was well worth the effort of such painstaking means. When Stella was content, his domestic life was paradisiacal. When she was not, the fires of hell leapt at his feet. In unprepared moments, an addled tongue could get him in trouble.

I don't suppose you do, honey, he managed at the arrival of this one. He put the car in reverse and backed out the driveway. I don't suppose you do.

Fortune was with him. Stella's mind had moved on to her speech, which she began to recite sotto voce.

Sometimes, Jackson reflected, he grew angry with himself for not insisting that his wife instruct her formidable powers of reason to service her emotions on certain occasions instead of the other way about. Her mind was a steel trap when she devoted it to a cause. Why did she let the dogs loose every time her innumerable sensitivities felt violated? Not that Jackson resented her for this. Stella was who she was. During their courtship, she made no bones or apologies about that. Her very family tried to warn him, waving enough red flags to equip a Stalinist rally. He'd wanted her anyway. He'd wanted nothing more than to make Stella Godwin happy, in effect, to protect her from herself. He was prepared and avowed to suffer to achieve that lofty goal. When it came to the part of his life that he feared looked to outsiders like enslavement to feminine caprice, he never blamed his wife. He blamed his mother. He blamed Missy Fine Sassaport.

Two

Spring, 1947

THE YEARS BEFORE JACKSON'S BROTHER, Ray, was born were the idyll of his childhood. True, Mama was often preoccupied—with what, he never learned—but whenever he asked Eleanor, the cook, or Sukie or Big Bokay why he had not seen her that day, the answer was always the same: Your mama's preoccupied. Other days, she hovered over him like a haint and just as relentless. He was her doll, her darling. She caressed him constantly and made him laugh. The morning after his experience with her husband's version of medical school, she told him she'd a great decision to make and a week after that grandly announced she'd made it. I now know what I want you to be when you grow up, she said. I will make you the perfect husband, the prince of every woman's dreams, and you'll be loved and tended to forever. Your profession will come to you through your nature, she went on while he attempted to cipher the meaning of "profession," but a man needs the gratitude of a contented wife to thrive.

To begin with, she taught him the rudiments of domestic chores. While these might not be the lessons young boys crave, the chance to be close to the body of his mother, to catch the odd embrace and the smell of her, good on some days, not so on others, to be, in fact, her day's preoccupation, was a heady wine for the child. Though the broom was too tall for him, he learned to sweep expertly just for the touch of Mama's hand across his brow when he was done. He learned to be careful with china and was soon trusted to polish silver. He couldn't hang the clothes, he was too short. And he couldn't carry the clothesbasket, it was too large. But he grew expert at churning the wheel of the wringer with two hands while Mama fed the wet clothes through and Sukie gathered them for a good shaking out at the other end. They shopped for groceries together, visited the pharmacy together, the bank.

After he had an appreciation of the work it took to run a household, Mama made sure Jackson was current with the pursuits women enjoy. They played cards, casino and Hollywood gin rummy. She taught him how to brush her hair for her, how to rub the kinks out of her shoulders. She introduced him to the joys of gossip. They listened in to conversations on the party line and pulled apart every nuance of their neighbors' calls. Once they chanced to eavesdrop on Miss Welty, but it was only an idle chat with a Mrs. Brewster about the downturn in their butcher's quality of meat. Rumors of a new polio epidemic about to erupt furthered Mama's schemes. Under the protests of her husband, she kept Jackson from starting kindergarten that fall lest he become infected. They ceased to leave the house much and spent yet more time together. Cosseting him in her lap, she taught him to read and drilled him in his numbers, had him memorize the capitals of Europe, of all forty-eight states, and the major tributaries of the Mississippi. Since Mama held the conviction that women of quality admired music, she played the piano and taught him Stephen Collins Foster songs. That Halloween, she sooted his face and dressed him up as Old Black Joe, which he sang for his neighbors on the swankest streets of Guilford when they opened the door. He was a big hit.

Mother and son spent so much time together, he had no other friends but she. To the people of the town, he looked to be a complete sissy. Missy's Sissy a tribe of pint-sized ruffians called him behind his back as he and Mama traversed Main. Although he did not know what the word "sissy" meant, he knew it was an insult and complained to her. Mama said: Don't you mind anything that comes out of the mouths of common children, Jackson. They are ignorant and cruel. Common children don't have the faculties to appreciate the things we do. They're just jealous, is all. Remember you are from one of the town's leading families. You must rise above, rise above.

It took a while, but Jackson eventually realized this claim to local nobility was a spurious one. While their address was desirable, smack in the middle of a swell gentile neighborhood, they remained Jews. Daddy may have been a doctor, but the rest of the family were trades-men in a town where only landowners with a history going back to slave times could claim the highest rungs of the social ladder as their own. Jackson's extended family was old, vast, and spread over three counties, but despite their retail empire, despite their town's proxim-ity to the state's capital, there were few Jews in Guilford, Mississippi. The twenty or so Sassaport Jews there were amounted locally to a glut. None of these were particularly observant, most ate shellfish and pork. In an orgy of ancestor worship rather than the fear of God, they spent major holidays together, feasting at New Year's, fasting and apologiz-ing to one another on Yom Kippur, asking the four questions at Pass-over. At least twice a year, rarely more, they organized a bus to trans-port the clan to Jackson and the synagogue there. Sassaport women lit candles on Friday night before supper, but there was nowhere for their men to read Torah in the morning, so they slept in on Saturday or opened up shop. Not only did they have no synagogue as their family traditions became muddled, peculiar, sporting accents and melodies of a hybrid Ashkenazi-Sephardic strain that even the Jews of the capital could not decipher, but they failed to found one. When they married or passed, they hired a traveling rabbi to officiate. Like most Jews of the era and region, they did not bar mitzvah their boys. The custom made them stand out too much when their goal was to blend in. The gentiles of Guilford respected them enough to patronize their outlets and offices and were unfailingly polite as well, but it did not often occur to them to drink bourbon or break bread with the murderers of their Lord Jesus Christ. Be that as it may, no one threw stones through their windows or attacked them in the street or rounded them up. Occasionally someone, usually a preacher from his pulpit, lamented the Holocaust or praised the new state of Israel. On civic holidays, they were not only invited to all celebrations but also honored on occasion. Whatever slurs were made against them were made behind their backs, out of hearing. For the Sassaport clan, this proved the glorious difference between America and Nazi Germany. A Jew could make a living in America, unmolested, even in the great maligned South, they told each other. Best country in the damn world, they said, thumping one another on the back. Uncle Benny, who owned the ironworks and gun shop outside of town, was so convinced he bought stars and bars posters for his shop windows and changed his name legally to Benny Lee, retaining however his patronymic.

When Jackson's special relationship with his mother was over, it was over in a hurry. First he was informed that a brother or sister was coming. Then one day, his mother sat at the piano to teach him patriotic songs from the First World War and the next a music teacher appeared on the doorstep to take over as Mama was close to her time, and needed her rest. Just as suddenly, there were no more reading sessions, no more cards. A waiting stillness fell over the house. Daddy and the servants spoke only in whispers, and Jackson wept quiet tears. He suffered a misapprehension. He considered he was such a failure as a child that Mama had grown weary of him. Or he considered if her pregnancy turned difficult, it was because he had worn her out. When January semester came, Jackson was sent to a private school. The doctor had sworn to his wife that not a single student or student's family member from Stonewall Elementary had contracted fever accompanied by paralysis. But for Jackson, it felt like the last boot of banishment planted up his backside. He complained to Mama with tears streaming down his cheeks. He didn't want to go. Lonely as he was, he wanted to stay home. By this time, his brother, Ray, was in residence.

Oh, if I was two women instead of one, I'd keep you here, darlin', Mama said. But there's just the one of me still, and I can't educate you and take care of Ray. Ray's the baby, she explained, adding that babies needed their mamas a bushel and a peck more than half-grown boys.

Jackson studied his little brother, wondering what that fat, greedy child needed so much. As far as he could see, Ray thrived just on eating and sleeping. And Mama didn't nurse him herself. She'd tried, but Baby Ray was born with teeth and bit while he sucked. She gave up after a week. I swear, she testified to her husband, that child could chomp the paps off a bobcat. I am havin' no more of it. There followed a succession of wet nurses who each bore him as well as she could before making excuses and passing him along to the next young mother desperate for income. The teeth fell out within a handful of weeks, but Ray had such strong jaws the wet nurses continued to complain. He turned out likely the fastest weaned child in the county.

On January 5, 1949, Jackson entered the world of Stonewall Elementary. There were other schools closer to home, but these were either public, Methodist, Baptist, or Episcopal. The doctor hoped a private, nonaffiliated institution would keep their child safe from commonplace anti-Semitic remarks, uttered though they might be from the mouths of babes with no appreciation of their sting, a fate none of the cousins had managed to avoid completely no matter what school they attended. Missy Fine Sassaport considered her eldest son a blessed child, given his sterling health and lively interests. She was confident the darling little ladies and gentlemen who attended Stonewall, being of excellent families, their neighbors, his father's patients, would exempt him from the usual rites of passage of the time. We do not live, she announced imperiously to her husband, her chins tilted upward and her eyes aggressively narrowed, in some Yankee factory town stuffed with Polish and Italian hooligans. We are an established family in a bedroom community of the capital of Mississippi. He will be reminded who he is, which might be a good thing, but no one will bully him on that account alone.

Nothing, however, could exempt Jackson from class prayer. In short order, he memorized the Lord's Prayer and a handful of children's hymns, which his mother hastened to inform him he should consider fanciful poems and ditties much like the stories in his Aesop's Fables. As for his classmates, once they figured out he was a Jew, they were curious but respectful enough while in class, though at recess, soft-spoken, polite young boys in white shirts and red ties approached his solitary station outside the building door to ask if they could please rub his head to feel his horns. I don't have horns, Jackson insisted, thoroughly confused. Sweet little girls in navy blue jumpers and crisp white blouses with peter pan collars asked him if he'd like to know more about Jesus. For the latter, Jackson blushed and declined, saying he was learning a lot already.

The doctor dropped his son off at school on his way to rounds every morning, so going to school went smoothly enough, but coming home alone and on foot proved a trial of major proportions. On Wednesday of his second week, he was halfway home when set upon by a clutch of ragtag children, truants and troublemakers, elder brothers of those who'd whispered Missy's Sissy behind his back, only these preferred to call him dirty jewboy and made true their point by pelting him with mud balls. When he got home, he told Mama he fell in a puddle. He was a painfully honest creature. Prevarication destroyed his digestion. Mama kept him home on Thursday to nurse his bad stomach. Jackson felt even worse then, for it seemed he had profited through mendacity. On Friday, he determined if his tormentors appeared again he would run like holy heck at the sight of them, but they lay in wait under the cover of sidewalk shrubbery to pop out and pounce upon him, stealing his books and juggling them in the air. Sissy jewboy! they called him while he scrambled about in the street for his texts then fled, with the pack chasing him until they got winded. This time, there was no lie required to prevent Mama from discovering the truth. When he returned home, Eleanor, shucking butter beans while rocking Baby Ray's cradle with her foot, told him Mama was preoccupied.

As it happened, that Saturday a Cousins Club picnic was held on the grounds of Uncle Jordan's sprawling estate downriver. Cousins Club—a creation of Missy Fine Sassaport to sustain family relations in the next generation—met every other month, usually at one of the aunt's or uncle's homes. On special occasions, the whole crew went to restaurants if they managed to find an establishment willing to accommodate the entire noisy mess of them. Though they accepted him because he was blood, the cousins had about as much use for Jackson as the neighborhood boys. They teased him mercilessly, pulling at his longish hair, sneezing at him or spitting close to his feet then taunting him with assurances he was now infected, not just with polio, but with diphtheria and TB besides.

Ordinarily, Jackson would not ask the cousins for anything. To do so was an invitation to trouble. But that day at Uncle Jordan's, he was desperate. There, under the arms of an ancient red oak, he reached deep inside his trembling heart to ask advice of the boys who, until his second week at school, had been the chief tormentors of his puny existence. Blood is blood, he told himself, repeating one of Daddy's favorite maxims, and cleared his throat. What do you all do, he asked the cousins while they chomped chicken legs and tossed the bones at one another, about the bullies that call you jewboy and the like? There followed instant silence, then the clatter of dozens of bones hitting tin plates as a generation of Sassaport males abandoned their lunch to surround him and pepper him with questions. Who you talking about? What'd they say? What'd they do? Jackson told them what happened, ending: I don't know who they are, but I believe they are blood related to that gang that runs around the post office all day long in summer.

Mickey Moe, Aunt Beadie's boy, was the Cousins Club leader, as he had achieved the age of eleven and was bigger than the rest. He was further fatherless, as Uncle Bernard had taken several Nazi bullets in the Ardennes. Aunt Beadie forever referred to Mickey Moe not by name but as "the man of the house" which had an effect on the child. In perfect imitation of every good old boy who ever breathed, he hitched up his pants and wrinkled his brow in an attempt at gravitas. Jackson waited for his response, admiring his every manly move. The others kept respectful silence waiting for the boy to speak. Eventually, he spit on the ground and announced: That'd be those Hicks boys and maybe some of those Turners, too. White trash, the whole lot of them. Must have got tired of harassing the Negroes. Stand up, Jackson, and come over here in the open. We need some room for this. Now, here's what you do.

Mickey Moe stuck out his foot and planted it in a grassless spot of clay. Jackson's eyes widened about as far as they could as he anticipated his first lesson in the art of self-defense. He gulped down the anxious tide of bile that rose to his throat at the idea of violence and made tight fists of the hands that hung by his sides. Meanwhile, the man of Aunt Beadie's house swept his foot through the dirt in a wide arc, then tapped its starting point with the toe of his Buster Browns. This here, he said, punctuating again with his toe, is Stonewall Elementary. And over here—he tapped his toe some inches over to the left—is Walnut Street. And that leads to Hickory Hill, don't it? Yes, indeed it does. Well now, that's a very fine neighborhood. Nothing but people of quality from end to end. They don't tolerate white trash lurking around. So you just walk down Walnut and then to the Hill and about over here, if you cut through Mr. Jenkins's backyard, you can get to your own street without ever having to mix with those boys again. Although Christmastime and Eastertime, they'll be hunting you, and you best be careful especially then. Mickey Moe brushed his hands together, then wiped them on the seat of his pants as if they and not his shoe had just diagrammed the route to safety. He ruffled Jackson's hair under his palm and marched back to his chicken with a trail of Sassaport cousins behind.

Ok, thought Jackson, looking at his cousin's map. It hardly seems enough, but I'll try it. I'll try it on Monday.

And on that day, Mickey Moe's advice worked a charm, and the boy himself was enshrined a hero in Jackson's book, someone to look up to, someone to trust. Previously, Jackson felt Mickey Moe a drop of blood apart from the likes of the Hicks and Turners, but now he reveled in a newfound affection for him, sticking close by his side at all subsequent family gatherings, pestering him with whatever questions of social consequence might be troubling him, for Stonewall Elementary was a mine field of difficulties and he needed all the help he could get. Being the runt of Cousins Club was worth the price of the many jokes of which he was often the butt end, if he could glean from them strategies to manage his struts through the halls of Stonewall Elementary without a misstep that might blow him up.

The fact was that even if he hadn't been Jewish or his mama's pet, his classmates would have considered him an alien creature, as Missy Fine Sassaport's instruction of him proved contrary to the curriculum approved by the state of Mississippi. His reading was advanced, he knew where Bavaria was, and he could read music as long as it wasn't very complex. Otherwise, he proved either ignorant or wrong. His manner of writing letters was full of embellished loops and curlicues that Missy Fine Sassaport had taught him to form, because she thought it would make the task of writing more fun for him. His teacher found it impossible to read. He could count up to one hundred, add, and subtract, but had never attempted to write figures. The concept of fractions was as foreign as Babylon to him. After the first few weeks, weeks of constant embarrassment and correction, Jackson decided to accept the assessment of his classmates and teacher. He was, undeniably, stupid. He was, undeniably, alien. He would never fit in. He would never have friends.

The only bright spot in the vast field of darkness spread out before Jackson until he could achieve the far-off summer, when at least he could remain at home all day, far from the classmates who ignored him, occurred damn close to it in mid-April. That was the day Daddy decided Baby Ray was not developing properly. He's too fat, he told Mama in Jackson's presence, he's nearin' nine month old and he just got strong enough to roll. 'Til now, he hasn't even tried. He don't babble. His mouth is too lazy to do anything but suck. He's way behind schedule there. I've heard no attempts at vocalization coming from that child, Missy, nothing but grunts. Mama disagreed. His eyes follow me wherever I go, she offered as proof of Baby Ray's alertness, and I know when he approves and when he does not of my actions. He understands everything I say. Daddy turned his back on her. So does the sheriff's dog, he muttered, but only Jackson heard him. By now, Mama was crying. Daddy sighed and went to comfort her. As usual, his blunt verbal outburst was followed by clumsy concession. Missy, darlin', he said with his arms around her from behind. Baby Ray may turn out the sweetest, most sensitive child, beloved by all. I'm just saying he's another one not about to follow in his daddy's footsteps. You'll have to give me more.

It was a joke accompanied by a nip on the back of the neck and a trill of chuckles, but his humor was not appreciated. Missy Fine Sassaport erupted into her legendary denial of physical stamina to accommodate the expansion of the clan and huffed into the kitchen where for three months she laid exclusive claim to the ice chest, the oven, and Sukie's cot. What made this a bright spot in Jackson's annus horribilis was the realization that Ray was defective, a dunce, more stupid than he. Mama might have abandoned him, but she'd quit Ray, also. As far as Jackson was concerned, his own abandonment was a misunderstanding, a mistake, but that fat, immobile stranger deserved it.

In the brief span that stretched from April to July, a tiny patch of time given the course of a life in full, a mere season in the green years that everyone forgets, two important things happened. Number one was that Baby Ray perked up. He gurgled and stood, his reflexes turned quick. Since he screamed for all he was worth until Mama came out of the kitchen to soothe him, Daddy decided he hadn't really been slow before, just supremely spoiled. Number two was that Jackson first experienced a wound of injustice while he watched Mama give over entirely to wailing Baby Ray what few tender moments she dispensed daily to her family before she re-disappeared into the kitchen, a formerly warm, convivial spot that had overnight grown a lock on its door, the rude click of which terrified him. If he'd not been terrified also of blood and death for most of the past year, he might have strangled Baby Ray in his crib for being a devil, for sucking the life from their mother. Five minutes with the greedy brat and she was too exhausted for anything else. Jackson had no explanation for her apparent preference of her tormentor over him, he had infrequent acquaintance with concepts of guilt and none at all with depression. He only knew that he did not like Baby Ray, hated how his arrival had transformed his cozy, closed-off world, and could not conceive of loving him, especially in the dopey big-brother way he'd been told for nine months he surely would. On the contrary, his most entertaining pastime was imagining a variety of accidental deaths for Baby Ray, some swift, some slow, depending on his mood.

His attitude improved when Mama at last returned to her family. Full of grits, satisfied she'd made her point, weary perhaps of a life devoted to pots and pans and dishes and cutlery and the things that disappeared too quickly from them, she emerged from the kitchen one day and never returned again except on holidays. At last, she took note of her firstborn, saw immediately his loneliness, and devised remedies. You're pale as a widow's cheeks, boy, she told him. You need fresh air. Now, I'd love to go out and play with you, like we used to do, you know I would, but Baby Ray needs me here. So I want you to be a good boy and play every day with Big Bokay's grandson, Li'l Bokay, instead. For your health, darlin'. His granddaddy's bringing him by today. He's going to take you fishing. You've never done that before, have you? Well, he's a big boy, ten years old, and he'll teach you things, just like Mama. Won't that be fun?

Jackson wasn't sure of that, but his mind was excited by the prospect of having a playmate, especially an older boy. The knowledge that his companion was a Negro tinged events with mystery and heightened his anticipation. Everything Jackson knew about race up 'til then, he knew on a subliminal level from the social cues around him. He saw that blacks and whites were intimately related, dependent on one another, sensed that each was aware of that fact, aware of an economic contract of uneasy peace between them, and after spending all their long workdays together, rejoiced in spending off time free from each others' race and its burdens at last. Jackson knew the staff of his home and Daddy's office well. He knew the man who packed their groceries, both the man who swept up the bank and the woman whose job it was to perpetually polish its abundance of brass knobs, lamps, and the balustrade that graced its marble staircase, knew them well enough to call them by name. He knew instinctively not to use Mr. or Miss before their given names when he addressed them as he was taught to address white people. He knew by sight the black children who popped in and out of their mothers' skirts at Sassaport Bakery and the older ones who spent most of their days at the banks of the Pearl making mischief. He could not imagine a world without black people. Yet if he knew a name to go with a small round dark face that was not of Eleanor's, Sukie's, or Big Bokay's families, it was rare, a social accident. There were, of course, no black children at his school. The Negro school was on the other side of town, through the woods and past the hollow, where those who did not live in an employer's home or at the back of a store lived for the most part on heir's property without electricity or indoor plumbing. When Jackson and Mama took nature walks, during which she taught him the names of trees and what berries he could safely eat, they always stuck to their end of the woods and never ventured onto that opposite side, epicenter of the unknown and undiscussed. That summer everything changed. His adventure that summer was the adventure of Li'l Bokay. In his memory it shone like the golden apples of Diana, a treasure so pure and irresistible even a virgin pursued by a horde of men would stop to marvel at its beauty.

Jackson enjoyed celebrating his youthful friendship with L'il Bokay years later when he entertained the Yankee civil rights crowd at college the year they all got ready to march down to DC. Accustomed to hearing him declaim in class, they accepted his bona fides as a political liberal and expected to get the real deal when they inquired with varying degrees of subtlety what was it really like to grow up Jewish in the deep South, in such a community that would murder him if given an excuse. Had he ever had a cross burned on his front lawn? Had he ever been inside a Negro home down there? Sitting in an espresso café in

New Haven, he told them alright, exaggerating his silken drawl, dropping his final consonants and elongating his vowels more than usual, the better to captivate them.

Missy Fine Sassaport's efforts had not been in vain. Jackson made quite the picture, despite his wardrobe, which would have appalled her. In those days, he had a preference for worn-out Jimmy Dean–style blue jeans, pegged at the bottom. His shoes were usually black leather boots with motorcycle straps. Mama would agree wholeheartedly that his demeanor was completely charming, he had the gallant's touch of self-deprecation. The way he sat, the way he gestured, would have been suitable in the parlors of kings. Three seasons a year his Yale colors were knotted around his neck in the form of a wool scarf knit for him by a coed who'd captured his attention for six months in his first year. He wore it ascot-style over dark turtlenecks and often wore a navy blue blazer over all, as his terms at Stonewall Elementary and Stonewall High had given him a fondness for such. In those days, he had a pencil-thin mustache, black as the forest of wild hair on his head. For a time he'd considered sprouting a goatee as well, but in the end considered additional facial hair too theatrical a statement. He didn't need it. He'd dropped into this sea of ambitious, competitive sharks like an eagle skimming its surface. Women liked him. Men asked his opinion. He had never been so happy. In other words, he took on the mantle of Southern raconteur with the vivid grace Mama had instilled in him, having the good fortune to find the role in vogue.

When he spoke about his first friend, he said in full knowledge of the sophistication and political passions of his audience: I'm sure you all can imagine how it might be for a young, friendless boy raised so close to his mama's teat suddenly to find himself in the intimate company of a rough-and-tumble country Negro three full years older than him. From the first moment, I was in heaven, chasin' after him in all his rambunctious pursuits with the fidelity of a Jack Russell puppy. He took me deep into the woods. We scrambled over rocks and splashed through streams, runnin' headlong deeper into the woods than I'd ever been before, to way over the Negro side of town. He taught me how to bait a hook and, you know, I do not recall what we used for bait that day except that it was slimy and squished between my fingers so that I was disgusted and thrilled at the same time. We propped up our poles with rocks and lay back in the soft dirt of the riverbank and let the dappled light daze our eyes. Li'l Bokay fell asleep almost immediately, but I was too excited by the day's events to do likewise and studied him instead.

He did not look at all like Big Bokay, his granddaddy, who, despite his name, had not been big since first the rheumatism then his only son's death in the war got hold of him and bent him over. Big Bokay was a soft-spoken, genial man—at least he was with me and mine— with a full head of white, wiry hair and large, knobby hands. I never heard a harsh word nor so much as a sigh of resentment from that man. Big Bokay was the color of Mama's coffee, which she liked sweet with plenty of milk, while Li'l Bokay was as pitch-black, tall, and beefy as he is today. Throughout our ramble in the woods, I felt like beanstalk Jack chasin' the Giant. On close inspection, I noticed his hands were small, the fingers short, as were his feet. I thought that a wonder, given his size. I puzzled over how he managed to stand upright on those feet. He looked to me as if he should bobble over every time he tried. His hair fascinated me, as it was smacked down close to his head with brilliantine. If I squinted my eyes, it sparkled like a king's crown in the sun.

When he woke up from his nap, Li'l Bokay declared he was bored with fishin', nothin' was bitin' anyway, and why don't we go steal hors-es instead. My eyes near popped from my head. Why? I asked. So's we can ride 'em, was the response. I gulped down my anticipated guilt and asked: Then what do we do? Why, shoot. Return 'em, he said. What you think, chile? I'm gonna kidnap you and lead you in a life of crime? And the look on my face as I considered this uncontemplated possibility caused him to burst into loud, rolling laughter so infectious I rolled with laughter too, there on that summer day by the riverbank where the fish weren't bitin' and a boy just has to do somethin' to amuse himself. All that afternoon we ran through the Negro side of town, stealin' scrawny mules and bony drays, which meant hoppin' fences and jumpin' on the backs of grazing animals, the two of us on the same one, kickin' its sides with our heels until the startled creatures trotted aimlessly through their pastures with us holdin' on to raggedy mane and each other for dear life. It was the most exhilarating day of my young life. I was returned home dirty and stinking of animal, bursting with all the boyish wisdom Li'l Bokay had taught me that day. Mama, I rattled, do you know that a horse can see out the side of his head but not at all directly in front? And Li'l Bokay says this and Li'l Bokay says that.

Now, this conversation took place in the kitchen, where Big Bokay had deposited me at the end of the day. He and Li'l Bokay were lookin' through the screen door, regardin' my excitement with big smiles, and Mama nodded over my head to Big Bokay: Well, I guess today was a big success. Might as well do it again tomorrow, that ok with you, Li'l Bokay? Yessum. Then Mama told me to go wash up for dinner and I ran off to the bathroom, but just before I reached it I realized I'd not said good-bye to Li'l Bokay and that seemed rude, so I raced back to the kitchen in time to see Mama place two quarters into his small, black hand with its pink palm, and I understood Li'l Bokay was my hired companion. Hired. This stung me in a place I'd never been stung before, but I buried the sting right away, piled Mississippi mud right on top of it, buried it deep, because there was nothing I wanted more in the world than to spend the next day with Li'l Bokay, then the next, doin' whatever he wanted to do. Which we did. Yes, Mombasa Cooper was my first friend and paid to be so. Only then, as I said, we all called him Li'l Bokay. I'm sure his mama still does today, despite his notoriety.

Jackson told this story often, as often as Mombasa, né Li'l Bokay, Cooper was in the news. Due to Jackson's popularity, he traveled in a crowd, an entourage if you will, and there were always people fresh to the scene around him who hadn't yet heard it. One afternoon, directly after "despite his notoriety," a honeyed voice, husky and sweet, rang out from somewhere in the back of the room: Was he as angry back then as he is now?

A good question, Jackson asserted, leaning forward and craning his neck, looking for the source of that voice, which from its first syllable affected him in a startling way, prickling his skin, making the hair of his head lift. As he looked over the heads of his peers, they parted like the Red Sea to afford him an unobstructed view of the incredible creature to whom that indelible voice belonged. Instantly, his mouth dried and his throat constricted, making speech impossible for the moment. It's doubtful Jackson understood his reaction as anything more than a spike of lust, if a particularly intense one. In later times, he came to comprehend that that day, in that café, while he was busy foolishly feeding his pride with the transitory adulation of those who could never hope to understand who he was or where he came from no ·matter how brilliantly Missy Fine Sassaport had educated him in the role of interlocutor, those who were too full of their own assumptions to even try to escape the provincialism which stained their opinions of what the South was and how it got that way, those for whom he wasted his breath, he had met his fate. He had met Stella Godwin.

There are few left who remember, but there was an odd sort of creature who sprang up in the nanosecond that ticked between the seminal movements of young intellectuals of the 1960s, between the beatniks and the hippies, a creature conceived in the smoke-hazed caverns of jazz and beat poetry, those black-clad cradles of generational incomprehension and rebellion, whose birth took place in the light, on the mountaintop, whose first scream was a howl not out of Ginsburg, not out of that anguish, neither of anger, whose first scream was a howl not out of Summer of Love orgasmic joy, not out of that chaos, neither of psychedelic daydream, but was rather a howl of grief. Grief, prescient and keen, for the good things of the old world that the new world worked so hard to obliterate. These were the creatures who listened to Mahler and not the Beatles, who admired the technique of Tintoretto more than the invention of Warhol, who read Jefferson not Mao, who were, by God, capitalists, whose mantra "change the system from within" was crushed between the nihilism of the worn-out and the exuberance of the self-indulgent. These were the true outsiders of their generation, these justice-hungry anachronisms, whose boundless pure energy was doomed to extinction by the time they could clamorously crawl, and Stella Godwin was their priestess. What's more, she looked the part.

Stella: glittering ropes of flame red hair, broad, pale forehead, oval eyes of a brown so deep Jackson's soul fell into them at once as if into a boundless well, plump, purple lips bowed at the center, a nose he knew instantly as the thin, long nose of a Jewish aristocrat, and that neck, ah, that neck impossibly long with its cluster of sweet freckles at the base, a neck made for tender bites. She wore a full-length belted trench coat with a tartan scarf and the neck, the head, that was all he saw at first. He had no knowledge yet of her full breasts and tiny waist, of the pert little rump from which grew thighs so slender they reminded him— once he did know them—of the stalks of irises they were that slim, that long, but the face, the hair, the neck popping up out of a mass of plaid were enough to inspire him to mute desire. He tried to elocute, but his throat remained clogged. He could not speak. He could only stare.

If it's such a good question, why don't you try answering it, Stella Godwin stated more than asked.

He coughed so that he could articulate something, anything, lest she write him off as a dumb hick. Twice he coughed then found it necessary to cough again.

Yes. Yes. Alright. No, I wouldn't call Li'l Bokay angry then, although he did have a temper.

The conversation took a turn to angry black men, to Malcolm X particularly, and Jackson was left running an internal dialogue with this woman he did not know, a dialogue about Li'l Bokay's fiery spirit and Katherine Marie and Bubba Ray and Daddy, too, about what happened among them all. This was a story he never shared. Katherine Marie had made him swear by his mama's blood he would never speak of her part in those matters. He'd not been sure even then if making that pact was honorable, but he'd kept her secret for three years anyway, no matter how he'd burned from time to time to let it all loose. For reasons he did not comprehend, he longed to relate all of it to this redheaded woman, this stranger who'd stolen his soul.

After minimal detective work, he discovered her name, where she was from, what she studied, where she lived. That is: Stella Godwin of Boston, a master's candidate in social work at Wesleyan, taking a semester off to lobby for the ACLU in New Haven. Yet more smitten by what amounted to an exotic background according to Jackson's lights, he arranged to run into her. After ten minutes of conversation, he was further sunk. Ten minutes of watching her lips move and he needed his mouth on hers, needed his hands on Stella Godwin's flesh. It was not simply a desire: he would not be at rest until he had what he needed. His friends teased him about his initial failures with her. What happened to Errol Flynn? they said when he shaved his mustache after he heard she did not like hairy men. They laughed and hooted as young men do when one of theirs succumbs to feminine power, telling him he looked like shit, telling him he'd met his match: She was eating him alive. He knew they were not far wrong. All day long he thought of her and at night, when he could sleep at all, he dreamt of her mouth, her hands on him everywhere. He about pined away before she had mercy.

It took maximum efforts of enticement, including coauthoring her petitions, standing in frigid temperatures collecting signatures, and accompanying Stella to the State House to deliver them, hoping every minute no one back home would somehow find out and proceed to make his daddy's life a misery. At last, he insinuated himself into her bed after a pursuit of five months and it was there, that first night they were home from the great march, their ears yet ringing with the good reverend's dream, that he told her about that summer night when the lives of Bubba Ray and Katherine Marie and Li'l Bokay and himself collided, crashing into poor old Daddy along the way. He told her in stutters, with blushes, with tears, and with sobs as the release of such a heavy burden demands. Stella Godwin listened, silent, poker-faced, huddled on her side of the bed with her luscious knees up and a gaze of utter attention for every guilty word. Just after he was done telling his story, she told him: I think I love you, Jackson. I think I just this minute fell in love. Up 'til now, I wasn't really sure about you. I only slept with you because you'd been so relentless in chasing after me. I figured I ought to give anyone who wanted me quite that much a chance. But now, after hearing all that, I think I love you.

And she opened her legs and her arms and folded him up in there while he broke down again, collapsing into her in a flurry of fresh tears, tears not of remorse this time but of gratitude.

THREE

Fall, 1963

AFTER THAT NIGHT, THEY OFTEN fell asleep entangled, and in the morning they bothered each other again. Stella liked to sleep in a bit afterward. Jackson would shower alone, careful not to make too much noise. Tidied up and properly bid adieu, he'd hit the street to walk from her apartment to his first class, thinking of how much he loved her, the adorable Stella Godwin, how much he continued to want her all the time every day and night, how he loved listening to her talk, how he loved the way she listened, how he loved her passion for him and for the general welfare of every other sorry-assed inhabitant of the planet. He considered her the most sanctified woman he'd ever met while the toughest-minded, the sexiest. Her apartment was a good distance away from campus, but Jackson enjoyed the time it took to get there as it afforded him the opportunity to think luxuriously of her legs both open and closed, their muscles flexed and relaxed, of her breasts, and that red hair. As he neared the university, he might run into a classmate who wanted to talk about their reading for the morning's lecture and, made bright and alive by love, he found himself expounding vigorously and insightfully on the lesson of the day. And he'd think: This is what Mama meant. A man needs a good woman's love to thrive.

Although his primary education had begun disastrously, Jackson caught up with his fellows, and once he started surpassing them, he never stopped. When Stella, applauding the job he'd done drafting one of her appeals, asked him how he'd got so smart, he told her the truth.

I didn't start out this way, I willed it. Until I was twelve, I thought I was slow, but looking back I think I was just bored. Then at twelve, I studied for my bar mitzvah. I knew very little a good Jewish boy should know by twelve years of age, I was half a heathen. I was the first boy in three generations of my family to be bar mitzvah, but the new rabbi over to the capital was on fire to get his flock consecrated, so it became the new fashion, and Mama was not one to be left behind where fashion was concerned. We didn't have a synagogue in Guilford. Daddy'd take me over to Beth Israel in Jackson for my lessons. My teacher was their new rabbi, Perry Nussbaum, who was very kind to me, patient and praiseful, which was remarkable for him. He had a reputation in the town for being blunt and, well, rude as a Yankee interloper to tell the truth. He was born in Canada, after all. People tried to overlook his rougher edges on that account, though it wasn't easy for them. Lord, no, it wasn't at all. It got even harder once he started in with the Freedom Riders. But this was before all that.

Anyway, it was unusual for me to have masculine approval. I lapped it up. I nearly got religion I loved that man so. One day I could not get through my Hebrew lesson at all. Every time I opened my mouth I made a mistake. I suppose I'd been lazy about my homework. Afterward, Rabbi Nussbaum left me for my father to pick up, and when he walked away he sighed. I know, I know it was just a sigh, a mere audible inhalation and exhalation of breath, but the disappointment in it stuck me like a Roman spear. First I grieved his former high opinion of me. Then I got angry. What made me angry was myself, that I hadn't studied. The level of my anger was unusually intense, which at that age was likely due to a hormonal surge. I recall I sat on the steps of Temple Beth Israel waiting for Daddy. He was running late, and I had plenty of time to pound the concrete with two fists until my skin was scraped raw. Right there, sitting on those steps, I made my first adult decision. I decided I was tired of being stupid. As a remedy, I was going to be smart. Then I simply willed my intelligence into being. Once enlivened, it took over.

Stella laughed and kissed him when he told her that story. Then she reminded him that smart as he was, she was smarter. It was true. It was another reason he loved her.

The day came in their romance when they discussed meeting the families. Stella's family was closer, in Boston. They planned a weekend with them first. During spring break, they'd travel south and meet his family. As the Boston visit approached, each grew more anxious. You don't know my people, Stella said. We ought to have a signal that means "I'm sorry" between us, then I don't have to be saying it all weekend, every time they embarrass me. Or you. You think the crowd at Yale is bad? They'll probably ask you if your family raped slaves. Jackson roared at that. She was so witty. He could not imagine she was serious about an old Boston family, philanthropists, factory owners, wielders of the means of production, the very thing that defeated the South. How could such a family make an inquiry that rude, that coarse?

On the trip to Boston, Stella squirmed in her seat, twisted her fingers constantly, sighed, frowned, making it impossible for Jackson to drive his Renault with anything approaching calm. Quit fiddling with your fingers, he said. Just breathe deep, in and out. Relax, for God's sake. The air in this vehicle is positively charged, and I cannot focus on the road. Do you want me to pull over? Do you need to stop somewhere? Stella burst into tears. Alarmed, he pulled into the next rest stop.

What is it, sweetheart? What is it? He tried to wrap her in his arms, but she'd only have a few seconds of it, and then she stiffened and slid out of them, fending off his reluctance to let her go with her gloved hands. At her best or at her worst, Stella had to keep part of herself to herself, there was something that never gave in that woman, but at that particular emergence of her boundaries, Jackson could only think he'd done the wrong thing and did not know what the right thing was. It was to become a familiar perception.

Since she could not stop crying, she talked between sobs. Her family, she said, could not stand her. She was their rebel, the conscience they could not hide from, the avatar of their error, for which they despised her. Her mother once called her a demon seed. Her father claimed he loved her, but he was a terrible hypocrite. Her two elder brothers had gone into the family business and closed their eyes to everything that went on within it, husbanding their intellectual powers for writing letters to politicians and stockholders. They never took note of her even as a child. Now that she'd gone off on her own, she figured they'd happily forgotten she'd ever existed. To make matters worse, as she put it, they were ostensibly pious, attending synagogue regularly and frequently holding office there and in the town. Her rejection of observance embarrassed them. He might as well know it: They were as likely to welcome her on their arrival as toss her out on her ear. She didn't know what had possessed her to agree to this visit. After he met them, she was certain he'd drop her on the spot.

Jackson listened to this story aghast. He could not bear to contemplate why anyone would make his adorable Stella suffer. Up 'til she divulged her biography, he'd been anxious about introducing her to Mama and Daddy and the odious Bubba Ray, now fifteen and turned out just as one might expect. He was the worst kind of mama's boy, lazy and sluggish with shifty eyes and a scheming mind. Jackson doubted there was a vice with which he'd not made at least a passing acquaintance. He feared how she'd absorb the South, too, how she'd take in Mississippi. He was afraid she'd misinterpret everything he loved back home and throw everyone into an uproar. He wondered on which street corner she'd get filled with a passion to stand with one of her petitions. He imagined with a dark mental quiver what Mama would have to say about that. Just what we need, she'd say, a dang Yankee communist attached to the family. All along, he'd been struck by how willing he was to bring Stella home anyway, despite premonitions of disaster. Then after hearing her family story, he felt an encounter with his own people infinitely benign compared to one with Stella's. Compassion overwhelmed him and nursed the first flames of his heat to serve as her protector against this insidious family as well as any other adversary who might cross her path. He muttered as much to the top of her head, to her throat.

Now that her fears were out there, flapping in the wind, Stella felt better and allowed herself to be embraced and petted within an inch of consciousness by the solicitations of a man who swore he would make up all the unhappiness inflicted on her by giving her everything she wanted forever and ever amen. He would work until he died for her. In other words, he proposed. She accepted. He was overjoyed. They started up their journey again, rode the rest of the way to Boston holding hands over the console. From time to time Stella fell silent, and when Jackson snuck a look at her she was smiling a straight, thin smile with just the corners of her mouth pointed up. He thought she looked satisfied, but also as if she was plotting something. His joy deflated a little until it struck him maybe she wasn't plotting so much as planning her wedding, a thought that made enough sense to restore him to buoyant happiness.

Jackson drove up Washington Street toward the great houses of Roxbury. His mouth filled with bile and his heart with both courage and dread. He stopped the car, got out, followed Stella's directions for opening the big iron grate to the courtyard of the family Victorian, then steeled himself for battle with his teeth grit.

They parked by the front door. Before they could get out of the car, a maid in uniform hurried out and grabbed their bags. A new one, Stella whispered to Jackson. I don't know her. Arm in arm, they walked up the stone front steps flanked by fir trees and into the foyer.

My, my, my, Jackson said, craning his neck to follow the slow curve of marble stairs that spiraled gracefully up a full three floors. Beautiful.

Something chimed twice loudly and his neck spun round looking for its source, a massive grandfather clock of a design he'd never seen before. Opposite was a fireplace graced by a mantel, also of marble, with interlocking sprigs of wheat carved into its face. There was a glass screen, a sparkling brass grate, and andirons. Orientals overlapped on the floor. Gilt-framed family portraits hung on the walls. Everything was heavy, dark, venerable. He felt oddly half at home and half in a fairyland. Foyers screaming history were not unknown to him. But foyers dark, heavy, and somber were. Yes, he thought, a winter's fairyland. As if on cue, oak pocket doors creaked open, and Stella's mother, a Snow Queen if ever there was one, stepped through them. Mildred Godwin was short and thin, her features sharp, coming to twin V's at the chin and nose. She was likely the palest woman he'd ever seen with hair a darker, flatter red than Stella's, cut close to her head and curled. It took him a second, but he saw it was a wig. Her eyes were mini versions of Stella's. On Stella, they were large, warm. On her mother, they were small and suspicious. She extended a limp, white hand in his direction. He took it.

Mom, this is Jackson. Jackson, my mother.

Stella's voice was dry, without emotion. Jackson would have noticed the mother and daughter barely greeted each other but he was too intent on delivering the most charming smile in his repertoire to the former. He bowed a little, just his head and shoulders, before releasing her hand.

You have a lovely home, Mrs. Godwin.

Stella's mother seemed more surprised by him than he was by her. Her voice had a tremor, a slight one, and she could not seem to look him in the eyes. Her head bobbed all around while she studied her foyer as if she'd never seen it before.

Well, yes, yes. We like it, she managed, and directed them to their rooms, telling them tea was being served in the library and in a couple of hours they'd gather in the living room for cocktails.

The way Stella described her relations, he'd expected everybody'd be at one another's throats before the second drink. But after he settled into his room, he ran into Stella's brother Seth on the stairs. A short, stocky man, prematurely bald and smartly groomed, Seth shook Jackson's hand warmly, telling him with a broad smile that his hat was off to any man who could make Stella happy and that due to unforeseen complications, he was the only brother Jackson would meet that night. He then kindly ushered him to the library, where Mr. Godwin himself poured him tea from a fine porcelain pot, then showed him a framed letter hanging on the library wall, a letter from Theodore Roosevelt penned to his grandfather thanking him on the production of uniforms for the Rough Riders.

How could this man be the tyrant Stella described in the car? Stella's daddy seemed a soft, befuddled gentleman who spoke very quietly with a lot of ums and choppy breaks in his speech. Frequently, his hand shot up to the top of his head to settle his yarmulke, although the blue circle stitched with silver thread appeared well anchored to his fringe of gray hair by bobby pins. Jackson considered Leonard Godwin's a humble appearance. He flat couldn't understand how these could be the same people Stella warned him about. They looked to be the salt of the earth. Meek, even.

They drank their tea and made small talk. When Stella did not appear, Jackson excused himself to freshen up for dinner. He tiptoed down the second-floor corridor until he found her leaving her bedroom to look for him. She put a finger to her lips and pulled him back into the bedroom, closing the door behind them swiftly, quietly. There they lay upon her bed awhile, fully clothed, silent, afraid to make noise, speaking in gestures and grimaces with an eloquence only lovers can muster.

Stella told him not to bother to dress for dinner, but when the couple entered the living room for cocktails dressed in their traveling costumes—the Jimmy Dean's, a denim shirt, and boots for Jackson, for her a turtleneck, cotton capris, and ballet slippers—Jackson was embarrassed. Mr. Godwin and Seth wore jackets and ties. As his mama would have wanted, he immediately apologized for not being attired properly for the occasion. Holding Stella's hand at the time, he did not miss the manner in which she stiffened as if his politesse were a direct affront to her.

We could wait while you change, but as it is Stella won't change, only a fool would ask her, and together you make a set at least, Mrs. Godwin said in a dry, cracked voice as tight as her white knuckled grip on a half full tumbler of Rob Roy.

Dinner was served in the formal dining room: oak paneled, heavy mahogany table and chairs, the latter cushioned with red velvet, a huge breakfront also of mahogany hosting a silver service fit for royalty, flocked salmon wallpaper and gilt mirrors, crystal chandelier. Two great silver candelabra graced the upper and lower ends of the table, which was set for five with china and service of rare quality. The snowy linens alone were finer than anything proudly possessed by Missy Fine Sassaport. Jackson was, in a word, intimidated by the room's magnificence. He'd been in grand homes before in the South, where the same grace notes were of the worn and tired type of elegance. The icy sparkle of the Godwins' riches awed him.

Once they were all sitting, Mr. Godwin blessed the bread and the wine, which Mrs. Godwin asked Jackson to pour. "Don't forget to twist the bottle when you're done, dear," she said after he'd poured for her without doing so. Now, if you didn't count Bubba Ray, the Sassaport family were not big drinkers. Mama had the occasional medicinal whiskey and Daddy drank bourbon straight on holidays and at parties but only the one. Wine etiquette was something alien to Jackson, who then poured for Seth, next up at this Yankee mama's left. After he was through, he dutifully turned the bottle upright and twirled the whole thing forcefully 'til it near sloshed out the top. Easy, cowboy, Seth said with a laugh while Stella turned purple. He's from Mississippi, not Texas, she muttered. Here, her father said, my wife meant like this. He took the bottle from Jackson and poured wine for Stella, twisting the neck so the last drop fell neatly in her glass. Jackson took color then himself.

The evening went downhill from there on in. No one asked him if his great granddaddy raped the household help, but they might as well have. After the wine debacle, the next bit of trouble Jackson got himself into was inquiring if he might please have the butter without checking first if the substance was laid on the table at all. We don't use butter with meat meals, Mrs. Godwin said. We're kosher Jews. She mistook his look of humiliation for confusion. Don't you know what I'm talking about? Aren't there kosher Jews down there? Well, not so very many, ma'am. The South is the birthplace of the Reform movement, you might recall, Jackson replied, which catapulted the conversation into an examination of the reason why Jews in the old South kept slaves. Perhaps, Mr. Godwin offered in his soft, halting manner, it was, um, a lack of foundation in the true tenets of Judaism. Perhaps, um, they didn't analyze properly the, um, ethical issues, being ignorant of halachic principles which would have guided them to, um, righteousness.

No, no, sir, Jackson felt compelled to reply. Race was a subject he'd been trained all his life to avoid in social discourse, but his classmates the last three years had no such scruples and pestered him constantly about it. He'd developed an instructive patter on the subject that he now delivered for the enlightenment of the Godwin family.

The Jews came to the South a lot earlier than they came to the North and in very sparse numbers, beginning around 1700, he told them. They were itinerant peddlers, providing a service needed at the time. Consequently, they were accepted as whites and participated in the dominant culture. The Bible had bondsmen, the South had slaves. They were part of their times, they didn't find a distinction. Perhaps you don't know this, but the majority of whites didn't keep slaves at all. It was a rich man's province to do so. Of the Jews in that category, some of them mistreated their slaves. Some of them treated their slaves well. Others were pioneers of abolition, but they didn't get very far and invited the wrath of the white population to fall upon their whole community. Basically, if Southern Jews disagreed with the institution, they practiced charity where they could and kept their philosophies to themselves to get along. My point is they were individuals like their neighbors, and each had his own take on things.

In other words, Mr. Godwin offered, they were just like any other, um, cracker with a few dollars to spend on human flesh. I'm sorry, lad, the lack of Torah is disastrously evident in your, um, people. I hear there are even Jewish members of the White Citizens' Council in your state. Pack of racists. Might as well be apostate, those, um, Jews down there.

Jackson nearly choked on his dry, unbuttered roll. Never in his life had he heard a judgment so rudely delivered to a dinner guest about his forebears. For a heartbeat, he was tempted to relate the story of his own daddy's membership in the WCC, how tortured a decision it was, how based in the desire to keep his family safe from the likes of J. B. Stoner and Admiral Crommelin. But how much could a man like

Leonard Godwin comprehend about the doctor's fear of Mississippi's version of jackboots in the night, of those unctuous agents of the scions of the town with their clipboards and door-to-door surveys asking which Jews were with us and which against? He looked over to Stella helplessly, unsure whether to confront her father or not. Should I tell him, darlin', why the Council came to existence? Created by peace-loving businessmen to guide social change at a pace people could handle while keeping the violent tendencies of the Klan in check? But Stella was occupied studying her lap while biting the inside of her cheeks. No help there. Well, sir, he managed at last, I regret I have not convinced you otherwise. Mr. Godwin snorted then patted his lips delicately with a napkin. Apparently, his gesture was enough to spark Stella's long-smoldering fuse. Tossing her glorious hair, thrusting her chest forward, she corrected him.

Dad, she said, you have no right to make such cursory statements, especially to Jackson. Why his best childhood friend was Mombasa Cooper.

Cutlery and jaws dropped all over the table.

No, really? Seth asked, incredulous.

Stella drew back to offer her brother that straight little smile she'd displayed in the car.

Yes. Really.

Lord, how they peppered him with questions. Stella told Jackson to relate the old story of his paid companion. Given his state of mind, he did not deliver it with half the charm or style he usually did. He rushed through, eliminating a host of details in his great hurry. Mombasa Cooper, Mrs. Godwin kept repeating every time he took a breath, imagine that. Paid? Seth asked, once again incredulous. How'd that make you feel?

Lucky, Jackson replied. Let them figure out on their own what that means, he thought, I am done tonight. He then helped himself to more wine without twisting the bottle and abandoned the conversation, leaving the Godwins to enthuse about the black separatist movement from Marcus Garvey to Mombasa Cooper.

Later on, after Stella had stolen into his room in the dead of night, she said: Didn't I tell you? Weren't they just awful? No, don't answer that. I can't bear the answer. The thing of it is they cry and cry about race, and they do nothing. If you knew what wages they pay at the factory! Believe me, if I were a man, I'd change all that. But no. I'm a woman, and my opinion doesn't mean anything, even though they sent me to Radcliffe and Wesleyan. Where's the sense in that? And Mom! Mom! She won't have anyone but the Irish in here to clean. Negroes are all thieves and liars as far as she's concerned. So much for civil rights no matter what lip service she gives.

Little as he knew about their history, Jackson didn't want to be the fuel that further enflamed his future wife against her mother. He tried to mend things.

But she seemed quite impressed by my relation to Li'l Bokay. I mean, Mombasa. And didn't I hear her mention donations to his movement?

Stella hit a pillow with her fist.

That's exactly what I mean! Hypocrites! The lot of them!

Shh. You'll wake somebody.

She was young, his caution made her giggle. They groped each other and made a hasty kind of love. Afterward, the first words out of her mouth were: Honey, what went on with you and Mombasa between the paid days and, you know, what happened later with Katherine Marie?

He pulled his neck back to study her with narrowed eyes. God, she was beautiful.

You want to hear all that?

Yes. I want to know everything about you. I want to know what separated you.

Howdy-doody.

What are you talking about? Don't tease me, tell me.

He sighed.

Ok then, ok, and he told her.

When Jackson reentered school the September after the summer of Li'l Bokay, he was a changed child. Gone forever was the shy, effete boy perpetually mourning the loss of Mama's company. He'd become vigorous in both mind and body, verbally confident, outgoing, perhaps too much so. His teacher was required to remind him repeatedly that the classroom was not the place for conversation. He tried very hard to obey her, but his efforts made him antsy. His teacher was further required to threaten him with a half-hour's standing in the corner or, worse, in the cloakroom, if he did not simmer down, stay in his seat, and sit still. At recess, he tore about with the swiftest, playing tag or red rover, or if it was rainy would often be found at the center of a circle of mesmerized boys while he told them tall tales from the village, which was what the Negro side of town was called when people felt like being polite, or informed them snootily of all they did not know about sex. All of this he'd got from Li'l Bokay, and much of it was the older boy's imaginative speculation or made up out of whole cloth to entertain his charge while they squatted in the dust under the blazing August sun and drew dirty pictures in the ground with sticks. If you grab a woman's titty, Jackson told those fine Episcopal lads, milk squirts out, and you gotta be careful it don't smack you in the eye or it might blind you. And don't put it in your mouth neither, cause it don't taste no good. They's a man in the village, and he called Walkie-Talkie cause that's all he ever be doin' walkin' and talkin' round and round all the day long. An' Walkie-Talkie he got an eye patch 'cause he got blinded from a squirted tit he didn't take the trouble to aim right. Now, that's a big secret I just tole you all 'cause not one saved soul in all the village knows the real reason why that patch be over his eye, but I'm tellin' you all to save you the trouble of titty blindness you own self.

On one occasion, a recess monitor snuck up behind a clutch of boys listening with both ears to Jackson's nonsense and wrote the whole business down. Just before the October break mandated by the State of Mississippi so that rural children both black and white could help harvest the family cotton, picking 'til their backs ached and their necks burned, a letter was sent from the headmaster of Stonewall Elementary to Dr. and Mrs. Sassaport, a letter of complaint about the obscene mouth their son had developed over the summer. It ended in a threat to expel Jackson if the situation was not immediately corrected. Included were quotations from the spy's notebook, which had Daddy in gales of laughter and Mama in a fit of outrage. Oh, all children get the facts of life wrong, her husband told her between guffaws, except when they get them right. Mama replied: Don't insult me, Daddy. This is not what disturbs me. What I am red hot about is the grammar our boy's picked up from that oversized pickaninny. All that low-life slang! This will not do. This will not do. We must find another way to socialize him.

The next morning was the last Saturday in September. When Big Bokay came by with his grandson to pick Jackson up for a Sabbath of riotous pleasure as was by now their habit, Mama put the kibosh on that day or any other day the one might continue to corrupt the other, saying: Jackson's a bit poorly today, he can't go out. Because she was on most occasions a fair woman, she gave Li'l Bokay his four bits anyway. Now, that'll be the last for a while, she told him. You're going to be helping your mama and granddaddy in that little field they've got the month of October, no? Of course you are. Well, then, we'll wait until November and see if we want to continue our arrangement at that time. Alright? Alright. You all have a bountiful harvest, now. And a very good day.

Meanwhile, Jackson came barreling down the stairs eager and happy. Since school started, he spent the whole week long waiting for Saturday when he would once again play with his hired friend. Mama, Mama, where's Li'l Bokay going? he asked. Is there something wrong? She bent over and gave him a hug. No, no, Jackson. Daddy and I have a surprise for you today, a big surprise. Just you wait 'til Daddy gets home!

Jackson was not the fool everyone took him for. He was well aware his father kept office hours Saturday mornings. But Mama, he won't be home for hours and hours and hours. Why can't I play with Li'l Bokay 'til then? She chucked him under the chin and lied to him as easily as she'd lied to the two Bokays. Because Li'l Bokay has some family business of his own today as it happens. Now, you go just read a book or something 'til Daddy gets home. Unless you'd like to help me with Baby Ray. You can play with Baby Ray. At her suggestion, Jackson decided reading had fresh charms and repaired to his room.

When the doctor returned home at the end of the day, he had Big Bokay with him, the two of them struggling together to bring a large wooden crate into the house. They tipped it this way, they tipped it that, and finally shimmied it through the front door while Jackson watched from the stairs, his head half stuck through the spindles of the staircase. The women of the house—Mama, Sukie, and Eleanor—huddled in a far corner of the living room watching with interest as intense as the boy's. Next came a lot of grunting and banging about until the men succeeded in freeing the crate of its contents: a brand-new console television, the first any of them had ever seen. Apparently a shipment of Zeniths had arrived to much fanfare at Uncle Izzy Joe's appliance store just that week, but for one reason or another this stellar event had escaped Jackson's ken.

Missy Fine Sassaport changed her mind four times about where the television should make its home. When at last she was satisfied,

Daddy plugged it in, set up the rabbit ears, and turned it on. After a bit of fiddling with the controls and ears, they all oohed and ahhed at the crystal clarity of the test pattern and sat around waiting for a program, any program, to appear. Eventually, they watched a wrestling match and ten minutes of news, then the test pattern reappeared with a printed message that *The Kate Smith Hour* would be on at seven p.m., followed by the inestimable Milton Berle. Though the attendant commotion of the day was at least distracting to the boy, Jackson couldn't figure out why the grown-ups were so excited or why they kept telling him how lucky he was to have such a fabulous invention in his living room sitting right there next to Mama's veneered credenza, formerly the prized item of furniture in the house. When he made their acquaintance, he found Miton Berle funny, and Kate Smith looked as warm and cushy as Mama herself. But he preferred the big color screen at the picture show to the one populated by tiny black-and-white figures at home. The Zenith, he decided, was a toy for grown-ups that had little to do with him. By the next day, he learned otherwise.

Late Sunday morning, Mama dressed him up in his blue suit and slapped a cap on his head. She hooked up her girdle, put on her navy funeral dress, her spectators and best hose, then topped it all off with a flouncy blue hat stuck through by an enormous pearl knobbed hatpin. Mother and child went for a walk past St. John the Divine Episcopal Church just as the congregation got out of service. While the families of congregants lingered chatting to one another on the steps and front walk, Missy Fine Sassaport patted Jackson's rear end and told him to skedaddle off and wish a pleasant Sabbath to this classmate and that. She remained behind to greet their mothers, taking the opportunity to bewail the dismal verbal habits her son had absorbed from unfortunate sources. She begged pardon of those he had so innocently offended, and assured everyone that all this amounted to a mischievous phase, now absolutely over. Then she dropped the confidence that by the way, the family had purchased a television.

Fresh from communion with the Celestial, the ladies of St. John the Divine extended Christian charity to the Sassaport family and forgave Jackson his sins of prurience largely due to what they considered the persuasive charm of his mother, who was quite refined for a heathen. When they further informed their husbands over Sunday supper that the family of Jackson Sassaport had purchased one of the new televisions, the children of the household invariably overheard. In screeches or wheedles, they badgered their parents to buy a television too, as well as to acquire them an invitation to the Sassaport home immediately. Considering themselves scientific-minded, their daddies to a man were curious about televisions. Confronted by the pleas of whining children disturbing the Sabbath peace, they raised their eyes helplessly, perhaps a bit pleadingly, to their wives, who replied: Dr. Sassaport's wife mentioned we are welcome to stop by any time at all to witness this electronic wonder.

That night the Sassaport living room was packed with neighbors. Children three deep sat cross-legged around the television with Jackson as their suddenly popular center. They watched *The Ed Sullivan Show*, where to the delight of all Julius La Rosa sang, Nanette Fabray made jokes, and a man juggled one hundred dinner plates for what must have been five entire minutes. Eleanor and Sukie made refreshments of iced tea and triangles of chicken salad between crustless bread. The two had never served quite so solicitously before, chiefly for the excuse to enter the room and catch a bit of old Ed themselves. From that night until Christmastime, when the congregation of St. John the Divine bought televisions from Uncle Izzy Joe en masse, there were friends of Jackson over watching television almost daily. Sukie began to badger Dr. Sassaport for a raise in her wages if every day there was going to be a party in the house. He refused. He was going broke enough, he told her, feeding the army of brats who had invaded his domain.

One Saturday morning just after this exchange, a gang of them was over, lounging around on the furniture and floor, mesmerized by Howdy Doody. Sukie was exasperated. It was supposed to be her day off. The kitchen was a shambles, two foot soldiers of Dr. Sassaport's army had spilled milk all over Miss Missy's plush red rug, and twice she'd been on her hands and knees mopping it up, and then a third had not only turned over his glass but jumped up and down at something Buffalo Bob said and ground brownie crumbs into it. She got down on her hands and knees again, praying to Jesus to bury the curses running through her head. Then she looked up, brush in hand from her chore, and shrieked. Frightened by the rude, sharp sound, the children all shrieked as well, disturbing the lady of the house who was upstairs working on her household accounts. Down the staircase she pounded, imagining a dozen catastrophes had occurred. What she found were six of Jackson's playmates once again staring placidly at the tube's screen, Sukie on her hands and knees, and Jackson himself on the other side of the room with his head stuck through the window talking to Li'l Bokay and some other village child.

Sukie! What on earth was going on down here? Jackson! Get away from there! You're ignoring your guests.

Sukie shut her eyes so she would not have to see herself reduced to relating to Miss Missy the following: I'm very sorry, ma'am. I was startled when I looked out the window, as it appeared to me in my tired and distracted state that Li'l Bokay and Don Edward standing there were grown men about to break in. I guess I frighted the children, but they're fine now.

To prevent herself from abusing the maid, Jackson's mama yelled at him instead. I said get away from there, Jackson! And you two get away from that window! Don't you ever sneak up on my house again. Do you hear me?

The dead could have heard her. Jackson jumped a foot away from the window at her first note. The children forgot Princess Summerfall Winterspring and went stunned and wide-eyed at its second. Li'l Bokay's cousin took off. But Li'l Bokay stood his ground. He waited patiently until she was through and said: Miss Missy, ma'am, I was just hopin' to see the new TV. No, no you will not see the new TV. My son has friends of quality now. I cannot, as I am entrusted with their care, expose them to you and your sort of vulgarity.

With that, Jackson's mother quit the room, the children being children burst into laughter. Jackson stood mute, frowning at the sight of Li'l Bokay marching toward the woods with a measured step, his head low. In the next moment, he heard the strains of the Post cereal jingle, which he liked to hum around the house, and lost himself in watching the advertisement that went with it rather than digest what had just happened to his first, beloved friend.

There was a sliver of time after the Howdy Doody massacre in which Jackson attempted to mend his relations with L'il Bokay. The very next morning, a Sunday, he left the house while his parents slept in and ran through the woods to the village to find the older boy and apologize to him for Mama's tirade. First, he ran to his house, a small clapboard structure cut up into seven tiny rooms to house with some pretense to privacy the three adults and five children who lived there, but no one was home. He ran to the Little Children of Jesus Baptist Church next, a place L'il Bokay had mentioned to him in the course of describing the largest female chest he had ever seen, a phenomenon which belonged to the congregation's choir leader.

The Little Children of Jesus Baptist Church was a square of cinder-blocks with no steeple, although there was a rail-tie cross painted red bolted over its metal front door, a door much like those found in school gymnasiums to keep the noise in and the ruffians out. It was still a warm time of year and the windows were open. Prayerful voices raised in song and recitation burst out of them like air from a bellows. Jackson crept to a window, hunkered down, and peeped. He searched through the mass of black faces within seeking L'il Bokay's but there were too many of them. Never before had Jackson seen so many Negroes confined in one place. He couldn't imagine how anyone could breathe in there, cheek to jowl as they were, let alone sing or dance like the group up front where the preacher stood with his arms outstretched. The preacher, a large round man in a white robe adorned with a rainbow of colored crosses embroidered along its hem, swayed from massive hips. His head bobbed up and down or side to side in sharp jerks to the rhythm of his people's worship 'til a heavy lock of slicked-back hair fell onto his forehead and bounced there. His lips moved, he seemed to be talking, but the folks he addressed clapped their hands and stomped their feet so loud it looked impossible any of them could hear him.

Giving up, Jackson walked from the church to the street and luck was with him. Big Bokay's truck pulled up, hauling a dozen or more children decked out in Sunday finery. They stood up in the flatbed so as not to get their best clothes dirty while hanging on to one another for dear life, and L'il Bokay was among them. Don Edward was as well. Jackson waited while the small ones were gathered and lowered to the ground by L'il Bokay's mama and a woman he felt must be an aunt, and the big ones jumped down. He took a deep breath and approached. L'il Bokay, L'il Bokay, he called out at least five or six times before the other slowly turned round to greet him. Why, Jackson, boy, L'il Bokay said, what you doin' here? He smiled. It was a cynical smile to match the tone he used, a tone that caused Jackson to furrow his brow in confusion. He sounded like a grown-up with a secret that mere children could not comprehend, like his teacher did when Jackson failed to get the point of a lesson. Beyond this, he wore a suit that aged him considerably. How had L'il Bokay grown up overnight? The question confounded Jackson's tongue. He stood puzzled and silent until the other said: Look, I got somewheres to go. He nodded his head toward the Little Children of Jesus Baptist Church, which all of his people had just entered. Unless you want to come with. How about that, Jackson? You wanna set in the water and be one with Jesus? Then he laughed a laugh with an unmistakable barb of cruelty at its hind end. Jackson couldn't find the humor in it. So he took another deep breath and said what he'd come to say.

I just wanted you to know I'm very sorry about yesterday. Mama shouldn't have talked to you like that. I don't know what got into her.

Oh, you don't.

No. I do not.

Then I'll tell you. She don't like me, Jackson. She don't like me at all. She don't want me ten feet away from you. She especially don't want me to be talking with you outside a Negro church on a Sunday morning. You better get on home now.

L'il Bokay gave him his back and walked to the church in the same measured step of the day before, only this time his head was not down but up. Jackson watched him, thinking: He's only three years older than me, but he is a man I do believe. Imagine that. L'il Bokay Cooper, a man.

After that day and until the year L'il Bokay, Katherine Marie, Jackson, and Bubba Ray crossed their threads of fate and made a knot as big and knobby as a tree-hole spider, Jackson ran into L'il Bokay once in a while, in the street or in some Sassaport store or other. They were polite, exchanging pleasantries about the weather and such, but that was all.

In retrospect, he experienced great guilt over the way their friendship ended almost before it began. He complained of it when he finished telling Stella everything. She kissed him, then reminded him he was barely seven years old at the time. Still, he said. Then she asked: Forget about Katherine Marie, do you think maybe that moment your mother booted him was it? The moment that made Mombasa out of him? The moment that planted the seed?

Jackson didn't even have to think about it.

Oh, I don't believe so. I believe he probably had an acquaintance with humiliation already.

He lay with his head on her breast, their legs entwined. She played with his hair and smoothed his brow. After a minute or two, he picked his head up and twisted to look in her eyes. All the hard, clear honesty of a young man in love for the first time was in his voice, his features, an intimacy that will devastate a woman's heart every time, and he said: I know it was cruel, but at the time I was a boy with the attention span of a newt, there was a lot of excitement around me, and it was just normal that Li'l Bokay would stand out there, it was just normal that he didn't knock on the front door like the other boys. I didn't understand the "have to" part. It was just normal. Same as me learning Christmas carols and the Lord's Prayer. I didn't see anything incongruous in it. It was just normal. Either way, I hate to think I'm in the middle of his anger. I know later on when push came to shove, I couldn't help him, and he was depending on me. But it wasn't my fault. Just like when we were children, there were powers at work stronger than me. So maybe I'm on the outskirts of his anger, but not smack dab in the middle.

Still, Stella the uncompromising said. Still.

Jackson fell to a miserable meditation then, recounting the various failings of his young life, when Stella sat up suddenly and said: My! We forgot to tell them we're engaged. Let's wake them up now and do it!

Her fiancé cringed. No, no. Let's wait 'til I get you a ring. It's just not right to make an announcement without a ring, and I don't think I can bear more opprobrium tonight. Let's get through the weekend. When I buy you a ring, we'll tell them.

Her face fell, her lower lip jutted out.

Please, darlin', please? he begged, and counted his blessings that for the price of ten minutes of attention to her most excitable parts, she relented.

FOUR

Fall, 1963

JUST AFTER FOUR A.M., STELLA slipped down the hall barefoot with her back against the wallpaper to go sleep in her own bed. Around seven a.m. there was a persistent cat's scratch at Jackson's door. Who's that? he asked, groggy and confused, unsure where he was or whether what woke him represented animal advance, a branch set against a window, or human interruption. A female voice that was neither Stella's nor Mrs. Godwin's answered: Mr. Godwin wants you to know he'll be ready to leave for services at eight fifteen. Dang, Jackson muttered, understanding immediately the implications of the announcement. He thanked the messenger and hauled his poorly rested limbs from bed with effort, calling up a vision of Stella in her most stimulating poses of the night to supply him strength for washing up and getting dressed at an uncivilized Saturday-morning hour. The more he thought of his fiancée the lighter, the more determined his spirit became. Jackson decided that if he and her daddy had started out badly, it was his duty to improve things. He would rise to the occasion to prove he held nothing but respect for Leonard Godwin despite his rudeness. Thankfully, he'd packed his blazer and a good pair of pants in case Stella wanted to step out in the city. He put these on, ransacked his mind for proper sabbath greetings, and descended the stairs.

He found Mrs. Godwin and Stella in their robes in the kitchen pouring glasses of juice and arranging thick cut slices of babka on a china platter. You're up early, honey, Stella said, pointedly going up to him, knife in hand, to peck him on the lips. Morning, Stella. In light of her mother's presence, he resisted an urge to kiss her back. Keeping his spine straight, stoic as a military-school graduate, he nodded over her head. Mrs. Godwin. She nodded back. Irene! she called out with a gravedigger's gaze fixed on Jackson and in a voice loud enough to startle. A robust Irish woman put her head through the pantry door. Plug in the coffee, please. For our guest. I'm going with your daddy to services, Jackson told his girl, who rolled her eyes at him.

Mrs. Godwin gave the couple a variant of Stella's straight, secret smile. I don't know why I'm asking this, but will you accompany your friend to shul, dear? I'm astounded he's going, her daughter answered, causing Jackson to wonder if he'd got himself tangled with her unawares by showing her father a son's respect. He tried to catch her eye, but she'd turned from him to get cups and saucers from a cupboard.

Leonard Godwin and Seth came to the kitchen in topcoats and fedoras. Mr. Godwin drank juice and ate babka with one hand, the other clutched a tallis bag close to his chest. Neither Godwin spoke but chewed and slurped mechanically like men on the run. Irene brought Jackson a black silk yarmulke, which he dropped on his head then patted with the flat of his hand to nestle it firmly in his hair.

Are we waiting for the ladies to dress?

Mrs. Godwin laughed. No, no. Usually I do attend, but today I want to stay here and catch up with my daughter, who won't go to one of the happiest places of her childhood without a bribe.

The men set off on foot. Mr. Godwin informed Jackson they were three blocks from the temple, he wouldn't live any farther away. Some of the local Jews, he informed, drove to shul, but he just couldn't do it. Jackson changed the subject. You have another son, I believe, sir. Will I meet him there?

My son Aaron is in, um, New York this week. On business. He met the, um, finance secretary of Mombasa Cooper's party last year, you know. Jackson took Mr. Godwin's confidence as an attempt at apology. Really, he remarked as if fascinated. Then Seth, who did not seem to Jackson to be such a bad sort, took over to explain the nature of Aaron's trip to the garment district, a subject in which Jackson feigned more interest, complimenting Stella's brother by asking intelligent questions about the quality and quantity of dry goods the ancestral factory produced.

Other early rising Jews walked briskly by them as they talked, wishing the Godwin family and their guest a good Shabbos, which wishes were returned as they passed. By setting the pace, Mr. Godwin managed to show off Jackson as the beau of a daughter the entire congregation thought too sharp a specimen to land any man at all. Jackson, of course, was not aware of his intent, but neither could he miss the stares that swept over him from head to toe. He checked his buttons, shirttails, and zipper several times in puzzlement over their attentions.

After a block and a half, two black men in somber suits much like those worn by colored funeral directors back home approached. Leonard and Seth Godwin immediately turned their heads toward each other and their conversation took on an odd intensity while they asked each other questions about minute details of Aaron's contacts along Fourteenth Street. Jackson gave the passersby a pleasant, down-home glance and wished them a good day. They were a few steps beyond them when Leonard and Seth Godwin stopped short.

Seth said: We don't speak to them. You shouldn't speak to them.

Why?

Jackson wondered if this was some arcane Yankee rudeness that refused to extend pleasantries to respectable-looking men of color on the street.

They're real-estate brokers!

Seth spoke in a contemptuous manner as if real-estate brokers were kin to murderers and thieves.

The trio walked the rest of the way in a grave silence Jackson could not decipher. But then he'd felt a traveler in a foreign land from the moment he'd stepped into the Godwin foyer. He tried to seize snippets of events to hold in his mind awhile 'til he could analyze them like those common phrases in an unknown language one picks up touring overseas.

He did pretty well during services. Inside the temple, seating was divided between men and women, the latter housed in a balcony facing the men on either side of the Ark. For Jackson, the Reform Jew of infrequent appearances in any house of worship, it was an alien arrangement. He raised his neck in amazement to regard the women, dressed in their Sabbath finest, perched like so many well-feathered birds up there behind a decorative grillwork, yes, altogether like birds in a cage. Seth elbowed him. With a jerk of his head, Stella's brother gestured toward their father to inform Jackson of the impropriety of his curiosity. Then the chazzan began the morning chants, and Jackson was able to demonstrate in his sterling tenor the lessons Perry Nussbaum taught him nearly a decade before. The Hebrew he flubbed here and there—Yankee Jews used so much of it—but where the chants were different from what he was accustomed to, Jackson employed the fine musical sensibility Mama had instilled in him. He absorbed just a few bars of melody, was able to anticipate the notes coming up, and let them out con brio. Stella's father and brother were suitably impressed.

After services, the congregation trooped downstairs to the basement function room to bless wine and bread and take a snack from an array of herring salad, egg salad, challah, and kichel laid out by the Sisterhood. Introductions to several congregants were made, but after the initial once-over, no one was sufficiently interested in the conundrum represented by a Mississippi Jew who could not see the difficulties inherent in a liaison with that Godwin girl. There were more pressing matters to discuss.

Leonard. Leonard. The Fassbinders put a For Sale sign up. And the Greens, both the father and his three sons! That's six signs in four blocks! You have to talk to them. They'll listen to you, Leonard. Or everything, all this, will be gone. It will be theirs, Gott in himmel. The shvartzes! Tell them what you told me when I was wavering. How we owe it to our parents and grandparents of blessed memory. That if no one sells, there's nothing to worry about. Tell them about nothing to fear but fear itself and how we stand together or we all fall down.

While he had no idea what everyone discussed passionately all around him, Jackson noted that Leonard Godwin appeared a leader of his community, a man armored with detailed knowledge and persuasive arguments about the subject at hand. He tried to follow the conversation so that he might reference it politely to Mr. Godwin later on, but there was too much Yiddish and Yankee slang bandied about for him to do so, and his mind wandered. It was far more entertaining to study his surrounds and imagine Stella at age four like that little darling over there clutching her mama by the leg, or twelve like that poor gawky child who looked so serious nearby, or seventeen like any one of that group eyeing the boys talking baseball across the room. This is where she grew up, he thought, this is where she first let go of her mother's skirts, where she first found that pure and generous ethos that drives her, where she first flirted with young men too shy to stop her in her tracks, which freed her to find her way to Connecticut and to me. I guess that makes this a holy place for me, Ark or no Ark. And he gave thanks.

When the men returned home, Mrs. Godwin and Stella were still not dressed. They huddled, heads together, at the kitchen table, which was spread over with open magazines. A bottle of champagne sat in a silver bucket on the countertop. The women held aloft empty flutes to salute their men. Their color was high, their voices loud. They made jokes to each other the men did not catch. Then Mrs. Godwin squealed: Stella told me your news, Jackson! and rose on unsteady feet to rush over to embrace him knocking herself into cabinetry along the way. She deposited a loud, sloppy kiss on his cheek while her frozen-in-place husband and son looked on with perplexed, open mouths. They're getting married! Mrs. Godwin told them over Jackson's shoulder. Can you believe it? Our Stella, getting married! Then she erupted into a loopy chain of chuckles, whispering into Jackson's ear so that he and he alone could hear her joyous claim: She's your problem now, son. All yours.

Seth rushed forward to clap him on the back. Brave man, he said. Brave man.

Leonard Godwin held his arms up as if to welcome Jackson to his bosom, but when he stepped up to receive that blessing, Godwin dropped them to his sides. I would have expected a Southern boy to ask my permission first, he said. It's the way we do things up here. Jackson turned forty shades of red and apologized. I am so sorry, sir. I meant to do so, he stuttered, gallantly taking all the blame for offending him until Stella's father reached out and clapped him to his chest anyway. It's alright, son, he said. Just do what you can to make her happy.

On their drive home the next morning, Jackson complained to Stella that she'd ignored his wishes completely on the matter of informing the parents before a ring had been purchased. You compromised me in your daddy's eyes, darlin'. And you'd promised me, you'd promised me to wait. It turned out alright, she told him. They're over the moon to get rid of me. I don't see what you can complain about. He had no argument there, only the nagging premonition that not to argue with her on this point constituted a dangerous precedent, one that would come back to haunt him. But as he began to expound on this to assure he had the authority men expected in those days over their wives, she gave him an upwards look of big-lashed brown eyes set above a wheedling pout. He found Stella's pose adorable, and thus put all misgivings aside.

Jackson was not yet old enough to possess the bit of self-knowledge required to inform him he was a flat-out sucker for the simplest of feminine wiles. His adolescent romances were one instance of manipulative disaster after another, although Jackson was the last individual on the planet to view them that way. When in tenth grade Amanda Riley dumped him the day before Christmas vacation so she could go to the Reindeer Ball with the dimwitted star of Stonewall High's wrestling team rather than the boy who'd done her homework all year with barely a kiss to show for it, Jackson was crushed but forgiving. Mama was not. The first morning of vacation when he arrived to the breakfast table late, glum and red-eyed, she won from him the sad tale of his broken heart at the first prodding.

Well, she pronounced, at least now I can rest easy that you're not stuck on stupid. I was worried how that yellow-haired sack of vacuity would affect your mind. You've got to upgrade your taste, boy. You need a gal with a little more upstairs and a little less down there. Someone who knows what you're worth and won't throw you over for the first mess of muscles wrapped around a stick that comes along.

Hot-cheeked and wretched, Jackson defended his Jezebel using much the same argument as Amanda Riley employed when she broke the news. Mama, I don't think she could help herself. She's a junior squad cheerleader. A cheerleader can't say no to a varsity man. Why, that would ruin her career before it half started.

Oh, you don't say? Are you sure it wasn't going to the big dance with the class Jew she thought might ruin her almighty cheerleading career? Now, don't give me that "Please, Mama" look. I know more than you think and my considered advice to you is to stick with your own kind. A nice Jewish girl would cherish a young man like you. Positively cherish.

Yes, Mama, Jackson agreed, mostly to end the conversation so that he could continue his bout of lover's grief in peace. What Mama didn't know was that Jackson harbored in his wicked heart a long and lasting lust for the idea of a Jewish girlfriend, principally because all the boys swore they were easy. Apparently it was as painless for a Christian boy to get his hand down a Jewish girl's blouse as it was to slice ice cream on a July afternoon. Mama's advice took root. He sought one of his own kind out.

First he talked to Mickey Moe to determine which of the girls of their tribe might soothe the torments of a young man gone mad from frustration. Mickey Moe informed that he wasn't certain, he didn't have personal experience here, but he'd heard from reliable sources that Frieda Mae Baumgold was easier to invade than a banana split was to swallow. Jackson set his sights for her.

The pursuit was the easy part. Frieda Mae Baumgold collected boyfriends like other young women collect hair ribbons. Curvaceous and big-eyed, black-haired, honey-voiced like Stella, she was more than willing to accept Jackson's attentions. But getting her to sit still long enough to be the object of his much considered, much rehearsed advances strained his imagination. She was one of those young ladies who hop out of chairs and flit across a room, who busy themselves at the turntable then bend over in their tight tweed skirts to pick through records on the bottom shelf of the bookcase just long enough to glaze the eyes of a virgin lad like Jackson Sassaport. They kneel and stretch their backs until their breasts point up and a young man's hands itch to shoot forward for a grab. But too late. In the last moment, they jump up to fetch something suddenly necessary from another room. Frieda Mae Baumgold was a temptress, alright, but tempting was about as far as she went. Jackson courted her for four months, until she tired of him and cast about for fresh bones to add to her collection. Not one to give up in this essential quest, Jackson pursued two other Jewish girls but neither of those would accept a third date. He tried another Christian girl, from his school. He struck out there, too.

The next time Jackson saw Mickey Moe, the two of them leaned against the back end of Great-Aunt Lucille's two-stall barn after a Cousins Club dinner smoking cigarettes. What if I never get to touch a girl, Mickey? he asked his childhood hero in the desperate notes of the hormonally tortured. Not in my whole life? Ah, his cousin said, you gonna get lucky someday, son. Everybody does sooner or later. Jackson went into a long rant bemoaning his piss-poor luck with Amanda and Frieda Mae, Sarah Celeste, Rachel, and Mary Rose. I swear to God, if I don't get to touch something female sometime soon it's gonna kill me. I can't think of anything else most times, I don't sleep right, and my schoolwork's suffering. Mickey Moe inhaled deeply on his smoke, blew it out in a thick blue cloud against the black night. That bad, huh? The family genius can't study? Ole Mr. Head of His Class? Well, don't you tell nobody I told you this, Jackson, but if you're in that much pain, you can always go down to the village. There's gals there make their living easing the pain of a boy like you.

Jackson was shocked and excited at the same time. I never did think . . . he started to say, then finished: Have you ever?

Me? Me? Mickey Moe, who by this time was twenty years old, strapping and handsome, a good old boy in flower, burst into gales of laughter, coughing out the smoke Jackson's question had surprised while still deep in his lungs. I don't ever have to feel that much pain, boy. A long time now I've got me a lady who is very kind, very kind. He reached out and ruffled his hair as if Jackson was still a kid. Console yourself! I'm older than you. I have my moves. Then he pushed away from the barn wall with one foot and sashayed down the path that led up to the big house as if demonstrating said moves, dipping his hips and twirling his arms. Jackson hollered and laughed until Mickey Moe was out of sight, then slowly slid down to his haunches. He sat in the dirt for half an hour, gazing up at the big house, smoking cigarettes, titillated by impure thoughts about the girls of the village.

Thereafter, constant images of those dark angels of professional mercy preyed upon his young mind. He pondered all the different body types and shades of them. He thought of whole rooms of them naked. He imagined the things they did to men, things the girls he knew didn't even realize existed. He suffered shame at his thoughts, squelched them good, but they were more potent than he understood and they always came back. Eventually, he was driven to ask questions as discreetly as he could to see what his classmates knew about hired love in the village. He determined a handful of names and a primary address. He found out the price of what he wanted, or rather a scale of prices ranging from four bits for the simplest of pleasures to five dollars for what the boys called the whole shebang. Fear of God and his parents forced him to redouble his efforts to tame his fantasies for a short while. But his unclean visions returned unbidden and with a vengeance. Once more, he tried to banish such thoughts and was successful in the daytime, although he reveled in them in the night when he was sure he was alone.

Months went by this way and then it was spring in Mississippi, he was sixteen, and the warming air, the thick scents of new growth and of the Pearl coming back to life, and the return of the insects—all of it increased his torment until he broke. Mama and Daddy went out one

Saturday for the annual Parents' Night Pot Luck Dinner at Stonewall High. Mama made her special seltzer brisket or, rather, made sure that Eleanor followed the old family recipe to the letter. She browbeat the poor woman all afternoon. Sukie was getting old by then, so they hired a babysitter for Bubba Ray, a rambunctious, sturdy little fellow of nine who ran rings around any sitter that took him on, had them chasing him from room to room, playing by a boy's rowdy rules and generally wearing them out. Once he had them good and tired, he'd sneak up on them from behind, snip at their hair with Sukie's sewing scissors, steal a dollar from their wallets, or barge in on them in the bathroom. Mama heard quite a number of complaints about Bubba Ray, but her judgment on the matter was tainted. No one could say a word against Bubba Ray in her presence. They were that tight. The least she could expect from those spoiled young heifers, she said, was that they earned their dollars down to the dime. Not every child was a Jackson, upstairs peaceably reading a book from the time he was four. Some had spirit to get out of them.

That night they were breaking in a new sitter. Rebecca Headly was a college sophomore home for Easter vacation. Big-bosomed, big-boned, and red-haired, dressed in a pink shirt, a gray poodle skirt, and saddle shoes, she looked like she could take on Bubba Ray and have a chance at keeping up. Jackson was introduced to her. He stood tall with his chest puffed out when Daddy informed her that her charge was Bubba Ray, not this hulking lad. Jackson would be going out to the library most of the evening and return home likely after they did.

As soon as his parents were gone, Jackson warned her that Bubba Ray was a holy terror. He's so close to evil, I can't think around here when my parents are gone. The girl laughed and slammed a fist into an open palm. I'll take care of him, don't you worry. Jackson was much relieved. Well, then, if you think you'll be alright, I'll go on to the library.

Jackson stuffed deep in his pants pocket the five dollars he'd saved over two weeks along with a condom that Buck Deaver had slipped him at school for fifty cents. Conspicuously carrying a pen and bound notebook, he bid Rebecca Headly a pleasant evening and slipped out the door to run like heck into the woods that led to the village. Luck was with him. He'd had visions of tripping into a ditch in the dark, breaking a limb to lie there nibbled by bugs, gnawed by bobcats, but the moon was full and there was plenty of light, or at least plenty enough for him to wend his rapid way with safety. Somewhere along the path he dropped both pen and notebook and didn't care.

He was nearly there, panting, out of breath before the disgrace, the indecency of what he was about to do ravaged his tender side and slowed his progress. How exactly does your desire, however strong, bestow upon you the right to buy a woman's dignity? his better self asked. He took one step forward, turned, and took two back. Then he answered himself: They don't have dignity! They're whores! He turned again, stepped forward. But his conscience pestered him. He wondered what it was that made a woman a whore, whether nature, necessity, or despair. He stopped, stepped back, considering. At last, he raised his arms to the heavens as if at prayer and rationalized. My lust will put food on someone's table, he told the moon, some little child who'd go hungry will not because of me. It's alright. It's alright. Dropping his arms, he marched on with the gravity of a soldier entering battle.

And immediately froze.

For a cloud had covered the moon and in the darkness the strangled cry of a creature unknown to him rang out. It was high-pitched, a shriek of inconceivable pain, the sound of a death struggle. It dried his mouth. A shiver afflicted his spine. Someone's eating someone else, he thought. Eating 'em raw, still living but with its guts falling out. And he thought about innocence and victims and whether or not a man could be better than an animal and he shouted out: Alright! Alright! I won't do it! At that precise moment, the cloud over the moon parted and he found himself smack in the center of a broad shaft of silver light that made his very clothes sparkle along with the leaves of the trees and the grass at his feet.

A miracle has saved my soul, thought Jackson, and he muttered a blessing Rabbi Nussbaum taught him for the sake of the creature that was eaten, nature's consecrated offering made to rescue him from sin. He resolved then and there that no matter how hard up he got in life, he'd never ever seek the company of bought women. Still, he figured he was out in the night with time on his hands and it wouldn't hurt to just continue on his way to the whorehouse and observe as part of his general education what went on in such a place.

The shack he sought was unmistakable, set off from the rest of the village by a long dirt road, draped from its tin roof with a string of Chinese lanterns that lit up the place brighter than neon. Over the front door, which was painted haint blue, a mess of chicken bones tied together and hung with string clattered in the night's soft breeze to keep bad juju away. There was a little cleared yard surrounded by underbrush behind which Jackson crouched to study his surrounds. Two pickups and a Chevrolet sedan were parked along the road next to trees disguised in kudzu bordering the woods. There were smells, too, wafting toward his hiding place, the scents of strong perfumes, liquor, and what seemed to him to be fresh biscuits and gravy, eggs, and bacon. He checked his new Timex watch, a gift from Aunt Gertrude Ann for his sixteenth. It was eight o'clock. He guessed sex made men hungry, and they cooked up light suppers within so the clientele could fortify themselves.

A new terror set in. There were men in there, real men, having their needs satisfied. What if they came out and found him? What if they laughed at him hiding there or, worse, what if the gals laughed?

How exactly was one supposed to behave while spying on a whore-house anyway? He began to sweat crouching there in the brush when a whooshing noise not three yards away nearly startled him into a yelp. He flattened himself against the ground in a heartbeat and there was a pounding as of heavy feet chasing the whoosh, following its path exactly, then all came to a sudden halt. Slowly, Jackson picked up his head to peer over the top of a bramble of thorny branches bursting with thick, waxy leaves. He gasped, then held his breath.

It was L'il Bokay and a young woman he was certain was Katherine Marie. Jackson'd had even less to do with Katherine Marie than he'd had to do with L'il Bokay in recent times, but he'd seen her around town all these years, watched her grow into a lithe beauty, and always with a proud stab of fondness.

L'il Bokay had her by the forearm. She winced and struggled but he gripped it in his strong right hand and twisted. He spoke fiercely to her, quietly but with command.

You are not going in there.

Lemme go, lemme go, I'll do what I want.

L'il Bokay twisted harder.

No. You won't.

Katherine Marie whimpered, gave up the struggle, and collapsed onto L'il Bokay's chest long enough for him to relax his grip and then quick as a cat she scrambled away from him, crouching in the pose of a defensive tackle while she stretched out her throbbing neck and pointed chin in a mad, angry taunt.

You don't own me. Ain't nobody owns me. It's kitchen help they want. No one's going to touch me in there. I won't let 'em. And Mama can't work no more, the twins need medicine and clothes. What exactly do you expect me to do about that? What? It's not like I haven't tried for other jobs, you know that. There's nothing else I can do and stay in school.

With that, she gave him her back and marched slowly toward the shack's back door with the same determination and pride Jackson remembered from their original encounter.

He was on the verge of jumping up and saving her himself, although how he could he had not the slightest idea, when L'il Bokay called out: Stop. I'll take care of you all. I've got a strong back. I don't need school like you do. I'll get two jobs and I'll take care of all you all.

Katherine Marie stopped and turned. In the moonlight, the tears streaming down her cheeks were like ropes of jewels loosely strung.

And why would you do that, Bokay? Why?

The big brute of a man fell to his knees and held out his arms.

Because I love you, Katherine Marie. Because I love you.

She went up close to him then and he wrapped his arms around her legs and she bent down and covered his head with kisses, telling him things Jackson could not hear. Eventually, she helped him up off his knees and the two of them walked down the dirt road past the two pickups and the Chevrolet sedan all bundled up in each other.

When he was sure they were gone, Jackson got up. He was moved beyond words by the sights he had seen, and all the long walk home he considered the nature of love. He discovered that he envied L'il Bokay, envied his apparent possession of a woman like Katherine Marie whose naked breasts he had managed to half-glimpse during their struggle, an image he simultaneously locked away in a secret place and attempted to erase from his mind.

When he reached his house, he wanted to go straight to his room and be alone with his thoughts, but Rebecca Headly lounged on the living room couch in front of the television and gestured to him. Her shirt was unbuttoned one or two notches more than necessary for comfort on a hot night. Come set with me, she said, moving her feet to give him room. I'm all bored. That li'l brother of yours sure is a pistol, but I got him tuckered out. He's sleepin' now, up the stairs. I've just been all alone forever with nothin' to do. Your folks won't be home for what? Two more hours at least. Good thing you showed up. I welcome the company.

Never one to offend a lady, Jackson did as he was told, and before he knew it, he was rubbing Rebecca Headly's tired feet and then her calves and then her thighs. When he got to the upper portions of the latter, they were both breathing heavily, but he wasn't sure what he should do next. Rebecca Headly took over and covered him with kisses and sly embraces until he thought he would pop off fully clothed right there on the couch. Then her hands were on his pants zipper and, sighing and giggling, she took him out and put him in her mouth and then he did pop off in a way that made him groan out loud in a deep, rumbling man's groan and she put her hand on his and guided him to the place she needed and he rubbed and rubbed like she told him to until she too groaned only in a light, high-pitched lady's groan and then they were done.

Jackson fell back on the cushions stunned and amazed. He couldn't believe his delight, his exhaustion, or his good fortune. He could only conclude that Rebecca Headly's randiness was a divine reward for his act of moral courage in rejecting the idea of buying flesh. Over the next few days before she returned to college, Rebecca and he met in the woods or she picked him up in her daddy's car and the two of them investigated all the possibilities of each other with barely a conversation they were that bothered. Then Rebecca went back to school. Although he wrote her letters, she never responded. In fact, he never saw her again. He'd hoped that during the summer Mama might use her as a babysitter, but when he casually asked whatever happened to Rebecca Headly and why was she not invited to sit for Bubba Ray, Mama replied: That gal was a filthy little thing. She spilled something on my best slipcovers and denied it. All I know is there was a wet stain there as big as Texas, and nothin's ever got it out.

In college, Jackson learned how to court a woman properly, meaning he could flirt and flatter his way into favors of all kinds. Yankee coeds practically threw themselves at his feet, because, as one of his conquests told him, he was an exotic. He knew that meant he was Southern, recited Kipling, Poe, and Dylan Thomas in his smooth, dark drawl, knew good music when he heard it, and was willing to listen to them talk, run their errands, and help them with their assignments. They called him handsome, a gentleman, and he gladly accepted that exalted mantle as his due. Stella was the only one who'd given him more than a month's worth of trouble before satisfaction. For her reluctance, he thought her wise, decent, worthy of the greatest respect. In fact, he respected her more than any other woman he'd ever lusted after with the possible exception of Katherine Marie.

FIVE

Spring, 1995

JACKSON PULLED UP TO THE country club behind the great snake of cars waiting their turns at the valet station and frowned. This is the price of being late to your own party, Stella. Weren't you supposed to be in a receiving line or some such? Stella rolled her eyes. Yes, I think I was, but I thought it was a stupid idea. I'm very glad we're late for that particular foolishness. She flipped down the vanity mirror to check her hair and face. Satisfied, she flipped it back up then gripped his wrist with such force he winced.

Look, look, it's her! Oh my Lord, it's her.

It was a misty night. Jackson squinted to peer through its veil. Who? he asked. His wife punched him in the shoulder. Katherine Marie, you big dunce! Katherine Marie. Oohh, look at her. I can not believe what she's wearing. Do you see what she's wearing? Jackson could barely make out more than the outline of the woman in question: tall, thin, hair pulled back and twisted in the French style, which accentuated even in the fog the long, sleek slope of her cheekbones and the point of her chin. As to what she wore, her dress seemed entirely appropriate for a gala evening. She had on something sheathlike, with high-heeled shoes. A formal jacket of some kind. What are you talking about, darlin'? he asked, sincerely confused about what was riling his wife. His shoulder suffered another assault. I swear, Jackson Sassaport, you have blinders on when it comes to that woman. She's wearing fur. Fur! That is a fox fur draped around her shoulders, I'm sure of it.

What Jackson wanted to say was: Now, Stella. Katherine Marie is a country woman at heart. You can't expect her to view the animal rights movement the same way you do. If her people didn't hunt, they likely didn't eat when she was a girl. What he said was: Imagine that. For his delicacy, his wife wound herself up into a huff.

I don't have to imagine anything when it's right there in front of me. What I can't imagine is that little miss PC's got innocent animal blood on her hands. Her ethos has suffered out of my influence, that's certain.

Jackson wouldn't be able to tell if what he said next was meant to defuse Stella's temper or to vent his own anxiety over the imminent reunion of Stella and Katherine Marie. Certainly, had he time to think about it he would have put his commentary in the Cautions column of his usual list, and found the most diplomatic way to express himself, but he had no time for the luxury of contemplation. It all came tumbling out.

Look. It's not that I don't fully empathize, don't fully understand and support your side of what happened with Katherine Marie. I do. If you'll recall my very first, instantaneous reaction, you'll agree about that. But, honey, a lot of time has passed. And all of those dire predictions we had, all of those fears of what she might do, of what Bokay might do, why, not one of them came true. Not a single one. And surely that must have been hard for her.

Then he added a thought he immediately regretted when it met his own ears. It sounded dyed-in-the-wool paternalistic once it was out there. As soon as he was done, he mouthed "fuck" to himself, so certain was he she'd pound him for it even though her original comment was mind-thumping paternalism itself. There were two standards of judgment in Stella's world when she was riled up, one for herself and one for everybody else. What he said was:

Think about it. She held back. She didn't tell him. That counts for something not insignificant. So you can say all you want about her ethos, yet I cannot help but think your influence over her continued from that day to this uninterrupted. Her reluctance to carry out her threats should prove that. You shouldn't feel all your work was for naught. Not by a long shot.

To his surprise, Stella swayed her head back and forth as if ruminating on his words quite seriously and said, Well, maybe.

So he moved in for the kill.

Then it's likely a little forgiveness is in order, darlin'.

But all he bagged was: Hmm.

She changed the subject: I hate all this fuss. They could've mailed me a nice plaque, and I would've been happy.

But they wouldn't have raised any funds.

Still. They could've found any number of ways to do the job. I could've given them thirty ideas just as profitable.

Perry used to say sometimes it's a mitzvah to let people do something for you.

Perry! Poor Perry. Look where all his mitzvahs got him.

The two of them fell into a saddened mood then, thinking of Perry Nussbaum. To comfort himself, Jackson reached over to squeeze her hands. He glanced sideways and noted the tears welling in her eyes. He picked up her hand then and brought it to his lips.

Her words still hurt, don't they.

She nodded and brushed a tear away before it could ruin her make-up: And you want me to forgive her.

It's not . . . it's just . . . he floundered, then gave up, inching the car forward in a deflated state until the valet arrived to deliver him from his discomfort before his wife commented on it. Another, seeing who sat in the passenger seat, rushed to Stella's side of the car, swung open the door, and held an umbrella over her head against the drizzle. Jackson joined them under the country club canopy, shaking hands while Stella put on her confident public face to greet the attendees gathered around her. You look fabulous, they said. So wonderful to be part of your celebration. It's a privilege. An honor.

Stella glanced over their heads to her husband. Although her mouth was stretched into a wide smile, her eyes said: This is ridiculous, isn't it? He gave her a look of agreement in return, shrugging his shoulders a little by way of punctuation. Inside, he was bursting with pride and happiness that at last, after thirty years, Stella was receiving acknowledgment from her peers for all her good works, works largely performed without fanfare, undercover you might say, with wisdom, strength, and courage. For all everyone had to say about her temperament, it was part of what made her what she was: passionate, determined, unrelenting in the service of those who could not speak for themselves. Yes, her tongue was sharp, but so were her wits. Yes, she was a bulldog in petticoats as Mama had once famously called her. But in the old days, only a woman who chomped at injustice with the jealous concentration of a bulldog gnawing at his bone could do what she did and live.

A voice reached through the night to disrupt Jackson's loving reverie. Jackson! it called out like a horn blown at midnight. Jackson! Get on over here! I require assistance. Yes, Mama. Yes. Steeling himself, Jackson turned toward the car from which Missy Fine Sassaport struggled to extricate herself while her sister and driver, Aunt Beadie, struggled equally to extricate her walker from the backseat. Mama's thick ankles spilled over the orthopedic shoes planted on damp concrete, her arms held on to either side of the car's open door while her hips twisted from side to side shimmying her massive rear off the passenger seat inch by treacherous inch. Hold on, Mama, wait for me. No, no, no don't even try that, Mama. Wait for me.

Of course, she did not listen and it was in the nick of time that Jackson arrived to grip her forearms and prevent her from tipping forward to fall flat on her face. Oh, thank you, son. That was a close one. Beadie, go on in and get us a good table. Now, where's that wife of yours. I must congratulate her. Jackson searched for his wife under the canopy where he'd left her, but she'd disappeared. I guess she's gone in, Mama.

'Course she did. She saw me comin'. I realize she is the local saint of all mercies, Jackson, but not much of it ever extended to me, did it? Missy Fine Sassaport dropped her handbag into the walker basket and pushed the mechanism forward, keeping her head down so she could be on the lookout for obstacles in her path. There's a step there, Jackson warned, earning only irritation for his thoughtfulness. I can see that, son. I might be stove up, but I'm not blind yet. He tried flattery: That's a lovely dress you have on, Mama. It would be silk, no? Such a pretty color on you . . . It new?

New? When did I last have a new dress your wife didn't get me? And if she did, wouldn't you've been the first one to hear about it and more than once? No, no. Bubba Ray found this in the back of my closet. He ironed it for me too. Such a good boy your brother is, Jackson. So good to me. I cannot understand why he's not invited to this affair. Family's family. Didn't I teach you that?

Because he loved his mother, Jackson tried never to bad-mouth Bubba Ray in her presence despite plenty of provocation. He knew Bubba Ray had no such reciprocal sensitivities and bad-mouthed him at every opportunity, real or imagined. Never mind the miserable history between the brothers, why did Mama think he could easily forgive him just for that or that Stella might? The answer was she didn't. She knew the bad blood between them was old and thick. That didn't stop her from trying to make him feel guilty about it. There were many times he wanted to tell her the whys and wherefores, just blurt it out and devil take the hindmost. But he didn't.

Yes, Mama, but—

Don't even try, Jackson. Obviously, I did not. Must've forgot that lesson somewhere between your ABCs and my labor pains.

She rattled on in this vein until Jackson had her settled in her seat next to Aunt Beadie at a table just beneath the dais with its wildly flowered head table. Her other tablemates were an assortment of black and white women her age, including his two remaining aunts. Everyone knew one another and exchanged warm greetings, asking after the welfare of whatever spouses yet lived, the children, the grandchildren, the greats. As he quit their company to deposit Mama's and his own coat in the cloakroom, he watched his mother's eyes search the room as she chatted and smiled and nodded to her companions. He knew who she was looking for: Mildred Godwin. He shuddered at the thought of those two knocking heads, Mama with her list of ancient grudges and Mildred with her fractured memory. There was a reason why Stella's family sat way the hell over the other side of the ballroom.

Meanwhile, he'd lost his wife. Striking as she was, he couldn't see her. There were a good two hundred people in the room and another thirty or so at the bar and at least fifteen servers bustled about. The noise around him deafened: shouted conversations, shrieks of laughter, howls of surprise, music from a five-piece orchestra the chair of the board herself had insisted upon and of which only every twelfth note could be discerned, providing it was struck ensemble and in a high enough register. He might not have worried about her whereabouts at all—Stella was more than at home in a crowd—except that he'd noticed something else in his search. Katherine Marie was nowhere to be found either.

Then he saw them. Together. They were next to a corridor that led to the kitchen and the restrooms. They faced each other, each with a grim expression on her face. Their mouths moved, but not, he judged, particularly passionately. For the longest time, neither moved a muscle. Dear God, he thought, this is terrible. Stella is never without something to say. Yet she stood there, motionless. Gotta defuse that, gotta defuse that, he muttered, and rushed through the crowd to separate the women before something awful, something shameful happened. His last sight of them was Katherine Marie speaking, then Stella speaking too and the two of them walking off together down that corridor. A loose and ugly heat swam around at the pit of his stomach. The crowd joined up, separated, cut off his view. He lost track of them completely.

Visions of the two women tearing out each other's hair in the ladies' room afflicted him. He reached that place and loitered by the door until he was certain nothing amiss was going on within. He poked his head in the kitchen and found only cooks and waiters hard at work. Perplexed, he returned to the ballroom, searched some more. After stopping by Mama's table, which he was constitutionally unable to pass without inquiring if she needed anything, he mounted the dais for an eagle-eye view of the room and searched again, glancing only briefly at the corner where Mildred Godwin and the brothers sat, as he figured this was the last spot where Stella might linger. Stuart Cahill was at his shoulder whispering thoughts that might be Jackson's own: Where is she? We've got to start. These are her rules, remember. We've planned accordingly. Where is she? Where is she? Jackson ceased his vigil to turn and look at the vice chairman of the town council. The man sweat from the crown of his head, rivulets of sweat dripped down the sides

82

of his great red face. Jackson found himself in the familiar position of calming another over the thing he feared himself. Stu, it's alright. She'll be here any minute.

It took three. Three long, anxious minutes during which the rest of the head table assembled and questioned him: Where's Stella? Where's Stella? At last he saw her coming through the service entrance of the kitchen in the company of Katherine Marie. What had they done, he wondered, hide from him behind the pots? They put their lips to each other's ears and whispered. They smiled or frowned in unison, as in the old days, assessing whatever it was they discussed so intimately with complete agreement. They were holding hands. Will wonders never cease, thought Jackson as he nearly shuddered with the relief of it, whereupon a great warmth spread throughout his chest. He longed to wrap Stella up there, and he wanted to wrap Katherine Marie up there, too, realizing in that instant how much he'd missed her, how very much. Yes, there they were: the two women he'd loved most in the world, under the same roof again, nearly in each other's arms. Then he remembered Mama. Her head was turned in Katherine Marie's and Stella's direction, a look of skeptical amusement on her face. Poor Mama. Poor Mama. Alright, he thought, the three women he'd loved most in the world under the same roof if not exactly conjoined in a triad of appreciation, at least not killing each other. That was worth a word or two of praise and thanksgiving, which he promptly offered the heavens.

A flash of red, green, yellow, and black burst into the left-hand corner of his field of vision, startling him. It was the head wrap of the board's chair, Adella Thompkins, a mountain of a woman who, thanks to her bulging eyes and dusky skin, looked not so much the African queen her gear intended but more the psychic swami of some renegade carnival out of Mumbai. Get her up here right quick, Jackson. Everybody's hungry and on the verge of drunkenness. We've got to feed these people. Like his wife, Adella Thompkins was a woman accustomed to immediate compliance from the men around her. A lifetime of matrimonial conditioning to her very tone of voice compelled Jackson to mutter yes, ma'am, yes while he rushed to the end of the dais, ready to trot on down through the ballroom's length and herd his wife to her seat. Stella saw him just then and gestured that he wait, she'd be right there. He stopped short. She and Katherine Marie bussed each other and parted. Stella took a proud, straight-backed walk toward him in that determined, self-possessed way she had. As for Katherine Marie, she hesitated briefly at Mama's table to extend courtesies, after which, just as Stella had predicted, she made a beeline to Mrs. Godwin and the brothers and settled herself in.

Jackson shook himself and met Stella on the floor. He put his arm around her and whispered: What happened? His wife radiated her public smile. Through her teeth, she said: She apologized.

No.

Yes.

I can't believe it.

Neither can I.

What did you do?

What could I do, I forgave her.

Stella was mounting the steps of the dais now, still talking through her teeth while smiling and waving to the crowd: And then I apologized too.

Adella Thompkins embraced Stella on her arrival to the head table, then pushed her into her seat, glaring at Jackson as if daring him to dillydally before parking his own ass in the chair next to. Stuart Cahill, who still sweat buckets, thoughtfully mopped his face with a handkerchief before leaning over to kiss Stella on her proffered cheek. Adella coughed. He hurried to his seat. The chair rapped a gavel on the podium to still the crowd. She began her speech. Half of it, Jackson couldn't hear. The words that echoed through his brain were the ones he couldn't believe he heard: And then I apologized too.

He shook himself. Tried to pay attention.

Ladies, Gentlemen, Adella said. I am so very happy to see you all here tonight. Are you all havin' a good time?

Women applauded lightly, forks hit the sides of wineglasses, a handful of men standing by the bar shouted: Hell, yes! And everyone laughed. Adella continued.

You know, it's never been our custom to deliver the speeches before you all have had your meal, but our honoree tonight demanded that we get the speeches over with at the beginning of our supper so, as she put it, when you all start nodding off during the tributes she can take her rightful blame tomorrow rather than puttin' it down to bellies bustin' with fried chicken. I pointed out to her that the noise of you all eatin' and clatterin' your silverware might drown out the speeches and she said: Well, thank God then.

Adella paused and waited for chuckles from the assembled to come and go. Then she sighed, dramatically, for effect.

That's just like our Stella Sassaport, isn't it? Always dodging the spotlight. Doing all her good work behind the scenes. Never pausing to rest for accolades, just on to the next worthy cause. Those of you who have worked with her know that she is a fiery spirit. She is not one you want to cross. I've been at meetings where grown men twice her size— here she glanced pointedly at Stuart Cahill, earning herself another round of titters from the audience—have trembled in their seats at the thought of doing battle with her. Yes, we are grateful that spirit has been on the side of fairness and justice, as it has served us well. Stella Sassaport's commitment to the welfare of our poor and downtrodden has never wavered since the day she arrived here in our fair state on the arm of her brand-new husband, our own Attorney Jackson Sassaport, and I know you all are aware that in those days and in that time the reception of her ilk was often neither gentle nor kind. She came to us at a pivotal point in our history, when her work was both difficult and perilous, but she did it and continued it long after others abandoned us, thinking the job done when it had only just begun. I'll let some of the other speakers enumerate her achievements. For now, to get the ball rolling, I just want to say to you all: Welcome, welcome to Hinds County, Mississippi's Unsung Civic Hero Award Dinner of 1995, honoring at long last our own Stella Sassaport, MSW, LCSW.

The applause was vigorous. People all over the room, people from the Rotary Club, people from the State Department of Human Services, a coterie of local philanthropists, all of them clapped away, but the people Stella had helped locate grants for their education or their surgery, keep their children, find shelter, enter rehab, get a job worth working at stood up and clapped the loudest, the longest. Though their affection brought a certain damp to Jackson's eyes, Stella herself kept her head down as she turned a deep, self-conscious red. She gripped Jackson's knee under the table. Her fingernails dug in. He tried not to wince. The first speaker was a former inmate of Parchman Prison during the Freedom Rider days who spoke more about Perry than Stella, but that was alright, Stella didn't mind that at all. The next was a middle-aged black woman, a Vietnam War widow, whose three sons won scholarships to Morehouse in the early '80s thanks to Stella's tutelage during her nights and weekends off. The last was a young white man infected with HIV for whom Stella had spent the last year lobbying Pfizer to provide him the drug cocktail that kept him alive. When he was through, Adella presented her with the traditional framed award, hand calligraphed, adorned with a gold seal and blue ribbon glinting under glass. It was Stella's turn to stand up and speak. With some reluctance, Jackson felt, she released his knee and stood while the room exploded with applause. This time everyone got up, even Mama, even Mrs. Godwin, although neither of those two clapped with the rest but stood there nodding like queens of England with twin expressions of modesty plastered on their features as if they and not Stella were the cause of all this boisterous appreciation. Stella gestured that everybody please sit, which they did, and the room quieted waiting for her to speak.

Thank you, Adella, Jim, Althea, Bobby for those gracious remarks. You all are too kind. She unfolded the sheets of paper she'd carried in a white-knuckled grip to the podium. I mean that. I did not fight these fights alone. However I may have facilitated your accomplishments, they belong to you, not to me. She gave a sweeping look around the room, pausing pointedly at her mother's table, where Seth and Aaron had sandwiched Katherine Marie between them, each leaning over and murmuring into her closest delicate ear remarks one might surmise were bitingly witty for the way she rolled her twinkling eyes and grimaced in reaction. Oh Lordy, thought Jackson, following his wife's gaze and knowing too well what the prompt folding-up of her speech meant. Lordy, she's going to wing it. She's going to wing it on wings of fire.

I am frankly stunned to see so many old friends and associates here, Stella continued. In fact, there are those here I would have sworn would attend a party in my honor only if it occurred directly after my burial. Oh yes, that includes a certain someone tryin' to hide behind his napkin over there.

Heads swiveled all around the room, looking for the object of Stella's attention.

Yes, you, Doctor, she said. I've not forgotten the time you had your nurse sweep me out the door with the rest of the dust under your feet. Bobby here remembers too. It wasn't so long ago. And let's see, ah yes, my girlfriend over there lookin' all febrile, or is that a blush, dear? You're the one stopped your daddy from giving Althea's second boy the books we needed, don't think I don't know about that . . .

Mouths dropped open all around the room as she continued calling out in veiled fashion those who'd crossed her.

And you, you with the green thumb who thought your wife's white roses were a more important crop for the community garden than vegetables for a mess of hungry, ill-fed children. I was so amused when they got the blight, especially when I heard you blamed me personally.

Stella went on. Although she chose to speak in pronouns, careful not to identify anyone outright, several of the guilty parties huffed and puffed and betrayed themselves immediately, to the great entertainment of their enemies. Others plastered frozen smiles on their faces to avoid detection. When she paused, shielding her eyes with her hand to study the assembled more carefully, picking out victims with the studied patience of a hunter huddled up all night in a blind, one prominent couple in the back left their dinner half-eaten and made tracks for the cloakroom before she could get to them. At her wits' end, Adella Thompkins reached up from her seat next to the podium and put a hand on her arm as if to arrest her scandalous litany, but Stella shook it off.

Oh, I know, Adella, these are the people whose ass we need to kiss every day of the week just to get poor little children places to sleep at night, but they need shaming. They've needed it a long time. Don't worry, I'm almost done. I'm moving on from Hypocrites I Have to Grovel Before to Secrets I Want to Share.

She paused to take a long drink of water while the room waited with all the dread fascination of rubberneckers at a traffic pile up. Jackson, do something! Adella whispered fiercely. She's bidin' her time, she'll use given names any second! Jackson whispered fiercely back: What can I do? and Adella said well, you could put your arms around her and squeeze so tight she has to shut up or suffocate.

What secrets do I know? Oh, they are legion, my friends. I know who's battered their child, who's diddled the maid, who's cheated some poor man of his pay because he assumed his victim was as stupid as he was powerless. I know who those greedy bullies are. I know about this one's drug problem and that one's gambling. I know who's dipped in the public till. I know who the takers are, the scammers, the ingrates.

She looked straight at Katherine Marie then. Katherine Marie tensed her neck and threw her shoulders back so that the yet hovering Seth and Aaron went off balance and swayed in their seats. Oh, Lordy, Jackson thought, here it comes. Only it didn't. In the next breath, Stella launched her summation.

I've heard it all in my day from sources none of you would suspect. Well, maybe some of you would. Those who have suffered the fallout from all that battering, diddling, drugging, and theft. The ones I've tried to lend a helping hand to in my career. The ones who weren't too proud or too far gone to take it. And I would like to say that it's you all who deserve this award, not me. A hero. Me. I was just doing my job. But you all. You survivors. You whose song has not been sung and likely never will be. You who demand so little from the world and so much from yourselves. I'm going to take this lovely little award and put it in the bottom drawer of my desk, the one I put my bag in in the morning and the one I take it out of when I leave. Every time I do that, I'm going to make you all a blessing. Because it belongs to all you all, not me. And I thank you, I thank you from the bottom of my heart for the gift you've given me. The gift of pride, of hope in my fellow man. Because those other bastards nearly killed it.

Stella sat. There was a second or two of silence and then the assembled burst into long, sustained applause, up on their feet again, beaming more, Jackson thought, with relief that they'd not been explicitly exposed than with appreciation of the fortitude of Stella's most successful clientele. He reached over to embrace her in congratulations but also for the opportunity to mutter in her ear: I thought for a minute there you were going to do it. That you were going to tell on Katherine Marie. And she replied: Maybe they'll let me speak again after coffee.

I could squeeze it in then if you'd like. Not a chance, he said, I definitely would not like, not at all.

After dinner, there was dancing. Stella had one dance with her husband and the rest with an assortment of civic leaders who suddenly burned to appear on her good side. Meanwhile, as instructed, Jackson worked the room soliciting pledges for Stella's latest project: a hospice house for AIDS victims. Of his own volition, he bypassed the inner circle of tables for the outer, thinking them the closest route to Katherine Marie. He smiled over at his in-laws' table every chance he got, making wave motions or holding up a single finger as if to say "just one more minute, I'm gettin' there, hold on" until Katherine Marie got tired of waiting for him, got herself up, and snuck behind him to tap him on the shoulder as the orchestra played "Can You Feel the Love Tonight" and she said: Dance? That was all, just, Dance? but her voice went through him like a bolt of lightning and immediately he stopped what he was doing to turn and grin and greet and hug hard then guide her to the dance floor with one hand on the center of her back as he had been taught at the age of nine was the proper way to escort a lady to such a place.

Though they were in each other's arms, face to face, both with full nostalgic hearts pounding wildly, neither knew exactly what to say. It's so good to see you again, Jackson tried. It's been too long. Way too long, Katherine Marie agreed, and then they were silent while each remembered the past from separate memory banks, aware their versions differed and wondering what to do about it. Finally, Katherine Marie said: Stella looks wonderful. She hasn't changed a bit. They both laughed then, with that note of sardonic camaraderie they'd always shared as two veterans of Stella's command. Katherine Marie leaned her head back and narrowed her eyes. She said she's forgiven me. Has she? Jackson was never disloyal to his wife. Yes, he guessed, yes, of course. It was a lifetime ago, wasn't it? And you? You truly forgive her?

Katherine tilted her head. If I forgave you, I had to forgive her, didn't I? Jackson felt a heat rise to his cheeks. And how's Mombasa? What's the word? Katherine Marie sighed. There's another hearing next month, she said, but we don't have much hope left.

Now, you can't ever give up hope, darlin', Jackson said, forgetting himself by using the endearment. He marveled at his indiscretion, although Katherine Marie didn't seem to notice or mind.

I heard about your daddy passin', she said. I was sorry about that.

Thank you.

I've been wanting to tell you that for thirteen years now.

Her condolence, however belated, touched him. His velvet baritone went deeper yet. Each word was a kind of caress.

It was a blessing. He was never himself after, you know.

Yes. I do know. I do.

The music stopped. The two old friends let go of each other. All of a sudden, Stella was there, putting her arm around her husband and nestling her head against his chest. It was a most unusual public pose for her whose intent escaped no one.

I'm sorry, but I need Jackson to do some politicking with me, girl, and you're going to have to let him go. We don't often get all these fat cats in one room feeling as guilty as they do right now. Why don't you stop by the house tomorrow and we can all catch up?

Of course, Stella, that would be nice, Katherine Marie said. About eleven?

Eleven's perfect. I'll make us a nice brunch.

Everybody kissed one another. Katherine Marie went directly to get her coat and pick up her car without saying good-bye to Mama or the brothers or Mrs. Godwin, a fact Jackson was sure he'd hear about more than once the rest of the night.

You think she'll come? Stella asked her husband while they watched her back.

No. No I do not.

Neither do I.

The party broke up after another couple of hours. It was a dancing crowd, or it would have been earlier. Jackson was working his way through a token dance with each of the female members of the school board when Mama rolled up, parting dancers with her walker as effectively as Moses the Red Sea with his staff.

Well, son, this shindig could go on 'til next Tuesday, looks like, and I've got the phlebotomist in the morning. Bubba Ray will be frettin' if I don't get home soon. Where's the guest of honor? I can't believe I've gone through the entire evening without more than a nod from her. But then you all looked so busy reacquaintin' yourselves with the distant past.

His mother gave him a squinty-eyed, pursed-lip look meant to rankle him into saying more than he should, but Jackson hadn't fallen for it since high school. Luckily, Stella stood nearby, chatting up the president of the Federal Credit Union Bank. He signaled her to come on over and see Mama off. The two embraced, but not warmly. They paid each other's dresses backhanded compliments. It was late, Mama was tired or she might have tried to push a few buttons, most named Bubba Ray. She settled for an easier mark.

And where's your mama, girl? I've been wanting to give her my regards all night.

Oh, you know, she's not well. She left a long time ago. And it's alright, she's not likely to have known you. Her mind's not right anymore. The boys watch out for her and thank God, she's quiet. Otherwise, I don't think she'd travel well. She likes to get out and watch the pretty lights and the colors, but she can't much add to a conversation.

Looked like she was enjoying one with that Katherine Marie Cooper.

Jackson had enough of her poking around looking to start trouble. He noticed Aunt Beadie's back a few people away. Oh, look, Mama.

Aunt Beadie's trying to find you. You'd best join up with her now.

Kiss me up then, children.

Jackson and Stella did as they were told. When at last they watched Missy Fine Sassaport's back, bent as it was, they sighed and squeezed each other's hands.

Katherine Marie surprised them both, arriving at their front door at ten thirty the next morning, her arms loaded with everything necessary for a hearty Sunday brunch: eggs, juice, bacon, sausage, grits, biscuits, fruit, a plastic container of rich brown gravy, and a little basket of pastries. What is all this? Jackson said, after answering the door in his bathrobe and slippers, newspaper in hand, which he promptly dropped to unburden her. Wuz it look like? I know Stella never has a thing in the fridge. Rather than go hungry, I thought I'd bring breakfast with. They smiled together at that, sharing unspoken memories.

She still asleep?

It was a long night.

Why don't we just get everything ready, and then you can wake her.

Alright.

Give us time to have a chat.

Alright.

The two of them set about unpacking provisions and assembling the tools Katherine Marie would need to cook everything up. Soon the room filled with homely scents redolent of comfort, family, of times gone by. Old habits resurrected, they worked together seamlessly without words, each anticipating the other's actions. She put out a hand, he filled it with whatever was needed. She cracked eggs and boiled water, Jackson set the kitchen table. They stepped aside or joined up as was necessary with the gracefulness of dancers long accustomed to their partner's slightest movements. Jackson's spirit brimmed with sentiment. Such a simple, silent collection of moments, he thought, a treasure.

This feels so . . . he said, breaking at search of a proper term.

Katherine Marie turned from the stovetop to flash him a bright smile: Natural?

Yes. I guess that's it. Natural.

He took a chance: I've missed having you around.

She sighed: I've missed you all, too. But you know, things being what they were between Stella and me . . .

She put down the spatula she'd been working with to emphasize her next words. Turned toward him and put her hands on her hips. Jackson noticed how slim they were, like a girl's. Good for you! he wanted to say. Good for you for staying damn lovely. But it sounded shallow or flirtatious or worse to voice such a compliment, and he kept mum waiting for her to speak.

I was angry with Stella, Jackson, but never, never for a minute was I angry with you.

I know.

He failed to expand on the subject, leading as it would to a discussion about his feelings on the incident in question. For quite some time, after all, he'd nursed a good head of steam about Katherine Marie's actions himself. Her disagreement with Stella he could understand, the cultural conflicts she'd underscored during their argument he could understand, but the insults, the threats—they were another matter entirely. At the time, he'd nearly raged on over to her place to put some retaliatory hurt on her himself. Only Stella or his breeding or—and thinking about it, this was probably the real reason—the past kept him from it. Oh, the past, the monstrous past he'd been enslaved to one way or another for thirty-five years! That night that colored everything he ever did. That night, that dammed summer night when he was nineteen and Katherine Marie twenty and Bokay nearly twenty-two and Bubba Ray, Lord, he was only thirteen, hard to imagine now that at a mere thirteen years of age he could have been the catalyst of all that misery, thirteen!

As usual when he suffered meditations on Bubba Ray, Jackson got lost. He started off wondering what that no-good layabout would do when he got down to Mama's last dime. He imagined his brother finding a way to tap him for support. His thoughts darkened then, churned like a twister with violent images. Completely unaware, he set to beating the spoon in his hand against the kitchen counter in a queer rhythm that matched the fantasies he entertained of pummeling Bubba Ray to an unrecognizable lump of blood-streaming flesh. Katherine Marie called him back to himself.

Jackson. Jackson.

Huh?

Where'd you go?

He blushed like a teenager: Don't matter. I'm sorry.

It's alright. Know what that spoon banging put me in mind of? Those days when we were kids. When I was first working for your mama after she got laid up. And you were memorizing poetry for school. You used to bang out the meter just like that, with a spoon on the counter, and you used to quote it for me. Remember?

How could I forget?

You were sweet on me, weren't you.

Well, I guess I was.

Then you might have chosen poetry a little more appropriate. I can hear you now doing Gunga Din. ". . .with 'is mussick on 'is back/'E would skip with our attack/An' watch us till the bugles made 'Retire.'" Oh, Lordy, it still makes me laugh. You'd pause there and give me this hooded look—fraught with meaning, I believe is the expression—and continue. "An' for all 'is dirty 'ide/'E was white, clear white, inside/When 'e went to tend the wounded under fire!"

Jackson was completely disarmed by her recitation accomplished in proper Cockney with dramatic gestures. He laughed at himself, laughed at her, the two of them collapsed into kitchen chairs with their laughter. Jackson tried to apologize for his young self between gasps for breath. He handed Katherine Marie a napkin and took one himself, as their eyes were running tears they laughed so hard and long.

They blotted their faces and calmed down, and when they could talk, Jackson said: "White, clear white, inside?" I recited that line to you? With romantic intent? Please, I don't remember ever being quite that stupid, Katherine Marie.

You were worse. Quoting such lines were your idea of racial liberalism back then. You'd get even more serious-lookin' and say slowly, making your voice deep as it could go: "Though I've belted you and flayed you/By the livin' Gawd that made you,/You're a better man than I am, Gunga Din!"

They burst out laughing again, kept at it until the grits burned and Stella woke up, came flying down the stairs wondering where the fire was and why all the racket. When she saw them so full of their own jokes, she laughed too, without knowing why, and the three of them stood in the middle of the kitchen laughing like idiots as if only in an excess of joy could the pain of the past be blotted out.

SIX

Spring, 1959

SIX MONTHS BEFORE JACKSON'S MAMA took sick at the age of forty-three, Eleanor died of her cough at last. The poor woman dropped dead, coughing up blood all over the Sassaport linoleum before anyone found her. At first, they found no one the lady of the house approved of to replace her, which left Mama on her own in a kitchen soon bereft of greens, legumes, fish, or fowl and awash in bacon, red meat, sugar, sour cream, and chicken fat. A backwoods blockhead could have predicted that she'd come down with diabetes, hypertension, glaucoma, or gout, but not all at once as it happened. The doctor had warned her of just these dangers ever since Bubba Ray was born, engendered as they might be by her dietary habits and family history. She paid no more mind to her husband on the subject of her health than she did anything else. No one foresaw that that powerhouse of will would take to her bed from shock at so much bad news, a cowardly act that threw the household into enough chaos that one afternoon Sukie declared she was too old to take care of things by her single self and nurse an invalid to boot. I am retirin', she announced, before you all kill me with the ever-flowin' river of your needs and whims.

Jackson's mama pitched a tearful fit at the declaration, and Daddy offered a substantial hike in pay, but neither could change Sukie's mind. She was done with them all, especially that rascal Bubba Ray, she told them, and though she felt sorry to leave Miss Missy high and dry laid up as she was and though she'd miss young Mr. Jackson, her family favorite, dearly, she was doner than done. She had her social security coming, her baby girl had come back home from that hotel she worked in Biloxi with savings in the bank and a hardworking husband in tow, so she didn't need the doctor's money quite so bad as she had in years gone by when she'd lowered her pride and begged for some, even though she knew he was tight as a nun's bedsheet with a dollar, she was that desperate. Despite the family's pleas and offers, she packed up her things the same day and was gone for good.

Once the dust of her leave-taking settled, Dr. Sassaport looked his wife in her panicked, cloudy eye and said: I can't quite fathom where all that sass comes from, can you? Weren't we always good to Sukie? Didn't you always give her your castoff dresses and the boys' toys for her children? It's not like your frocks were in tatters or the toys broken. Nothin' we ever gave her was but barely used. We gave her days off when she asked most of the time, as I recall, and presents on her birthdays and Christmas. Sure, she slept here four nights a week, but we wanted five, and dammit, we paid her well for that duty, didn't we? We paid her promptly a fair rate and never once cheated her out of her due. Call me stupid if you like, but I was attached to that woman. I thought she was attached to us, too. Well, I guess it goes to show. With Negroes, you just never know what they're thinking. Don't you worry, honey, I'll find someone to take Sukie's place. I've got a number of patients that owe me money, we'll find a bargain in the process, you better believe.

It took a month. The first candidate struck Mama as slovenly from her first step through the back door. The second she thought had the darting eyes of a thief. The third appeared too weak to handle the workload, and so their maidless weeks dragged on. During that time, Jackson was required to take over, to vivify the domestic skills he'd learned from Mama during their golden year before Bubba Ray was born. He cooked, he swept, he laundered, he polished and scrubbed. He ran up and down the stairs ten times a day before school and after to make sure Mama had her pitcher of tea, her medicines, her magazines, her fresh towels. His grades suffered, but as he'd already enjoyed early acceptance to college, no one cared. Meanwhile, Bubba Ray lay about on the couch with his hands down his pants like the great adolescent slug he'd become and laughed at him. He trailed crumbs through the house, wadded up filthy paper and shoved balls of it under the couch, puddled his milk on the countertops and yelled to his brother: Miss Jackie, you missed a spot over here! Jackson slapped the brat the first time he played such tricks on him. He didn't use anything close to his available force. It was a firm but slight slap to the shoulder such as one might deliver to the hind end of a toddler who was squalling because those fascinating matches had been taken away. Bubba Ray screamed like a woman and tore upstairs to hurl himself onto their mama's bed where he sobbed out grandiose exaggerations of Jackson's intemperance, presented his chubby cheeks streaked with tears, made his lying eyes round with damp pathos. Horrified, Mama rang the little bell she kept on her end table to summon the older boy to her side. Within minutes, he stood in front of her, hangdog, knowing what was coming while Bubba Ray sniffled amongst the bedclothes where he lay half-buried in Missy Fine Sassaport's lap, his one visible eye twinkling with victory and revenge.

Jackson, I know my convalescence is hardest on you, Mama said, breathing heavily with emotion and fatigue. I know what a trial keeping this old house in one piece is under normal circumstances. I know with your schoolwork and these new responsibilities, you're no doubt pushed to the limits of your endurance. But some things cannot be helped. And a man, a real man, bears with the frustration of the inescapable without resorting to violence against a hapless child.

Wide-eyed, Jackson opened his mouth to protest. There was absolutely nothing hapless about the unruly, mean-spirited creature in question, he wanted to say. He was as tall as Jackson was and thick around the middle. He looked like an Ottoman warrior, for Lord's sake. Jackson considered his brother's long, simian arms, his thatch of thick curly hair, the heavy-lidded eyes and lips like a fish. There was something not right about him, something barbarian. As if listening to his thoughts, Mama raised her arm with her palm held flat up to heaven like a Baptist.

No, no, no. Don't even try, Jackson. I will not hear a word against your baby brother. Whatever monkey business he may be up to, it cannot possibly excuse you from abusing him. Now, I want you to apologize this instant and swear before me, Bubba Ray, and God Almighty that you will never bully him again.

Oh, it was difficult. It might have been the most difficult task ever set before Jackson Sassaport, but he humbled himself to please his dear, sick mama. After choking out a much-detested apology, he vowed never to lay a hand on Bubba Ray again. It was the first of only two vows of his life that he ever broke.

Later on that night when Bubba Ray had gone to bed and Jackson checked in on Mama before retiring himself, it being one of Daddy's meeting nights with the Council, mother and son had a heart-to-heart.

You're a good boy, Jackson, Mama began, a mother couldn't ask for one better, and I am fully aware that on the other hand Bubba Ray is a ruckus and a half. As you know, I've lost my temper with him once or twice myself. But you have to understand, as Daddy and I do, that he's not like you. He's not very smart and he's not good-lookin', that's the pitiful truth of it. He does, however, possess a certain charm. Daddy calls it the shrewdness of the willfully ignorant, but your daddy's always been hard on you all. Lord knows, Bubba Ray can get outta me whatever he wants on charm alone, and I am convinced that will be his saving grace, how he'll get by in the world. Maybe he'll sell something in one of your uncles' stores. Or, as he's big and burly enough, maybe he'll be a sports star. That's what I like to fancy for him. Isn't that queer? A sportsman has to apply himself, and he requires a lot of sleep, don't he? but I can't get the idea out of my head nonetheless. Bubba Ray hurtlin' through the goalposts, Bubba Ray sailin' over the finish line, Bubba Ray knockin' one out of the park. That's what I think about when I picture your brother in days to come. Well, time will tell, time will tell. The thing of it is that I do believe Bubba Ray wishes he were you. Wishes he were smart and handsome. He feels his lack bitterly. But brains and looks were not what the Lord gave him. So I want you to try to be compassionate. Understand that when he torments you, it's out of jealousy, plain and simple. Rise above, son, rise above. Your brother does not have the capacity.

Considering his mother's delicate condition, there wasn't much Jackson felt he could do. He was old enough to know there was no arguing with a mother's love. He promised Mama he'd try, although he found her opinion of Bubba Ray to be maternal love gone delusional. By his lights, Bubba Ray was a selfish, lazy, good-for-nothing destined for penury and prison. He didn't possess charm so much as a blighted soul basted in snake oil. The only thing he was precocious in was growth: He seemed to have twice the body mass his elder brother marshaled and not yet twelve, he already shaved twice a week. Yet Jackson was too busy with the demands of home and school to dwell much on the subject of Bubba Ray's grotesqueries. Whenever he could, he ignored him, worked around him, and squelched the resentment he felt at having to feed and clean up after the greedy devil.

To Jackson's relief, by the time a month had passed, Daddy came up with a maid and cook of whom Mama could approve. The doctor announced her impending arrival at supper.

Well, while I thank you, son, he told his eldest, I thank you very much indeed for your efforts during the past number of weeks, I am delighted this is the last evening I have to chomp down on chicken drier than a boar's teat. I have located us a replacement for Sukie and Eleanor. She dropped by this afternoon while you boys were at school, and Mama liked her just fine. She'll start tomorrow. Jackson, you got clean sheets in the house? I think we ought to drag Sukie's old cot out of the basement and make it up nice and fresh to welcome her proper. She's a young one, never lived away from home before, saving up money for her wedding, so the story goes.

Jackson asked where he'd found her.

Actually, she came to my office lookin' for a way to repay me for takin' care of her two young sisters. Twins. Asthmatics misdiagnosed as tuberculars, can you believe it? I had those two pups in my office not two weeks ago on charity night croaking out what sounded like their last breaths after some midwife witchdoctor down in the village tortured 'em with mustard plaster and pepper soup. Why anyone with half their senses thought that would cure tuberculosis, I haven't a clue. I don't know who it was diagnosed them, but it didn't sit right with me, don't know if I can tell you why, it just didn't. I took 'em over to the hospital next day when I went for my morning rounds and had 'em X-rayed and blood tested on the QT, otherwise that gal'd never be able to pay for it, and I wanted to know, dammit, I wanted to know. Turned out I was on the money. Allergy-induced asthma. Both of 'em. One, two, three, I fixed them up with atomizers, and they breathed easy last week for the first time in a year, big sister tells me. Like I said, she was thankful, brought me over a home-cooked lunch. Catfish and spoon bread and Lord, it was delicious, much better'n yours. Better'n Sukie's, too. Little side of black-eyed peas spiced tangy. Don't know what was in it, but it was fine. Didn't bite your mouth, just nibbled it. I asked her if she could cook low-fat and low-sugar just as well, and she's a proud one, she said, Why yessir, I can cook anything on God's green earth. Well, we got to talking. Ipso facto, Jackson's reprieve. How'd you like that, son? Perhaps you can look forward to a carefree spring and summer before you're off to Yankeetown and the shining future of your dreams after all. Providing this little miss works out.

Daddy, I wish you'd stop calling it Yankeetown. It's New Haven. It's Yale.

Well, all I can say is that if it were Oxford or Durham, we might be able to afford a maid and a cook again rather than have to lay all our hopes on one skinny li'l gal.

Jackson held his tongue, but what he wanted to say was: Can't you be proud of me for once in your life, Daddy? If you were, maybe I wouldn't feel so cooped up in Guilford that I'd crawl to the ends of the earth just to get away from you. Doesn't it mean anything to you that I'm valedictorian? That the Ivy League wants me? But it'd been a long day of shopping and housework, school and study. He was too tired for the argument he knew would ensue, as they'd had it so many times before.

You're a Southern boy, Daddy would say. They won't be able to freeze that outta you up there, no matter how cold it gets. You'll be on display, like some circus monkey. They'll call you quaint and backwards and worse. I'm not denying you'll win yourself a fine education, but you'll be lonely, and you'll be homesick. It's not that easy to leave home, boy. You can't just turn your back on the familiar and embrace the foreign, which will not embrace you back in any case. Mississippi will haunt you. You'll long for down-home cooking and the smell of river mud, for a kind word from people who know who you are and take you as you are, no questions asked. They'll move too fast for you. Everyone up there wakes up hell-bent in a rush to nowhere. They're rude, too. They have no social graces. Employin' bad manners is how they pass the time of day. You'll feel slapped in the face five times an hour by damn Yankees, who haven't got the sense to know they just finished insulting you. Or they do and don't care. I know you think I'm a fool, don't know what I'm talking about, but remember I lived up there in Philadelphia PA for an entire month examining veterans after the war. Worst month of my life. I know of what I speak. Can't no one deny it.

After supper, Jackson and Dr. Sassaport got Sukie's old cot up from the basement, along with the Korean screen Uncle Max sent home from his war. Jackson felt the new maid might want to enjoy some privacy, a commodity Sukie never gave a fig about, but she was old, he figured, and this new girl was young. Even Daddy was impressed by his thoughtfulness and threw him a bone of praise over it. Encouraged, he sponged the dust off the screen, then sprayed it and the cot all over with Mama's lavender after-bath cologne to get rid of an odor of must. He made up the cot with clean sheets, a blanket, some pillows, and then, in a moment of inspiration, set down next to it a small table fetched from the front porch and on that he set a lamp from the same place and a bud vase into which he stuffed a branch of wisteria before he left for school.

Throughout the day, he imagined Sukie's replacement finding her corner of the kitchen all cozy and spruced up, and he felt pleased with himself. For the first time since Mama took sick, he was eager to go home at the end of the day despite the fact that Amanda Riley herself passed him a note during civics saying she'd like to talk to him about something after class. He sent Amanda his regrets through Booster Cochoran. He surprised even himself that he was that anxious to meet the new help. He imagined the reason was that he was deeply thankful someone had finally pleased Mama enough to release him from servitude. Such a creature must be truly rare, he thought, a special case, worthy of his curiosity and excitement. When he burst through the kitchen door, smiling broadly, about to make this marvel's acquaintance, he realized his intense anticipation was prescient. The new maid was Katherine Marie.

His first sight of her was a back view as she worked over the stove, but he knew her, he knew her instantly. It was her hair, he thought later, black and kinky like every other Negro girl's, but braided from the center high on her head the way the horsey girls at school did theirs and with a paintbrush of a tail, thick and shining and full, flipping up. Or her neck, maybe: long, sinewy, with a sweet constellation of moles forming a perfect circle at the nape. It was not her body, although images of those long muscular legs and the short tiny waist had plagued him frequently since that time a year earlier in the backyard of the village whorehouse. It couldn't have been, as she was dressed in a shapeless shift, gray-colored, modest as a cloister's habit, which ended past her calves. Whatever it was that sparked his knowledge, it caught him by the throat, and he stood there just inside the screen door speechless with wonder at this turn of events. He watched, slack jawed, openmouthed, while her slender shoulders rose and fell. She turned her head, giving him just the point of her elegant chin, a sliver of nostril, the half moon of one brown eye profligate with lash.

Mr. Jackson, is that you?

His heart pounded. She remembered him. She remembered him. She remembered him. He could only nod.

Home from school so quick?

Yes.

She turned to face him. Held out her hand. A bold move, completely unorthodox, he thought, as bold and as unorthodox as he was to take that dry fine-boned member in his own damp palm and give it a good, single shake as if it were the most common thing in the world for a white boy in 1959 in rural Mississippi to take the proffered hand of a Negro girl, a servant in his own home, to show her respect like that, as if there were no difference between them either in race or station. She smiled and raised her eyebrows. It was a haughty look and one of approval also, which for some reason pleased him enormously. He grinned back, showing all his teeth, every one of them, which must have made him look like an idiot or threatening maybe, because then Katherine Marie blinked a few times and abruptly turned back to the pot she was stirring. An uncomfortable silence dangled between them, which Jackson did not know what to do with, so he stood immobile, his lanky arms hanging by his sides.

Are you hungry, Mr. Jackson? Katherine asked at last. Shall I get you something?

Well, a little, but I can fix up something myself. And please, I'm just Jackson. There ain't no one ever called me Mr. to my face and under my own roof except for Big Bokay, and he's been gone now three years. He was a very polite man, of the old school I do believe.

Jackson suddenly remembered that Dr. Sassaport had said the new help was saving for her wedding, and according to what he'd spied last year, surely Li'l Bokay must be the one. Hopefully, she appreciated the awkward compliment he'd paid to a man who would have been her granddaddy-in-law had he lived. Lord, he felt like an imbecile as well as standing there looking like one. She turned to smile at him again, which caused a frantic flutter in his chest.

Alright, Jackson, alright.

Thank you, Katherine Marie. Thank you.

He then started whistling, as he couldn't think what else to do, and bustled about in the pantry for some bread and peanut butter to make himself a sandwich. By the time he finished, Mama's bell rang with all the force her muscled, if hypochondriacal wrist could muster. Katherine Marie brushed past him as she rushed upstairs. Though he ate very slowly awaiting her return, he was long done, patting a finger around his plate hunting for crumbs before she arrived.

Everything alright up there? he asked.

Katherine Marie held a hand up and shook it at him in a frazzled, "I'm too busy to deal with you right now" manner. One after another, she opened, searched, and shut cupboards with alarming speed. Dang, dang, dang, she muttered after each fruitless inspection. What's wrong? What's wrong? Jackson rose from his seat at the table to block her way and plead yet again, What's wrong? before she answered him, irritation studding her words like rivets.

Your mama needs her twisty straws or she cannot drink. Her throat is dry as a bone. It's time for her medication. She has collapsed against her pillows and swears she has not the strength to lift up her head.

Jackson responded with the urgency her irritation, if not Mama's request, demanded, obtaining the twisty straws from their drawer in the pantry with the speed of a champion sprinter.

Here they are, here.

Katherine Marie looked like she might kiss him, she was that happy at his find.

But she did not.

Thank you, thank you, she said with a smile Jackson considered as bright as a hundred lightbulbs switching on all at once, then she bounded back up the stairs to Miss Missy's sickbed.

His heart racing, Jackson sat again and waited. He waited quietly, without movement, so he could hear her approach. He held his breath at every creak of the old house in case it turned out to be her step down the stairs. He listened to the refrigerator hum. He listened to a branch of sweet gum buffet the beams of the back porch. He listened to a door open and close, which caught his breath, but then he heard water rushing through pipes in the wall, realized it had only been the bathroom door, and suffered disappointment. What was Mama doing to her? he wondered. What if Mama got all unreasonable and drove her away? The idea of having Katherine Marie living in his house one moment and banished the next terrified him. Why did he care so much? Although the answer to that question was swiftly becoming obvious to him, he examined himself on it in great detail. Was he simply thrown back by the unexpected sight of her to the moment they met, the panic he'd felt and how she'd saved him? Was it the old gratitude? His childhood vow to even the score with her? Was it that Katherine Marie possessed the only pair of Negro breasts he'd ever seen half-naked? Was it as venal as that? Did he lust after her? Any more than he lusted after every girl he met? Did he love her?

He was on the verge of admitting that last and contemplating the whys and hows and whats of it, when the object of his disturbance reappeared with her hair disheveled and little rings of sweat beneath the armholes of her shift. Jackson pretended he'd just finished his snack and rose to put his plate in the sink.

Mama alright? he asked with his back to Katherine Marie so he could feign a casual manner without betraying himself.

Sure. She needed a little help getting to the facilities and a back rub, is all.

She returned to her stewpot, where she set to scraping the bottom as she'd been gone so long it'd begun to clump up. Dang, she muttered, dang. Jackson looked around the room trying to figure out an excuse to continue hanging around. Then he hit on one he decided was perfect in every way.

Katherine Marie, he said, I'm accustomed to doing my homework in the kitchen. Do you mind? Will I be underfoot?

It was not as if custom allowed her to refuse him. She assured him it was just fine, that her job was to help the family, not get in their way.

They continued their little dance of politesse that first week until it appeared habit for Jackson to return home from school every day and spend as much time in the kitchen as Bubba Ray did in front of the television. He read his texts, scribbled his papers at the Formica table situated not three feet away from her screen and cot while his head filled with images of her sleeping there, in a nightgown if it were cool weather, out of one if it were hot, reading Mama's castoff magazines, listening to the transistor radio on the countertop next to the toaster. Katherine Marie had many duties that took her out of that room, and when she left it, he took a chance now and again to put his nose against her sheets and pillows for the joy of catching the female scent of her, and he was so quick about it not once was he ever caught.

Around suppertime, just before Daddy came home, Jackson would scoop up his belongings and head to his room feeling a reluctance he hesitated to name. Often, he'd forget a pen or a slide rule or some such as an excuse to return after the dishes were washed up so that he and Katherine Marie could exchange a few pleasantries. Or he might find her finishing her chores and help out by putting the silverware away, as, he told her, Mama was very particular about her silver, and perhaps it was best that he took care of it. Every chance he got, he tried to let her know by his comportment that he wasn't like other white boys whose acquaintance she might suffer, in that she was a person to him, not just a retainer or a Negro. He went so far as to engage her on the subject of her upcoming marriage, asking to be remembered to Li'l Bokay, underscoring his friendship with that man in the long-ago. The mention of Li'l Bokay opened her up considerably. By the end of the week, Jackson and Katherine Marie were as easy together as the oldest of friends.

On Friday night, Mama left her bed to come downstairs and have what she called a traditional sabbath dinner. This perplexed Jackson quite a bit. Unless it was New Year's or Passover, they'd never had a sabbath dinner that was in any fashion at all traditional, at least by the lights of how Rabbi Nussbaum described one during his bar mitzvah lessons. Usually on Friday nights, Mama lit candles whenever it was that Daddy got home, whether before sundown or after. Daddy would quick-ass mumble a blessing over the wine and bread, and then they'd have pizza or barbecue Daddy picked up in the city after his evening hospital rounds. Mama said that if it were forbidden to work on the Sabbath she didn't see why she or Cook should have to be scrubbing pots and pans after the family ate, whereas tossing away a pizza box or cartons of coleslaw and rib bones wasn't work at all. Still, in preparation for her first Friday night at the house, Katherine Marie spent much of the day chasing dust, washing table linens, baking braided bread, and roasting chicken. In addition, Mama instructed her to bring out the good crystal and china and lay a party table out for them all. When Jackson got home from school, he found her struggling to polish the giant silver candelabra Mama kept behind glass in the pantry, which hadn't been used in so long the tarnish made it look forged from iron. It was his pleasure to rescue the girl from such a mammoth chore. He sat at the table polishing away while Katherine Marie whisked eggs for vegetable kugel. Mama had unearthed the recipe from the back of a family photo album no one had looked at for as long as Jackson could recall.

This isn't how our Friday nights usually go, he assured Katherine Marie while he rubbed the long stem of the candelabra with a soft cloth. I don't know what's made Mama get these plans into her head.

She's testin' me, Jackson, Katherine Marie replied. Wants to know how much I can take.

No.

Yes.

No, I can't believe that. Mama's generally very considerate of others. Maybe her illness has inspired a religious streak. Yes, I think that's it.

Katherine Marie looked at him as if he were the slowest child in the county.

Alright, she said. If that's what you want to believe. Miss Missy got religion. Just so happens it's the week I start work.

That night at dinner, Katherine Marie served them with a formality Sukie never practiced. She didn't speak unless addressed first, and then it wasn't but "yessum" and "yessir." Jackson tried to catch her eye several times, and complimented her on the table and the chicken, but it was Mama who accepted his compliments and thanked him as if it were she who did the work, not Katherine Marie. It struck Jackson anew that the way he and Katherine Marie related was not usual neither in his house nor in the town, and this awareness both thrilled and touched him until Saturday morning when all his delusions and confused thinking came crashing down on him.

That morning, Jackson lay in bed past nine o'clock, trying to determine what would be a genteel hour to appear in the kitchen of a weekend. Every other day that week, Katherine Marie was dressed and fixing breakfast by the time he went downstairs, but he figured on Saturday she might want to sleep in. He waited until the scent of Daddy's coffee wafted up the stairs before he got washed, dressed, and descended.

Only she wasn't in the kitchen, although everything there was in spotless order. A coffeepot steamed over a shut-off burner on the stovetop. Waxed paper was crimped over a china plate of sweet rolls sitting on the counter next to, but there was no Katherine Marie. He stood outside the hallway powder room for twenty seconds, listening to see if she was perhaps within, but it was quiet as a sealed-up tomb. He stuck his head down the cellar door and said her name in case she'd gone down there for canned goods or some kind of cleaning supplies. Katherine Marie! he called, distinctly though not loudly, as he didn't want to wake everybody else up. She wasn't there, either.

Then Bubba Ray bounced down the stairs in his pajamas, grabbed a sweet roll in each hand, and remarked: Boo-hoo-dee-hoo-hoo. Miss

Jackie's got her heart broke. Li'l Bokay came a while back and took your lady love away. For her weekend home. Oh yes, they gonna be humpin' and gruntin' all weekend long. Poor Miss Jackie's gonna be all forlorn.

Jackson grabbed a broom and raised it to chase the brat out of the room then collapsed into a chair while four facts of life struck him one after the other like blows to the face.

Number one. He was hopelessly in love with Katherine Marie. She was like no girl he'd ever known, probably because she wasn't a girl. She was a woman. And he wanted her, like he'd never wanted anyone ever before. Number two. She was a Negro, a fact of life he could get over in a heartbeat given the strength of his desire. Didn't he hear that preacher on the radio the other day? Saying it was a new day in a new South? And if that day had only recently dawned and promised to be a very long and stormy one indeed, wasn't he moving North in a handful of months anyway? There, he surmised from the way Yankee newspapers, politicians, and social organizations pressured and castigated the South daily on matters of race, Negroes and whites mated every day of the week without raising the hackles of anyone at all. There remained, however, number three. Katherine Marie was a betrothed Negro woman with no romantic interest in him whatsoever, which pretty much took care of number two, although maybe somehow he could get her to change her mind. That left the worst fact of life, the most depressing one, the one a bit scary as well. That left number four.

Bubba Ray wasn't as dumb as he looked. Bubba Ray had him figured out.

SEVEN

Fall 1959, Summer 1960

AFTER HE MADE THE MOST discreet, the most casual of inquiries, Jackson learned from Daddy that Katherine Marie was due to return to work at six a.m. on Monday morning. On Monday, he was up chewing his fingernails in the kitchen by five thirty, full of anxiety that Mama had been too hard on her, and after a long conversation with her fiancé, she'd quit. To cover, he pretended to do last-minute studying at the kitchen table, cleverly choosing a seat that faced the back door. It was warm enough to keep the door open, so he could watch and listen through the screen for L'il Bokay's truck. When that ancient vehicle arrived, full of clatter and sputtering smoke, Jackson jumped up from his chair and stood by the window above the sink, watching Katherine Marie kiss her man good-bye. She kissed him once lightly, but after she'd opened the truck door a smidgen, he pulled her back in with one rough hand on her slender arm and kissed her hard and long, which caused Jackson the pain of a thousand straight pins jabbed into his heart at once.

Well, that sure is an unseemly sight.

At the sound of his daddy's voice, Jackson whirled about. Luckily, the doctor was too preoccupied watching the lovers neck to notice Jackson's agonized expression, which the boy masked as best he could.

I'll have to have Mama instruct that gal in proper behavior on our street. This ain't the village.

Daddy, they're engaged.

I don't care, son. It just ain't right.

I've seen Willy Bowers drop off Caroline Parkman across the way on Saturday night and carry on a whole lot worse than that. They steam up the windows, and then their heads disappear. And they've only been going out two months.

His father chuckled.

Now, if I was told there was a Peepin' Tom under my roof, I woulda sworn it'd be Bubba Ray. Oops, look. He's finally releasing her.

As Katherine Marie exited the truck, her spirits were high. She was laughing, rolling her eyes at something her intended said. When she saw the two Sassaport men watching her, she dropped her gaze. Jackson hurried back to a seat at the table and bent over his paperwork.

Dr. Sassaport, good morning. Have a nice weekend, sir? Can I get you something?

Daddy ordered a hefty breakfast for himself and a light one for Mama, which he instructed Katherine Marie to set on a tray and bring right up to her. He'd be in his study and would appreciate a call when his own was ready. Humming, she started in to fixing the coffee, boiling water for Mama's oatmeal.

How about you, Jackson? You must have played a lot this weekend to be up so early with your schoolwork.

Not really. I was just lazy, is all. And you? How'd your weekend pass?

Oh, it was wonderful, thank you for asking. My Bokay was anointed deacon of our church this Sunday. I was so proud. He's the youngest ever deacon in our church's history. He gave a sermon, you know, on the Book of Revelation and I swear he moved the congregation so they were weepin' and dancin' in the aisles and singin' Praise Jesus! 'til they was frog hoarse. Then we had a big ole church supper to celebrate. I was so proud. So proud.

Jackson's pin-holed heart dropped to the ground, where her joyous banter stomped it to dust. All his impossible dreams of conquering her, of stealing her from L'il Bokay lay stomped to dust next to. He reached deep inside his broken spirit and decided to be magnanimous, noble, and let her go. He said: So you'll be a preacher's wife. That's a very nice life, I would think. I truly hope you will be happy and prosperous.

Katherine Marie laughed. Well, she said, no. There's a heap of learning and service between being a deacon and being a preacher. And anyway there's not much money in it unless you've got the spark and go on the circuit. My Bokay's got the spark alright, but he's got me and two jobs already. He works over to the lumberyard during the day and over to the Tick Tock Diner at night. Once we've got the money together, we're going to send me to nursing school. That's the first thing. After that, I don't know. I truly don't. 'Course we don't know where I'm going to be able to go to school, either. Maybe Tougaloo will take me, but I'd have to take the entrance examinations, and my high school didn't offer them. I was lucky to have a high school that gave me a whole four years of education, never mind college preparation. It's a problem. Bokay says that's why it's a good thing for me to work for your daddy. Maybe he'll take a likin' to me and help me out later on. What do you think, Jackson? Do you think your daddy could help me?

She whipped around from her counterwork to face him, and her young face was so alive, so alight with what Jackson determined was hopefulness and love for her man and their future, that out of his own affection he could not disabuse her of any notion, however foolish, she might possess. Never mind that Daddy came home from his White Citizens' Council meetings every week on fire with indignation over the mischief uppity Negroes concocted at the prodding of communist agitators. Never mind that he swore his head off asserting that if they didn't learn to simmer down and be patient, allow change to occur at a natural speed so that the entirety of the social order would not be derailed and civility lost forever, there was no way the Council could continue to deter the Klan from acting out. Once out of the box, those kluckers would know no restraint. None at all, he'd say. And when they finish moppin' up Main Street with Negro blood, guess who, he'd say, guess who'd be next. Never mind all that. What Jackson said was: I'm sure Daddy'd help you in whatever way he's able. Once he gets to know you better, Katherine Marie.

His reassurance seemed to please her very much. To make good on his words, Jackson sought ways to ingratiate Katherine Marie with his daddy. After a time, Mama felt more secure about the household running along smoothly. She got out of bed and took up a few duties she enjoyed, like shopping and folding laundry. This left Katherine Marie with a little more time on her hands. Jackson, seizing opportunity when Daddy chanced to complain at dinner that he couldn't get any decent help on charity nights, suggested Katherine Marie work at the office on Thursday evenings. If need be, he'd help out Mama at home in her absence, which he wouldn't mind if it made life easier on the doctor. It would be a way, sir, of thanking you before I go off to college, he added, knowing Daddy wouldn't be able to resist the balm of filial devotion. Well, you seem to know her better than any of us, Dr. Sassaport said without the tiniest note of sarcasm. Do you think she's smart enough to handle some of the simpler tasks I give my nurses of an evening? Sterilizing the instruments, fetching the bandage, undressing the ladies, things like that? Jackson thought this an incredibly dense question, since Katherine Marie had been in charge of Mama's health care and all of them really for months now, but he pretended to take the time to formulate a thoughtful response. Daddy waited. Well? Why, yes, sir, I do. Katherine Marie's at the very least as smart as that.

In this way, Katherine Marie became grateful to Jackson and struggled to repay him without incurring the notice of family members who might not approve. She made him special dainties and packed them away in his school lunch. When she ironed his shirts, she sprayed them with rose water first to improve their scent. She always had a smile for him when he came home no matter how her day with Miss Missy went. She helped him with his homework by listening to him explain the theories of his history and science texts and recite the poems and essays he memorized for the public-speaking club. As time went by, she realized she was learning from him things they never bothered to teach her when she was in school, things she needed to know if she were ever to get to nursing school, things she thought Bokay ought to know as well, so she tried to teach them to him in turn on the weekends. In the meantime, the doctor was pleased with her work at the office Thursday nights and considered expanding the scope of her chores. He took to calling her "my best all-around gal." Once or twice, he teased Mama that he needed Katherine Marie more than she did and he just might steal her away.

It seemed to Jackson as if his life at home had obtained a golden burnish like that which adorned ancient treasure described in the Bible. Everyone was happy. Mama was happy. Daddy was happy. Katherine Marie was happy. One might easily surmise Bubba Ray was happy as well, since that hulking devil never played on Katherine Marie the tricks he'd peppered over his brother, his old babysitters, and Sukie. On two occasions, he overheard Bubba Ray speak to Katherine Marie in a honeyed voice and ask if he could help her with this or that. The first time, it made him clench his fists in the hallway. The second, he got in the kitchen right quick to see how Katherine Marie handled him. Bubba Ray saw him and shot him a sly look. Katherine Marie saw him a heartbeat later and told his brother: That's alright, Jackson always takes the garbage out for me, and here he is. Jackson could not resist a chin-up gesture of triumph over Bubba Ray, but then Katherine Marie ruffled the latter's hair like one does a much smaller child than he. It was a tenderness Jackson would have fought for on the field of honor. You go on and play, she said, and Bubba Ray handed off the garbage pail to Jackson with a snicker. He would have been angry, but at least the boy was gone now. He and Katherine Marie spent the rest of their afternoon alone, he with his homework, she with her kitchen chores. In the end, as long as Jackson could continue to focus his life on the Katherine Marie–filled Mondays through Fridays and distract himself on Saturdays and Sundays when her time belonged to Li'l Bokay, he was happy too.

The senior prom came and went. Jackson escorted Felicity Rose Carter. She clung to his arm all night tighter than a tree toad to a windshield in July, which should have pleased him but didn't. It irritated him until he couldn't wait for the last dance to be done and over with. Graduation came and went. Jackson was valedictorian of his class. That hot June afternoon, he gave a speech on the virtues of community service, which was well received. Later there was a party in his honor back at the house attended by the entire Sassaport clan and half the neighbors as well. Katherine Marie couldn't handle the workload for such a huge party by herself even with all the aunts bringing covered dishes, so L'il Bokay was enlisted to help serve along with his cousin Don Edward.

Now up until that very day, Jackson'd avoided any direct contact with his oldest friend, principally because he was afraid his envy would get the better of him. He did watch from behind a curtain whenever L'il Bokay picked up Katherine Marie and whenever he dropped her off. One day, he'd chanced to tell Katherine Marie he admired the way sawing wood and frying steaks had built up her man into a near colossus with arms as wide around as Jackson's own thighs. Sometimes foolish things like that just popped out of his mouth around her. On that occasion, he was trying to make himself look mild enough for her to tolerate a little more intimacy from him. There were times when he burned to clap an arm around her or grip her knee for an instant the way friends did without even thinking about it, but he was afraid how she'd react, so he said stupid things, hoping she might initiate such a gesture herself, which she never did. On that occasion, what she did do was put down the mop she was wringing out, place her hands on her hips, and say: What made you think Bokay was allowed anywhere near the saws at that yard, Jackson? That's a white man's job. He sweeps up the shavings and bags 'em, then he'll go take 'em around to stables and whatnot. He gets thirty percent of what he can sell and has to use his own truck and gasoline to do so. As for fryin' steaks, don't we wish it. He washes the dishes, don't you know. Really, Jackson, really. I think half your mind lives up north already. Must've been born there, 'cause it sure don't know what's what around here.

In any event, on the day of his graduation party, Mickey Moe plied him with celebratory bourbon, which lent him the combination of courage and sentiment required to approach the tall, broad Negro with chiseled jaw and eyes much like his granddaddy's, eyes as old as the earth itself. He wore a hairnet and white gloves along with a rented red jacket that buttoned up high as a priest's collar under his chin while he served silver trays of Aunt Bernice's famous stuffed mushrooms and Aunt Beadie's cheese pies in the God-awful humid air. Drops of sweat beaded his face worse than pox on a lecher.

Why, L'il Bokay, Jackson said, swaying on his feet a little from the bourbon and the heat along with the effort needed to crane his neck and look up at the man, a maneuver made difficult when liquor and dehydration are added to the mix. It's good to see you here. I've been meaning to catch up with you and congratulate you on finding yourself such an excellent bride. Katherine Marie is the treasure of our household, we all just love her.

Yes, Mr. Jackson, sir. I'm sure you all do.

Except for the eyes, the man's features were blank, his voice impassive. The eyes, though, the eyes. They bored into him, through him, and out the other side really. He knows, Jackson thought. He knows how I feel about her. Just then, the brand new graduate of Stonewall High suffered a guilt attack. It came to him as clearly as the death cry of an unknown creature in the wilderness. It wasn't right for him even to imagine poaching on another man's woman, black, white, or purple. He realized this all in a rush and blurted out: It's Jackson to you and yours, L'il Bokay.

Then because he was drunk as well as guilt-ridden, he added: Although it just came to me that Katherine Marie never refers to you as L'il, just Bokay, which name I must hear fifty times a day so I don't know why it took me this long to figure it. Well, it's understandable because you've grown up huge, you know, huge. So you call me Jackson from now on and I'll call you just Bokay.

Bokay wrinkled his brow then favored him with a gentle laugh no one else could hear.

You always were the strangest child, he said.

Mama lumbered by just then. Jackson, leave the help alone. We've got hungry people around here. Go on, L'il Bokay, get on with yourself.

Over that summer, they became friends of a sort again. When Bokay arrived to pick up Katherine Marie and had to wait 'til she finished this or that, Jackson kept him company out on the back porch. He offered fond reminiscence of Big Bokay and also of Eleanor, who, it turned out, was an auntie of Katherine Marie's—startling news to Jackson when first he heard of it. He asked Bokay about his work at the church, about

Katherine Marie's twin sisters, about life at the lumber mill, about the habitués of the Tick Tock Diner just outside of town. He asked his opinion of Charlie Jones's people's boycott that Easter of the white shops on Capital Street in the city, even though his heart raced while he did, since never before had he dared to voice a sympathetic word about the civil rights of Negroes from a chair on his own daddy's back porch. Bokay, for his part, responded politely and with as much candor as he felt wise. Every once in a while one of them said something that struck the other as pretty funny, and Katherine Marie would find them listing back and forth on the porch swing holding their sides and letting raucous guffaws spill out into the night as if the Sassaports were the only family on the street and could make as much noise as they cared to. She'd light into them, telling them to pipe down or Miss Missy was going to sack her for bringing a bad influence into the house. Then she'd plunk down between them, Bokay would whisper in her ear what was tickling them, and she too would start in to giggle and titter until she had to cover her mouth and drag Bokay into the truck to keep the peace.

Jackson worked that summer before Yale at the post office, selling stamps and weighing packages. It was a good job, paid well. He had one of Daddy's Council brothers to thank for it. He worked from eight a.m. to three p.m., pretty much the same hours he'd kept at school. During the month of August, it got stifling hot. Mama felt poorly and took to her bed again. To help out, Jackson did the food shopping on his way home from work, but one day, one very hot day, a day when the air was so thick the packages at the post office sealed themselves, he couldn't tolerate the idea of stopping anywhere on the way home. He decided he'd wait until after he'd had a chance to cool off some over a nice tall glass of Katherine Marie's sweet tea before he did. He walked home feeling he walked through a wall of water. The scent of jasmine and honeysuckle hung in the air heavy as a shroud, which made him yearn for all he was leaving at the start of the fall term before he even left it. The intimation of future loneliness surprised him, and he pondered whether Daddy had been right for once. He arrived home early, when no one was expecting him, which was why he figured no one greeted him when he strolled through the back door. He was about to call out to Katherine Marie to see where she was when he realized, why the cellar, of course, the cellar, where it's cool. And quietly, to surprise her, he opened the cellar door and crept down the steps. He heard something odd, something—he wasn't sure what it was—a tiny scratching sound like mice or rats or squirrels, only there was a grunting sound too, and the sound of feet shuffling against a floor. It was all odd enough that he stopped short and held his breath the better to listen, the better to judge. His eyes got used to the light, and then he saw them.

Bubba Ray and Katherine Marie. Bubba Ray and Katherine Marie locked in a mortal struggle. Bubba Ray had Katherine Marie up against the wall so hard the right side of her face and half her nose was squished against it. He had one raised knee and all of his great belly jammed against her kidneys. Her mouth was open, but his left hand choked her, and she could not scream. His other hand traveled from up high underneath her dress down her thigh heading toward the inside of his pants. He was getting ready to further violate the girl. Katherine Marie saw Jackson, and her eyes widened pleading with him to save her, as if he needed a plea, a cue, a signal with hot blood pounding through his ears. He bolted forward and knocked his brother down. At the time, he felt he'd not had to use much force, that Bubba Ray was imbalanced and the might of his own weight toppled him over himself. Years later Katherine told him he'd called out and charged at Bubba Ray like a goddamn champion bull.

Meanwhile, the adolescent would-be rapist was knocked unconscious and bled from his forehead on the concrete floor. Jackson nudged him with his foot, but the boy lay still. Jackson wondered if he'd killed him. He croaked to Katherine: Get out of here! Quick! Get outta here! And she ran. Ran up the stairs and out the house. He waited 'til he heard the screen door slam and he knew she was safe. Then, still croaking but loudly this time, croaking in fresh shock at the sight of the widening puddle of blood at his feet, he yelled for Mama.

Mama! Mama! Something's gone wrong with Bubba Ray! he yelled.

Hearing emergency in his tone, Missy Fine Sassaport hauled herself out of her nap and rushed to the cellar as fast as her gouty foot allowed. Seeing Bubba Ray sprawled there, spouting blood, frenzied her. She screamed, and Jackson ran upstairs to telephone his father, who told him to wrap up his brother's head and put pressure on the wound. He'd be there directly. What happened? O Lordy, what happened? Mama demanded, never taking her red and weeping eyes off her youngest son, while Jackson blotted his wounds with a dishrag, and Bubba Ray moaned and moaned. He fell, Mama, Jackson said, as it was all he could command his throat to commit to. Daddy got home before fifteen minutes passed, stitched up Bubba Ray's scalp, brought him to full consciousness with smelling salts, and together he and Jackson got him up two flights of stairs and into bed.

Daddy then sent Jackson to the pharmacy, as he'd fled his office so abruptly he'd not taken a full black bag. They needed more bandages, more antiseptics. Jackson hadn't run four blocks down the street when Katherine Marie popped out of some hedges and grabbed his sleeve. Her hair was wild, her eyes were wild, one of them scraped underneath. Her dress was torn at the shoulder, there was dirt and a raw, red mark on her cheek, another broad mark coming out on her neck, and her nose ran.

Do they know? Do they know what happened?

He pulled her back through the hedgerow and put his hands on her shoulders to calm her down. She flinched and shivered at his touch. He released her, put his palms a foot and a half away from her face, patting the air to make what he thought a soothing gesture, up and down, up and down. She batted at them with furious motions and asked again.

Do they know? Do they know what happened?

No. I told them he fell. But I have to tell the truth as soon as everything simmers down, Katherine Marie. It's the right thing to do. He needs correction, and you need justice.

She took his two hands in hers and held them tight: No, no, no. Listen to me. You can't tell. You can't. You don't understand what would happen to me if this came to light.

I'm not so sure, he murmured while his mind spun with about a dozen scenarios she might be referring to. He started to turn his back on her when Katherine Marie grabbed his shoulder and forced him to face her square. Her proud eyes filled up with tears.

Please, you can't. Swear to me, please swear to me. I'll be done in this town if anyone finds out. And Bokay, oh Jackson, I don't know if I could keep Bokay from killing him.

Jackson relented.

Alright, he said. I swear I won't tell. I won't tell a living soul. But I'm going to have to do something. I don't know what it is, but something.

He didn't have the chance right away. The day after Jackson split his brother's head open, Bubba Ray had a seizure. In the middle of the afternoon, he rolled off the television couch where he sprawled milking his convalescence and went klunk on the hardwood floor. His eyes rolled back in his head, his whole body shook, he nearly choked on his own tongue. Not two minutes later it was all over. He was just fine. He never had another seizure in his long, miserable life, but once was enough for Mama, who witnessed the whole episode and never got over the idea that, big as he was, Bubba Ray was fragile and couldn't quite do for himself. Katherine Marie was no help. She never got back to work. Mama decided the girl must have spilled something slick down there in the basement and didn't clean it up, which made Bubba Ray's accident all her fault. The reason she never came back to work was the guilt hung hard over her head. That left Mama to do for her young son.

At first, it looked like Bubba Ray was going to get away with his crime. He certainly thought so, anyway, and took to strolling around the house in his bathrobe casting smug, cynical looks at his brother as if he had something on him instead of the other way around. This was pure torture for Jackson. He spent his daylight hours avoiding home. He spent as many nights as he could sleeping over at Mickey Moe's or the house of whatever school friend's mama would have him. When he had to be home, he avoided his parents' conversation. His behavior did not go unnoticed. To explain it, his parents decided Jackson must be anxious about leaving Guilford for school in another week. For all the boy's bravado, Daddy suggested, Yankeetown prob'ly scares him as well it should, Mama, as well it should. He's never been far away before. He prob'ly doesn't want us to know how scared he is.

The nights he spent at home he spent tossing, turning, clenching his fists and resisting the urge to get out of bed and finish the job he'd started by crossing the hall to Bubba Ray's room and pummeling the pig to absolute death. When that idea got too tempting, he switched over to obsessing about the welfare of Katherine Marie. How was she holding up? he wondered. When would it be reasonable to stop by the village to find out? Five everlasting nights post-incident, he went over there and tracked her down working at a sewing machine at Annie Althea's place, which he knew well because Annie Althea did all Mama's dress alterations. Katherine Marie'd told her family swarms of lies in explanation for her injuries and reasons why she couldn't return to work. She told Jackson that the incident with Bubba Ray was just one of those things that happens to Negro girls. She was strong, she'd get over it as long as he kept his mouth shut, that was the only thing to worry about, anyone finding out. She was very grateful to him for saving her from worse harm, but if he didn't keep quiet everything would have to change. Her whole life depended on things staying the same, as much the same as they could since his brother lay hands on her. While he disagreed, and despite the torment it caused him to dissemble in front of Mama and Daddy and, worst of all, Bubba Ray, Jackson felt he had to respect her wishes. He kept his mouth shut.

Once he was in residence in New Haven, he avoided coming home. He took extra-credit courses and jobs on campus during vacation periods to make his absence look reasonable. Mama and Daddy applauded his industry and ventured up north to visit him during the winter holiday. He did not go home until he had to that summer of 1961, a scant stretch between the summer session and the fall. The night he could hold up to Katherine Marie as proof that she'd been wrong, that there were worse things than anyone finding out, that life was going to change no matter what any of them kept quiet about or exposed under the noonday sun, occurred during that fortnight, the one when all hell broke loose and nothing was the same for Jackson or Katherine Marie or Bokay or Bubba Ray or Daddy, especially poor Daddy, ever again.

EIGHT

Spring, 1964

AT SPRING BREAK, JACKSON AND Stella drove south for her premiere encounter with the Sassaport family. It was uncertain whether Jackson's car could make the trip. Stella itched to take the most favorable seat in a Southern bus or railroad car then give it to the first old black woman she saw and plant her own ass in the back. This was a desire her fiancé determined to thwart at any cost. We'll take the Renault, he told her. There's federal law and then there's custom, and I'd like to see us arrive in Guilford without unanticipated detours. Besides, he continued in what he considered a cajoling tone, freedom rides are old hat. Mama tells me people are startin' in to set wherever they feel they should, and you know all the white Freedom Riders anyway were released from custody before you and I ever met. The very second they were let go, they mostly scurried back north to hold forth in coffee shops and lecture halls. Freedom schools are the thing this year. If you want, we can stop by some of the churches around Guilford where you can sign up to spend time this summer improving the reading skills of those who need it to register to vote. Why, I'll bet you could become a canvasser and register folks door to door. When her eyes developed a kind of misty shine at the thought, he added: Of course, I'll be staying up north to finish school during the summer session. We'd have to be separated. That dulled her gaze right quick, an event that pleased Jackson enormously. He chuckled inside for days and days over it.

He'd figured out something about Stella. He'd figured out that he could manipulate her iron will if he tried hard enough, which he did without guilt if the occasion at hand was truly important. Not that there were many of those. He loved his Stella just the way she was. He had no plan to tame or subvert her in any substantial manner. He honored her remarkable spirit, her intelligence, her goodness. When it came to introducing her to his family and getting her in and out of Guilford unharmed, expediency ruled supreme over adoration or respect. The part that tickled him was that her Achilles' heel appeared to be her devotion to him, which struck him as a most felicitous miracle. If he'd been wiser, he'd have realized that this heel would begin to grow calloused directly after the wedding, at which time the process would advance with such alarming speed that Stella could jig over cut glass without injury before their fifth anniversary. But that spring, Jackson Sassaport was nowhere near as wise as he should have been, neither about Stella nor his family nor the township of Guilford, Mississippi.

He did not, for example, imagine that once they got beyond Washington, DC. Stella would spend the trip plastered to the passenger window, hands up against the glass, marking it with round puffs of breath. When the climate changed from cool to sultry, she opened the window and dangled her head out the car. Despite the guard of large black sunglasses, her eyes squinted against the wind, and her red hair blew in all directions where it was not confined by her Italian silk scarf. Undeterred, she studied the passing countryside as if she'd never been beyond the confines of New England, when he knew for a fact that she'd been to Europe—Paris and London, to be exact—and several times to Chicago, where her mother had family. Everything she witnessed she pronounced unexpected or beautiful or charming or mysterious. She laughed when a pickup full of good old boys and several dogs, too, nearly ran themselves off the road trying to pass Jackson's Renault on the right-hand side in order to get a good look at her. When the car indeed broke down just outside of Knoxville, Tennessee, she expressed awe at the kindness and superlative manners of the grease monkeys who happened by, gave them a tow and, amidst a great deal of head-scratching and hoo-ee's, straightened the engine out despite the fact that it was "furrin." Lordy, Jackson thought, pleased no end as the men doffed their various hats to bid a grateful Stella good-bye, you'd think I'd planned this trip after animal sacrifice to the gods of good fortune and amity.

Whenever she drifted off to sleep while he drove, a sense of foreboding rose up from his gut to threaten him with closure of the throat and suffocation. He had no confidence at all that Stella would keep the promises he'd extracted from her that she not confront Bubba Ray, especially in front of Mama and Daddy, and that she try her hardest this first trip to stand back and observe the way things were back home before she did something rash and made a damn Yankee fool of herself. Things are different there, he'd say. Things aren't always what they might appear. At the same time, first impressions mean everything. Oh, she shook her head and made her vows alright, telling him she just wanted his family to like her, that her love for him was stronger than her politics, stronger than her lust for social justice, it was the strongest entity in the world to her. The way he'd stoically borne the insults of her family inspired her, she would perform no less honorably with his. When she listened to him wax sentimental about Guilford, it was with such concentrated attention that he felt the sharpened tendrils of her critical capacities curl through his brain cells like tiny beasts of the night trolling for sustenance. That unnerved him, no matter what her oaths.

After they crossed the state line into Mississippi, Jackson's disquiet grew. It was not only his anxiety about Stella but also his own attitudes that unsettled him. He hadn't been home in three years. Twice Mama and Daddy had visited him up north, but since that disastrous trip home the summer after his first year at Yale, he'd not returned. Instead, he took such a heavy load of courses each term, including the summer one, he was already halfway through law school. He'd graduate and study for the bar in a year. Mama was too proud of her son the genius to question his motivations. Since Daddy's business had understandably fallen off since that terrible night during Jackson's one and only previous trip home, there were economic rationales for his ambition as well. The real reason he'd driven himself to achieve what few in the entire history of the Ivy League had managed was that he couldn't bear the idea of coming home and living under the same roof as Bubba Ray. He couldn't tolerate sharing a meal, a holiday—damn, a sidewalk—with him. He hated him. It was as plain and simple as that. He hated his brother. He hated him for everything he'd done, and then he further hated him for keeping him from home, which to tell the truth, he dearly missed up there in the frozen, rude, careless North. He wished his brother would die.

We'll be home in about ten minutes, darlin', Jackson told Stella once they'd crossed the Guilford town line. She came alert immediately, pulled down the visor on her side of the front seat, and reapplied her lipstick, brushed her hair, popped a stick of Dentyne in her mouth to sweeten her breath. She didn't speak but reached over to squeeze his arm with edgy anticipation. Nothing they passed, no detail however small, escaped the silent, studied gaze she cast over the landscape. They'd entered from the north end of town, where the farms were and the river and then the vistas of suburban variety sprang into view: postwar, redbrick ranch-style homes proudly perched atop manicured lawns, then Main Street with its shops and the site of Daddy's old medical office, which Jackson duly pointed out, and at last on the southern end, sprawling wood structures sinking by the sheer weight of their years into half-acre lots dotted with flower and vegetable gardens backed up by a forest of ancient, venerable trees. He pulled into the driveway of one of the oldest homes. He waited a moment while she took it in: the long portico with its vine-covered columns and rocking chairs, the flowerbeds at the foot of the wrought-iron staircase leading up to Mama's potted rhododendrons in early bloom, the balcony off the master bedroom. Well, darlin', he said. We're here. She took his hand and held it firmly, gently. It's like a picture book, she said. Oh, my darling man grew up in a picture book, fancy that. She gave him one of her piercing, steady looks. You know, everything's going to be alright, she said. Really, it's going to be ok.

Mama appeared on the verandah just then, leaning on her cane, a big smile planted on her face. Apart from the cane, she looked vital to Jackson—young, even. Her hair was arranged in large, loose curls, plastered with hairspray and dyed a sparkling auburn. She had makeup on. Thick brown pencil gave a vigorous arch to her eyebrows, waxen coral a glisten to her lips. Given her weight, her face was smooth, free of wrinkles, the eyes bright as new coins. She had her good watch on and her ruby cocktail ring, a crisp flowered dress. It touched him that she'd gone to such a troublesome toilette to meet Stella. He got out of the car, opened the opposite door, helped her out. Hand in hand they approached his beaming mother who opened her arms and jiggled her fingers, urging them into her embrace. Once she had them in her grasp, she squeezed them good, then let her son go, held Stella out at arm's length, cupped her face in her hands to study her. Oh, you're a pretty one, aren't you, dear? I can see what has besotted my son so. Well, welcome. Come on in, you must be tired and hungry. Sweetheart, your daddy and Bubba Ray are out. They had to go into the city for a medical appointment. They extend their apologies. They'll be home later on this afternoon, I do hope before dark.

Jackson, much relieved, inquired: Is Daddy doin' ok, Mama?

Well, he's better than the last time you saw him anyway. But, Lord, that was a while ago wasn't it? Well, you're busy, busy, busy outshining all your classmates day and night, I suppose. How on earth have you found time to land yourself a redheaded beauty? I don't know, Stella, dear, what made this boy of mine so industrious. He wasn't much of a student as a child, you know, but he sure has made up for it.

Mama continued to ramble on while they entered the house, deposited their bags in the foyer, and were hustled into the dining room, where the table was set for a formal lunch. It was half-past one in the afternoon, a good hour beyond Mama's traditional midday meal. Jackson thanked her for waiting for them and admired her service, the flowers. We'd like to freshen up a bit, though, he added, then showed Stella to the half-bath downstairs while he rushed upstairs to pee and wash his hands, splash cold water on his face, hurrying back down as fast as he could so Mama would have less time alone with his fiancée.

Too late. Stella and Mama were head-to-head practically, whispering about God knew what. They didn't hear him enter at first, and Jackson watched Mama take her arm and put it around Stella's shoulder then squeeze in a gesture he could only interpret as one of comfort or encouragement, a fact that mystified him completely. Then they noticed him. In tandem, both heads shot apart from each other as cheek to jowl they were 'til that moment, cheek to jowl, he registered, imagine that. Their two sets of eyes bored into him with an intensity that left him no choice but to wonder what it was exactly he'd done wrong. Stella broke the ensuing silence—a brief one, so very brief, but also tremendously heavy—first.

Sweetheart, she said brightly, your mother's been explaining to me her theory about Mombasa and what happened to your father.

Oh, Lord, Jackson thought. After the physical presence of Bubba Ray, this was precisely to the letter what he did not want to face before he had a chance to recover from the drive. He'd hoped it would take at least a day or two 'til Mama got around to pointing fingers.

Mama. Don't. Not a soul on earth knows what really happened except me and Bokay, and no one believes either one of us. Besides that, I'm hungry.

The accused's words are always suspect, dear, and you were concussed. What you think you know is all in your head.

Like I said, no one believes me, and I'm hungry. Why don't we just eat a calm and pleasurable meal as we're right off the road and maybe tomorrow, maybe tomorrow in the afternoon we can have us a good old-fashioned Sherlock Holmes hour of fact finding and conjecture. Really, Mama. I've bragged to Stella about Southern hospitality until I'm sure she's disappointed there wasn't a red carpet laid out on the front steps for her. So couldn't we indulge in a little of it first?

All sweet submission, Mama bowed her head then peeped upward at her son in angelic apology. Her upper lip pursed itself while the lower jutted out in a plump, pleading pout. It was, to be sure, a somewhat grotesque image she provided, like something twisted out of Tennessee Williams. Stella's eyes went wide watching her. A tiny guttural sound issued from her throat, representing the heroic containment of gargantuan amusement. Jackson widened his own eyes, cautioning her. At the same time, his chest felt a stabbing pain that was, he knew, embarrassment for Mama and anger, too, at his darling Stella for finding her ridiculous. Mama couldn't help what she was, and what she was was something deserving of respect. What could Stella possibly know about Mama's upbringing in the backroom of a warehouse, the bargains she made to achieve her status as a Jewish doctor's wife, the double-barreled burden of Bubba Ray and Daddy's reversal of fortune, the graceful way she bore it? Yes, she was a provincial with mannerisms as quaint, as antique, as they were comical to Yankee eyes. After three years up north, he could admit that. Hell, they were all provincial down here, but where was it written provincial was such a terrible thing? And Stella, he wanted to say out loud, what makes you think your self-righteous sophistication is any holier? These thoughts occurred in virgin territory of Jackson's mind. He was unaccustomed to criticizing either his mother or his lover, and the novelty of it confused him, made him breathe dangerously fast. His face turned a vibrant red, so he mumbled something about the heat and his blood sugar and sat down opposite Stella, touching his foot to hers under the table with more underscored warning than affection. Stella turned her head away from Mrs. Sassaport, offering him a clandestine expression: one eye half shut, the opposing eyebrow raised. Later, he muttered through clenched teeth, later. He fanned his napkin noisily in the air then placed it over his lap.

Mama was oblivious to everything, although Jackson suspected her apparent ignorance was a pose, a valiant nicety to spare her future daughter-in-law the pain of acknowledging her rudeness. Holding her hands aloft close to her left ear, she clapped them twice rapidly like a flamenco dancer. In a matter of seconds, an elderly black woman, as thin as Mama was portly, stuck her head through the dining room door. Eula, Mama said, bring on the dinner, please. Alright, Miss Missy, Eula said, then reappeared with a tureen and ladle from which she dispensed a cold cucumber soup into the china bowl set in front of each diner. Mama introduced her. Eula this is my son Jackson, of whom you have heard so much, and this is his fiancée, Miss Stella Godwin of Boston, Massachusetts. Children, this is our latest and greatest major doma, Eula Rawlins, who has taken the place of Nora Jean, who replaced Ethel the Red, as Daddy called her, who replaced Sister

Cynthia, who replaced Katherine Marie, who remains affianced I do believe to the infamous Mombasa Cooper, whom my entire family and this entire town knows as L'il Bokay. Mama flung herself back in her chair enormously satisfied with her recitation. Jackson smiled weakly, then turned in his chair to look about the breakfront for a bottle of just about any kind of drink, as he was beginning to feel a distinct need.

How do you do, Miss Rawlins, or is it Mrs.? Stella asked. This appears very excellent soup.

Eula glanced at Mama sideways, and the two of them shared a heavenly host of thoughts before Eula answered: Thank you, Miss Stella. As a matter of fact, I do have a husband of thirty-five years but please call me Eula, or I'll think my mother-in-law's come to call. If you'll excuse me now, I've got your next course to attend to. Mr. Jackson, you lookin' for somethin'?

A little white wine would go well, Eula, if there's some about. Or a beer.

Yessir. I'll locate you somethin' like.

Why, whenever did you become a drinking man, Jackson? Mama's voice had an edge of concern beneath its playfulness.

Stella laughed. Jackson? A drinking man? Hardly, Mrs. Sassaport. Every once in a while when he's tired or overworked or celebrates the unusual, I've seen him take more than a drink or two. But compared to the boys at the university, he's the soul of sobriety.

Well, it is the middle of the afternoon, dear, and there's plenty of ice tea on the table. You cannot blame me for jumping to conclusions. And I think you should get used to calling me Mama, don't you?

Eula reappeared with a dusty bottle of Passover wine left over from holidays past, which she wiped with her apron and set before Jackson along with a juice glass. Jackson twisted the top open, quickly poured, then quaffed four or five inches of the stuff. It was sweet, it was musty, full of silt. It tasted terrible, but he was feeling punky, damn punky, and he didn't care. He would've tried rubbing alcohol if that were all there was in the house. As he drank, the conversation between Mama and Stella experienced lulls in the course of which each glanced at him with a certain longing, the hope that he'd fill in the gaps. The wine tied his tongue. Or maybe it was exhaustion from driving all the way from Connecticut to Mississippi, their longest stop at the garage in Tennessee. Or maybe he was just annoyed with the two of them and in a punishing mood. In any event, he did not accommodate.

After clearing the soup bowls, Eula served the cheese grits and fried catfish, accompanied by a side of greens atop of which she'd crumpled up crisps of bacon. Mama watched Stella push the bacon aside with her fork. Oh my Lord, she said. It never occurred. Are your people kosher, dear? Stella blushed. Well, yes, they are. I'm not particularly, but still I've never eaten pig. Mama shot a look of reprimand in Jackson's direction. You could have told me, son, it said, rather than subject me to this highly uncomfortable moment. Jackson poured himself another few fingers of wine. Mama smiled bravely and launched into her safest topic: family.

Tell me about your people, she said to Stella, I hear they are quite established in Boston, going back how long exactly? I only ask because I do believe one of the Sassaportas of Virginia ventured up north around the same time the Mississippi Sassaports settled here. I recall hearing it was Boston to which he repaired and I believe it was a Goodman family he married into. That wouldn't be a variant of your own name, now would it?

Jackson nodded off in his chair.

A door slammed somewhere, and he came alert to a carousel of rotating roses from Mama's tablecloth. His head hurt, his mouth was jammed up with dust. When his vision steadied, he watched Mama's torso twist backward and Stella's face turn similarly toward the dining-room entrance. Stella's gaze was especially bright, radiant with the light of her hard, clear intelligence. It was that intense look she had when she analyzed something foreign to her, something that excited her curiosity. Oh, Lord, he thought. Lord, it's Daddy and him, isn't it. I am not ready. But he slapped a smile on his face anyway and, stoic as a Christian martyr, rose to his feet, reeling his aching head in the direction of the table's attention.

Daddy went directly to a spot between Mama's and Stella's seats at table, bent over to kiss Mama's cheek, then bowed a little and took Stella's hand. The eye patch he wore together with his seersucker suit and thick head of gray hair gave him a rakish look. For half a second, Jackson was sure Daddy was going to go Prussian, click his heels, and kiss her hand. But he did not. Instead, he took his gloved hand, the one that stuck out from the edge of his silken sling, and cupped her chin. So this is my new daughter, he said. Ain't she pretty, Mama? Here, stand up for me, girl. Turn around so I can get a good look at the whole of you. Oh my, Mama, she's a bit thin, don't you think? We're going to have to fatten you up, child, if we're ever gettin' grandbabies out of you.

Daddy had his first sight of Jackson in more than a year, nearly two. You look well, son. Glad to see they haven't worn you down to a nub. The two maneuvered around the table to hug each other briefly, after which Jackson returned to his chair and Daddy sat down at the head of the table opposite Mama, calling out: Eula! Eula! The man of the house would like sustenance! Then he took to banging his good hand against the table, which he apparently intended to keep up until the woman appeared. Mama looked at Jackson and said: Ever since the accident, you know, he's become downright effusive. She turned toward Stella to further explain her husband's boisterous manner: I believe he sincerely thought he bounced off of death's door, and this gave him a renewed, no, a redoubled zest for life. We can hardly contain his spirit.

No, Mama, Jackson wanted to interrupt. He does not have a renewed nor a redoubled zest for life, he's just gone stone-cold crazy is all. And it was not an accident in the sense you describe it. Not at all. But he could not say this in front of the damaged man that was his father. He and Stella exchanged a look of understanding. She knew what was what. He'd told her enough. So she smiled at Daddy and put her hand on his good wrist to keep the racket down and asked: I hear you had an appointment today. How did it go?

Bubba Ray's voice, a low, slurred rasp, a caricature of a gentleman's drawl, came from the hallway. A steel claw took hold of Jackson's nerves and rattled every inch of him.

He's comin' along, Bubba Ray said. Well as anyone can expect.

The great hulk of his brother stood in the doorway, filling it up, each arm spread out to grasp the frame, supporting his heft there, so that he looked to Jackson like nothing so much as a gorilla about ready to swing. Mama made introductions, and Stella got up again to give his brother a kiss on his cheek, an incomprehensible act that flummoxed Jackson into mute awareness of the changes in Bubba Ray, the changes that three years had wrought.

Bubba Ray, the detested, the dark, the devil, was bigger than ever, adult-sized yet soft-looking, with a full beard of stubble. It struck Jackson that there was no member of his family the boy resembled, neither immediate nor distant. As far as he could tell, there were no such heavy eyelids anywhere on the Mississippi Sassaport family tree or on the Fine, no such curlicue hair or long baby jowls sloping over a stubbled jaw. Surely, thought Jackson, and not for the first time, there was a clever, lively teenage boy handsome and fine-boned who was living somewhere in Hinds County with a tribe of dull giants, that unfortunate child who'd got mixed up somehow in the hospital with this alien, Bubba Ray. Hanging on to the lintel by one overlong arm, the creature in question then gestured to him with a wide sweep of the other.

I would say it's good to see you, brother, he said, but we both know that's not true.

Jackson would have agreed, but Mama erupted into a chain of giggles as if Bubba Ray's rare effort at honesty was an example of great wit. Those boys of mine, she said to Stella, who had returned to her chair, always joking each other. Always.

Eula appeared with a plate full of fish and grits for Daddy, asked Bubba Ray what he wanted, and soon the whole family was seated together while Mama chatted about the Cousins Club meeting she'd organized over the weekend to introduce Stella to the extended clan. Daddy busied himself eating, Bubba Ray slurped his soup, and Jackson poured himself more wine.

When the meal was over, Stella required a lie-down, and it was time for Mama's daily nap as well. Mama took Stella upstairs to Jackson's childhood bedroom and instructed him that he would be spending his stay downstairs on the couch in Daddy's study, which Eula had taken great pains to set up. Something told him he didn't want Stella up there at close quarters to Bubba Ray without himself positioned as buffer, but he was too groggy to express an objection. After he was ensconced in the doctor's study, Jackson found Daddy's store of bourbon quick enough and hit that bottle as well, feeling a wild sense of incaution so uncommon to him it amounted to rebellion. He found this satisfying without in the least comprehending why.

A soft voice in his ear woke him, but when his eyes fluttered wide apart, there was no one there. He was unsure what time it was, but it was dark, and the house was still. His head pounded, his throat was raw. He headed toward the kitchen for water and saw the lights were on. According to the living-room clock, it was just after eleven. Now, he distinctly recalled Mama telling them that Eula slept at her own home, that it was impossible to get a good girl to live in anymore, failing to mention the equally relevant fact that the family could no longer afford a live-in. He remembered that conversation for the bristle in Stella's spine at the word "girl" and how he'd nudged her under the table to silence any wisdom she'd try to dispense to Mama on the subject of the proper way to speak about women of color. He arrived at the kitchen, wondering why it was alight, when to his utter shock and dismay he saw Bubba Ray and Stella there at the breakfast table chatting over tea in their bathrobes. Much perturbed, he said: What are you doing? and the two of them looked up startled, uncomprehending so he repeated: What are you doing? And Stella said: Why, getting to know each other.

Bubba Ray rose and made a great display of yawning, then slapped his flabby arms against his sides. I am very tired after taking care of Daddy all day. You've been gone so long you cannot know what I mean by that. So I leave you to your lady. He nodded his head to Stella then quit them with a sharp turn, flourishing the hem of his bathrobe, as if he were a knight errant soaked in manners and nobility and Jackson was a no-account peasant, lending emphasis to his crack about Jackson's prolonged absence, making him out the bad son and Bubba Ray the good. The insult caused Jackson's fists to clench, his jaw to stiffen. He was about to shout at his brother's back when Stella put her hands on him. She pushed him into a seat, the effect of which was to cause him to swallow his words and silence him. She took his tortured face in her hands and spoke in a voice of command: Do not get so excited. It's ok, I have experience in dealing with these characters. Remember, I'm a social worker. I know these troubled young men, and I've been trained in how to talk to them. He doesn't frighten me. Oh, Lord! Jackson said loudly, only out of luck not waking the entire household. Oh, Lord! you do not know of what you speak!

Horrified with himself, he started to weep and then he started to blubber in a way that humiliated both of them. To blubber was unmanly. To blubber took every dictum of Southern chivalry and tossed them into the landfill. But he could not help himself. There was so much he hadn't told her. That first night they spent together in New Haven, the night he'd put a chink in the stone wall that was his vow to Katherine Marie, he'd only told her that someone had threatened Katherine Marie, that he rescued her, without mentioning exactly who the villain was and how he'd hurt her. Over time, he convinced himself that was alright. He hadn't named names nor given gory details. When he told her about that event's repercussions the next year, he left more out than he told, so that seemed alright, too. Only on that warm night under his family's roof did he tell her everything. Every last bloody detail. He felt terrible about betraying Katherine Marie in this way, but while he was talking he convinced himself that she had been wrong to exact a vow of silence from him in the first place. Who was he telling, after all? He was telling his beloved, his future wife. Wasn't a man entitled to have no secrets from his wife? And he told her about the vow part, it wasn't as if he forgot that in the telling. In fact, that was the part most difficult to get out of his mouth but also the most exhilarating to reveal. Stella petted him and kissed him, telling him she understood, that there are secrets so hard to bear they cannot be kept, reminding him he could trust her, she would not talk, who could she tell? Her voice, her touch was like a balm spread over a wound that had never really closed, a sore wound he'd got used to bearing until that balm was spread cool and soothing over it and the healing of it stood in contrast against the soreness like day does against night.

Oh, I need this, he thought. I need to tell someone. This secret is killing me.

Then it all came out. He told her everything he'd omitted before, told her what happened that night three years before, the summer after Bubba Ray's assault of Katherine Marie.

NINE

—◇◇◇—

Summer, 1961

JACKSON CAME HOME FROM COLLEGE late that summer before the fall semester of his sophomore year. Much as he longed to embrace his mama and bask in the admiration of his daddy, which given his grades he was certain the man could no longer deny him, he did not venture home until he knew Bubba Ray was gone to summer camp like all young people his age who could were that time of year. Jackson couldn't handle being alone with Bubba Ray. It was the second week of August and dreadful hot. He slept on the hammock on the front porch rather than inside the house, which would have killed him after a whole year up north. He'd got used to that thin air, how the day's warmth died at night sudden as a thunderclap. His very first night home he was sleeping hard by the light of a full moon when a hand on his arm awakened him. It was L'il Bokay, snuck up in the night. When he saw him, he tried, he tried like hell not to look in any way startled or annoyed, because the foremost thing in his mind that summer was finding out how Katherine Marie was. He would have thought his trip home a failure had he not determined how she was, that sweet, wronged girl who rose up like a ghost between him and all his conquests of the preceding year, conquests not inconsiderable in number. He was hoping to run into her or L'il Bokay so he could find out if she was alright, and here her future husband was crouching by his side with a finger held up to his pursed lips to caution him not to cry out. Jackson's throat was dry as a Nevada desert and his muscles were tight, ready to spring should the need arise, but he said as if it were high noon and the occasion a lunchtime meeting planned well in advance: Why, Bokay, how are you?

Bokay answered in an urgent whisper.

Forgive me, Jackson. I've been waitin' and I've been watchin', ready to swoop right in and talk to you whenever you got home and the moment seemed right. I guess this moment ain't quite right, but here I am anyway as the moon's so bright I saw you from the street when I passed. It appears my courage and the very stars have aligned in a moment of opportunity. I cannot wait another second. There's somethin' I must ask you, somethin' I need quite desperately to know, and I believe you and you alone can give me the answer. May we talk, Jackson, in honor of all past friendship?

Jackson rubbed his eyes, smacked his lips, nodded, and stretched although his heart raced.

Let's go to my truck and talk, then. It's just there, down the driveway, where I thought it might escape notice from the house.

Alright, Bokay. Alright.

He pulled the blanket up from his feet and wrapped himself in it. Not because he was cold but because he was dressed only in his shorts and felt without armor in the presence of this man and needed some. They got in the truck.

Bokay. Oh, poor Bokay. Although the windows were down, his presence in the cab overwhelmed Jackson. He was large, large like

Bubba Ray, and then there was his scent—the sour, pungent scent of a man in panic, a scent that blended with the scent of the night, of honeysuckle and gumbo mud, heavy, confusing in the nostrils. It was a scent that forced one to breathe shallow because it seemed as if it might kill you contained in full in the lungs, it would kill you all at once, like a gaseous poison. It was the scent of masculine despair, of a man's heartbreak. It was a very different scent from that of a woman's comparable extremes. A woman's emotion blends with the earth in a natural way, Jackson thought. They become part of the whole instantly, connecting to it without resistance, like a child that fastens to its mama's teat moments after birth, without being shown where or how or why. For a man there is a rending to contend with and it comes out from his pores in fumes. This is what he smelled when he breathed Bokay in. He stiffened his back. He knew from that scent what he was going to ask.

Jackson, he said. Jackson, I believe somethin' happened to Katherine Marie in your house last year. I don't know what it was. I only know that somethin' happened. She's been different ever since she left your place. First, it was just a little. First off, it was in a way only I would notice, because I love her and she's my own. But it's grown. Doubled itself or maybe tripled. See, she started out just kinda jumpy. She quit your family after fallin' down the stairs at the library where she'd stopped on her way home to return a book for your mama, least that's what she said, and the very next day went jumpy. She went jumpy always when it was dark, sometimes in the daylight if it was especially quiet, and she went jumpy whenever we went into town, day or night. Next, little by little she froze out on me. It might be a kiss she did not return, then it was an arm around her she shuffled off without cause, then it was any kind of touch. Doesn't matter who touches her—me or her auntie or one of the twins—if she gets touched she shudders or flinches. I don't know if you know this, Jackson, but this is a gal warm by nature, hot-blooded you might say if you'd a mind, headstrong and independent, suddenly gone cold and frightened. And I can only think after analyzin' the timing of everythin', analyzin' 'til I am sick at heart, that somethin' happened to her in your house, Jackson. And I want you to tell me right here, right now, exactly what it was.

Jackson shifted in his seat. He squirmed. He wrapped the blanket more tightly about himself. He blushed. He stammered. He denied all knowledge of anything amiss. He told him he was very sorry to hear that Katherine Marie seemed troubled, but there was nothing he could add to his knowledge about what was wrong with her. He asked: What does she say the trouble is? Does she acknowledge it?

He didn't answer. He stared instead, leaned over and put his large black self not ten inches from Jackson's face to peer at him with the sweat rolling down his brow and the scent of him nearly choking his childhood friend.

I don't believe you. You know somethin'.

Jackson made his eyes as innocent as he could and dragged up from the deep, warm place where he had buried all the love he had for Katherine Marie, the love that honored his vow that he not tell a soul what had happened in the basement that afternoon a year now past. It evened his voice and he swore again:

I do not know what you're talkin' about. I do not know anything.

The other man searched his eyes a second time. A silence stretched out between them with those tortured features stuck in Jackson's face for what felt like forever while he wondered if Bokay would blow up and kill him.

Dang it, I believe you, Bokay said at last. I believe you. You're the only one in your house she speaks kindly of, Jackson. Mention anybody else and she curls her lip. So I'm going to believe you. Dang it, I have to.

Suddenly, the man let out a strangled sob and fell back against the driver's seat. He grabbed the sides of his hair and tore at it, then crossed his arms over the steering wheel and buried his head there and his whole body shook.

I'm nothin' without her, Jackson. And I've lost her somehow.

Jackson didn't know what else to do so he put a hand on Bokay's back, made circles, and patted as if he were an infant needing a burp.

You haven't lost her, Bokay. She loves you, he said. When she was working for us, if somethin' went wrong and she got down, all I had to do was mention your name and she picked right up. Half her conversation was about you and your future. That kind of affection doesn't just up and die. Maybe she got the weddin' jitters. Is your date soon?

Bokay picked his head up from the steering wheel and studied him again.

Thank you, Jackson, for those words, he said. Suddenly, his features lit up with hopefulness. Listen. It occurs to me that you two always talked easy. Maybe if you kindly spent a little time with her, she'd tell you how she feels, tell you what's wrong.

I don't know, Bokay. It's been a long time . . .

His face crumbled. It hurt to see a proud, strong man ruined like that, especially the hero of his long-ago. And the idea of spending time with Katherine Marie was definitely attractive, especially now his fears for her state of mind were more or less confirmed. Jackson switched gears. But I don't see how it could hurt.

Bokay brightened in a heartbeat. How about right now? She got a night job over to the rest home on Dalrimple. We could stop by. There's not much that goes on in there at this hour, everybody's drugged-out and sleepin'. How about it?

Jackson laughed and waved his blanket around.

I go over there like this and they might admit me, Bokay, against my will.

He smiled and said, Ok, then tomorrow night?

Alright, Bokay. Tomorrow it is. Around eight, how's that? We can meet here at the end of the driveway. My folks will be watching the TV. They won't notice.

The men shook hands and quit company. Jackson spent the next twenty-one hours in a state of extreme, if conflicted, excitement. The idea of seeing Katherine Marie again was thrilling in itself, but the specter of all that had happened the previous year, his vow to her, and the difficult task Bokay set before him colored that thrill considerably. He wondered if he went to embrace her hello if she'd shudder or flinch. Preparing all manner of speeches for her mentally, Jackson took a shower after dinner, put on a clean shirt, and pants. Got a hot date, son? Mama asked. No, Mama, just gettin' together with some old friends tonight. Jackson believed she would have asked more questions, which might have left him in a pickle, but Daddy called out, Missy, honey, *What's My Line*'s nearly over, and she hurried off. Jackson walked down to the street at ten to eight to wait for Bokay, but he was already there. They nodded gravely to each other and Jackson got in the truck.

Maybe they should have waited until later in the night. It was still light out, the sun had just begun to set. They stopped at a traffic light and next to them in a green Ford Maverick drinkin' beer were Joey Hicks and Earl Bob Turner. Those two had not changed a hair since the days when they'd torment Jackson on his way home from school, push him in the mud, and steal his books. They were white trash then and they were white trash to that day without a stop in between. They saw Bokay and Jackson together and this struck them as funny. They set in to whoop and hit the dashboard with the palms of their hands and Joey Hicks gunned the motor. Jackson had learned a few things about defending himself since he was six years old and he'd learned more up north. He was about to give them the New Jersey finger when Bokay spoke up.

147

Do not look at 'em, he said. Do not meet their eyes. Remember where you are and who you're settin' besides.

Aw, come on, Bokay. They're rilin' me.

His hand rose from where it rested. Bokay reached over to grip his wrist and hold it down. Jackson winced under his force.

What's the matter with you, Jackson? Didn't you read a newspaper or listen to the radio up there in Yankeetown? Watch news on the TV? Don't you know what's been goin' on here all summer? You wanna get us killed? Those boys are kluckers. I know that for a fact. How do you think they got that fancy car? Ever know either one of 'em to hold any kind of job longer than a week? Lord knows what kind of mischief they're up to tonight. I know for a fact they spent most of the month of May holed up in the Busy Bee Inn out there on Route 55 makin' forays over to the bus station in the city every day lookin' for heads to crack. They found 'em. Believe you me, they found 'em.

Chastened, Jackson stared ahead and mumbled: I thought things were quiet since the riders were released.

Quiet. That's a good one. Quiet.

Bokay's tone stung. Jackson felt ignorant. Disloyal. It was true he'd kept his nose out of the news from back home as much as he could get away with. Current events made sore his heart. They frightened him on behalf of all his loved ones back home, embarrassed him in front of his college peers. He relied on telephone calls from Mama to keep up. She was more anxious to talk about Daddy and Bubba Ray than racial politics. That's Jackson's heartache, she'd say. Guilford's a whole other kettle of fish. The day things change around here is the day the heavens split open and the Messiah comes. You can thank your daddy's Council for that. They make sure the Klan's lid's screwed on tight. Jackson was young. He chose to believe her.

Bokay clearly fumed beside him. He attempted to defend himself: Mama told me things were much the same in Guilford. There were no incidents here.

What makes your mama think she'd know if folks in my part of town get harassed and worse by the likes of those two boys? Everything that happens in Jackson just fires 'em up. There's more trouble for all of us, and I include your own people in that. Most of those civil rights workers are New York Jews. Don't think that little detail escapes the minds of our neighbors here, tiny as those organs might be.

The light changed. Laughing their heads off, Joey Hicks and Earl Bob Turner peeled out, leaving them their dust to eat. Bokay drove under the speed limit awhile giving them a chance to get a good distance ahead. The Riverside Rest Home on Dalrimple was situated over on the outskirts of town. Jackson knew one way over there, straight down Main Street, right at the feed store, but the roads Bokay took were foreign to him, stretches of dirt lined with nothing but deep, weedy trenches and trees. They went over wooden bridges past fence lines Jackson never knew existed. Bokay was taking an evasive route in case those boys were up the road waiting to trap them. But at the time, Jackson began to feel a tad uncomfortable wondering where all in the backwoods Bokay was taking him. He wondered if Bokay already knew everything and was going to take revenge on the Sassaports through him, that his skeletal remains would be found years hence with no forensic evidence left intact to tell the cruel tale of his unjust demise. He'd heard the anger in Bokay's voice, anger he'd never heard outta him in all his life when surely there were occasions in the past when a public display of anger was called for, even fools such as Jackson readily acknowledged that. Then he recalled that vengeful fantasies were unlikely in the man, since Bokay was a churchgoer, a deacon, a pastor in training, and the song he was humming under his breath, presumably to calm himself, was "I'm So Glad," which Jackson happened to know. To calm his own self, he started singing it over the accompaniment of his basso hum.

> *I'm so glad, Jesus lifted me,*
> *I'm so glad, Jesus lifted me,*
> *singing glory hallelujah, Jesus lifted me.*
>
> *Satan had me bound, Jesus lifted me,*
> *Satan had me bound, Jesus lifted me . . .*

Bokay turned to stare at him in surprise, then laughed out loud and joined him in full voice. He slapped the steering wheel with his hand to guide their rhythm and they sang together louder and faster verse by verse until they quit the woods and came out all of a sudden onto the battered blacktop of Dalrimple Street with its strand of streetlamps. There weren't so very many, it was a poor gal's adornment, but what there were gave off what seemed a sunburst of miraculous light after the darkness of their way and Jackson sighed and said: Well, praise the Lord, here we are! And they both broke out into huge grins, Jackson with relief, Bokay with genuine humor. How'd you know that song, Jackson? You meet Jesus up north? And Jackson grinned then with genuine humor of his own. No, no, no. But you can hardly grow up 'round here without learning a gospel song or two. Bokay pulled up to the back entrance of Riverside Rest Home and parked his truck in the service lot with the other cars belonging to the night workers. Well, you sang it right fine, he said.

He told Jackson to stay in the truck until he signaled. He thought it might look suspicious he was bringing a Yankified Jewish boy to visit with Katherine Marie, and she needed her job, couldn't have a whiff of trouble with the home's administration. Not that there's likely to be any bosses around at this hour, he said, but it never hurts to be careful.

Jackson sat in the truck, waiting, more nerved up than he was willing to admit. He tried to regulate his breathing, which had become labored despite all that singing. He looked into Bokay's rearview to pat down his trip-tousled hair with his hands.

When the back door to the rest home opened, Bokay's long arm reached in to keep it ajar. Jackson held his breath. Katherine Marie strolled out and stood on the landing. She had on a white uniform and her hair was braided the way she did, in one long central braid. One hand was on her hip and the other was up shielding her eyes searching for no one else but Jackson settin' in her fiancé's truck in the dark. She looked magnificent. She looked like she did that night by the river when they were children, like an incandescent angel of the Lord, complete with wings outstretched. It was the uniform, he supposed. With a little help from the moon. He jumped out of the truck with as much grace as he could muster and approached her. He felt certain his smile rivaled the moon in luminosity. He bounded up the steps to the landing. Demonstrating enormous restraint, he stopped short in front of her and, with a dumbass smile on his face, put out his hand for her to shake. What she did next was a moment from Jackson's dreams. She laughed, slapped away his hand, put her arms around him, and gave him a quick hug, thumping him on the back with her hands. It was a chaste hug, sororal in character, but for Jackson it felt like the satisfaction of buried hopes. Nor was there the slightest trace of shudder in it. His spirits soared. He hardly had time to register his feelings when she released him and Bokay joined them. Jackson recalled his mission on Bokay's behalf and studied the ground to hide his pleasure.

I've got an errand up the road, Bokay said. You all catch up. I'll be back in say an hour to take you home, Jackson. He lowered his head to kiss Katherine Marie good-bye on the mouth. She turned her head at the last moment, and his lips hit her cheek. As he left them, he pulled an expression behind her back that said: See what I mean?

Riverside Rest Home fronted Dalrimple, but its rear faced the Pearl. There were rockers lining a hillock of land above its banks. During the day, the ambulatory residents fought over them. Katherine Marie suggested they go sit and rock and talk, which they did. Right away, Jackson asked her how she'd been.

Oh, fine and dandy, she lied initially, fine and dandy. This is a good job, the pay's not bad, and I can study for the college entrance examinations during the night when everything's quiet. During the day, three days a week, I do piecework for Annie Althea. Then, of course, I'm helpin' Mama with the twins and Bokay up to the church the rest of the time.

All that means is you're occupied, Jackson said. He turned his chair around to address her eye to eye. How are you really. You holding up?

He didn't know why, but Jackson felt there was no reason on earth why this woman at this time should give her deepest trust to him, but she did. At his words, the floodgates burst and everything that was vulnerable in her flowed in a tearful river of misery down her dear face. There was nothing for him to do but try to put his arms around her for comfort. Trying meant nothing. He reached out, enfolded her, got the preemptory flinch, the fierce tearing away, the presentation of her back. It broke his heart. He pulled back as far away from her as her need directed and listened to a garbled sobbing release on the subject of her previous year, dwelling in a peculiar variety of Mississippi hell.

It would've been alright, she told him, she could've got over what happened except that Bubba Ray wouldn't leave her alone. There wasn't anywhere she could go that he didn't show up sooner or later. And every time he did, he caused her some kind of trouble. He'd stare at her back at the post office until she dropped everything she carried. He'd walk up and down outside Annie Althea's until she lost stitches or cut along instead of against the bias. There was one time in the early spring during Holy Week just after evening services. She was collecting prayer books from the pews over to the church when she swore she saw his round sweaty face staring in at her from the window. The only time she felt safe was when she was at work at the rest home, because at least then she could pretty much depend he was home asleep in his mama's house. I don't think he ever goes to school, she said. Because he's always doggin' me durin' the day. People notice, you know, and they laugh at him. The black folk make jokes about his bein' in love with me. The white folks too. The whole town seems to know how he dogs me. Well, except Bokay, and it's a sad old story there, ain't it? Old as Moses: everybody but the black man knows his woman gettin' put upon by a white man. Oh, I know it looks ridiculous, she said. He's only thirteen. That I should be afraid of a thirteen-year-old boy, even one as big as him. That's why folk laugh at him, 'cause he's so young. Plus he's got that reputation of bein' a bit tetched. Everyone say he's just not right because of that seizure he had. But you and I both know what he's capable of. You and I both know what he's got in mind. And I'm sorry, Jackson, but that boy is evil. He doesn't care about anyone but himself. He doesn't care what folks say about your parents behind their backs over him. He hears 'em, and he pretends he don't. The kluckers say the doctor and his wife got one Yankee niggerlover son and a redneck one to boot. That it's only a matter of time before one of you gets your daddy kicked off the Council. Oh, it's terrible, terrible. He means to finish the job he started, Jackson. And I don't know what I will do when he tries. I carry a knife now, you know. That's right, I do. I want you to know I'll hurt him, shoot, I'll kill him if I have to. Then what's gonna be? What's gonna become of us all then?

Jackson wished he'd had the right words for her, but he was out of luck there. His heart was too sick with shock and dismay, so he said the first thing that popped into his head: Well, maybe I should kill him for you, Katherine Marie, before he has the chance to cause you more harm.

That stopped her in her tracks. She whipped around in her seat and stared at Jackson as wide-eyed with horror as he must have been that night they shared on the riverbank, the night of their first meeting so many years ago.

Oh, Jackson, she said. I couldn't have that. I couldn't cause you to murder your own brother, much as he deserves it. I couldn't carry that guilt on my soul.

You need to tell Bokay, Jackson suggested next. But no, she was having none of that, either. Bokay really would kill him, she was convinced, and their lives would be ruined. They discussed whether she could charm Bokay into leaving town, starting fresh somewhere else then. Katherine Marie turned that idea over in her mind. She felt he wouldn't go for such a plan, since they were established in Guilford. They had good jobs. Bokay was rising in the church, and they'd family here, family who depended on them, but maybe it was worth a try, she thought, maybe it'd work if she found a good enough excuse. Jackson asked her how close she was to applying to college. He nearly broke in two from the tide of sentiment that washed over him while he watched the old pride return to her spine. Her back straightened, she held her sweet point of a chin up, told him they had about enough money saved for two semesters but figured it'd take another year or more before they had tuition for the whole two years a practical nurse's training would require. They batted back and forth the wisdom of waiting when college was the perfect reason to leave town. Bubba Ray's only going to get older and bolder, Jackson cautioned, then immediately regretted his candor, for she'd just about recovered from her outburst, her eyes were pretty dry, her voice clear again when the very idea of an older and bolder Bubba Ray seized hold of the weakest part of her and, mute as a stone, she trembled from head to foot imagining such.

Bokay's truck came up the drive just then. It never ceased to amaze Jackson the talent women have for dissembling. He knew of no man who, once the rage or the fear took hold of him, could slap on a pleasant face or a calm demeanor without a hairsbreadth of hesitation if occasion quite suddenly demanded, but that's exactly what Katherine Marie did at the sight of her beloved Bokay's headlights turning into a parking space. Not a word to him, she hissed at Jackson out one side of a frozen smile. Promise me, on your life.

He did.

Naturally, as soon as they were alone in the truck, set to drive home, Bokay asked: What did you find out?

Now, Jackson had been ponderin' ever since Bokay pulled up exactly what he was going to tell him, and what he decided represented a chance taken, the chance that Katherine Marie would take his advice to heart and hurry up her college plans, making sure she'd have to relocate for her education, as what Jackson told him was just that. He told Bokay she'd discovered a Baptist nursing school in Detroit that would likely give her a scholarship as they were reaching out to rural students, principally ones of color, and the idea of leaving home made her fraught with anxiety, so much so that she was fearful of bringing up the subject with him. Oh, Jackson told whopper after whopper trusting that Katherine Marie would be quick enough to answer Bokay's questions later on with the proper amount and type of detail. Luckily, his pack of falsehoods nipped around the heels of Bokay's chaotic emotions about the state of Katherine Marie's commitment to herd them to a safe, comprehensible conclusion. In other words, Bokay bought it. He shook his head in agreement, said: Why, thank you, Jackson. Thank you very much. It sounds very like her, worryin' about her mama, no doubt, and the twins as much as myself in her absence. I'm going to talk to her. Let her know that she shouldn't sacrifice her dreams to us. We'll manage. We'll figure it out. I hear there's a lot of good work up in Detroit. I can go with and still take care of things down here both. Isn't that what a man does, Jackson? Take care?

Bokay was much relieved. In fact, judging by his behavior, his relief was heroic in proportion. He sped down Dalrimple with his left arm out the window. He used it to thump on the roof in a heavy rhythm that made the cab shake while he shouted out: She loves me still! Thank you, Je-sus! Thank you, Jack-son! over and over again as if they were the same entities. He'd whoop and holler and then start it up all over again: Thump! Thank! Thump! You! Thump! Je-! Thump! sus! Thank! Thump! You! Thump! Jack! Thump! son! It struck Jackson as loony. He wondered if he was entirely safe being driven by a man made mad with love when something else happened that gave him a real reason to worry.

That is, from out of nowhere, a green Ford Maverick was behind them, churning up dust so close to their rear end that if Bokay slowed down even a tad to make a turn, disaster would ensue. Bokay! Jackson called out as warning, Bokay! But trying to get his attention proved futile while he was burstin' with a young believer's visceral expression of gratitude to his God, a gratitude that tied him so tight to the divine source it drowned out everything else around him, including those good old boys tailgatin' the truck to no wholesome end. Jackson was shouting now, pulling on Bokay's arm, trying to tell him that danger pursued them and the worst kind at that, for it was drunk, full-moon Mississippi danger. Horrified, he watched the Hicks and Turner boys through the rearview as they passed a bottle. Everybody's windows were down. He could hear their wild-assed shouts, their harrowing howls of delight at finding a nigger and a jewboy alone together driving in the night on a dark deserted road at the end of the Freedom Ride summer. It was a time that rankled and enflamed them to such a degree, no matter how many heads they'd cracked over to the bus station in the city there plain weren't enough to satisfy.

Jackson didn't know when it was that Bokay finally noticed the predicament they were in. He didn't feel the first hit from behind, he knew that. They both lurched forward, but Bokay demonstrated not a moment's break in his thumpin' and praise to Je-sus and Jack-son. The second time, though, he could not help but feel. The second time, it was harder, drove his free hand from the wheel, and the truck maneuvered on its own volition, according to the laws of impact and motion and torque and Jackson didn't know what else. He plastered himself back against the seat and gripped tight the bottom of the seat cushion. It was all he could do as they swiveled to the left, and then the direction they went was up. They flipped all the way around, landing sideways against the pavement on the driver's side. Bokay was out cold and Jackson, he was piled up more or less on top of him. Probably Bokay's bulk saved him. Jackson was conscious, he was alert, he climbed out of the truck somehow, he had no idea how. He only knew one moment he was all crumpled up into Bokay and the next he was outside the car, panting, hurt, bleeding, and not knowing what the hell to do next.

The green Ford Maverick was gone. Jackson saw this right away, processed its absence as a good thing, as a thing that meant maybe the worst had happened and all he needed to do was figure out how to take care of what was in front of him: Bokay unconscious, stuck in a smoldering heap of metal on an untraveled road in the middle of the night. He tried to waken him first, tried to pull him out. He couldn't do it. He was too weak on a good day to haul a man that size. So he stumbled up the road looking for help, and thank God it wasn't very far he had to go before he came upon a phone booth in the middle of nowhere. Why on earth there was a phone booth on a stretch like that without homes or stores or gas stations or buildings of any kind nearby, he did not know. Perhaps it appeared there for him that night, perhaps it disappeared the next day, he couldn't say. He thanked God for it as if it were the miracle he perceived it to be and found it another miracle there was a dime in his pocket. He called his daddy and he told him there was an accident. He told him where he was and told him he wasn't too bad, there was someone who needed his help more than he, and then he went back to Bokay and sat like a fool next to the smoldering truck and waited for his father to arrive.

Daddy came. Looked him over. Said: Well, you'll live, son. Now, why exactly are you and that devil Bokay alone together on the side of the road in a wrecked-up vehicle in the middle of the night? Jackson had no idea what he told him.

Somehow, they got Bokay out of the truck and into Daddy's car. Then they went to Daddy's office on Main Street. By this time, Bokay was awake, although he kept slipping back into unconsciousness then breaking out of it again. The first thing he expressed was concern over his truck, which was his livelihood, after all, and concern about who was picking up Katherine Marie from work later on. Daddy soothed him the way doctors do, telling him he needed a once-over and he was happy to do it for him, that Bokay was lucky to be alive and not to have killed his son as well, that if push came to shove, Jackson would go pick up Katherine Marie in the doctor's very own car so he needn't worry. And as Daddy found Bokay required at the very least taping of probable broken ribs as well as stitches for the gashes on the top of his head, his right knee, and left hip, this is exactly what happened once Daddy patched up Jackson's more minor injuries and determined he was recovered enough from the shock and jostling he'd received to drive a car.

When Jackson got to the rest home, Katherine Marie was waiting outside looking for Bokay's truck. Jackson called out to her from Daddy's sedan and told her there'd been an accident, Bokay was hurt but not so's he'd need a hospital, and he was there to take her to him. Oh, no, oh, no, oh, no, she said, tears filling her eyes and voice. When she got in the car, she knocked into the door frame as she was unsteady on her feet and her eyes were clouded by fear. What happened? What happened? she said, and Jackson told her piece by piece because he didn't want to send her into some kind of hysteria. We were driving home, he said, and we were run off the road. Oh, no, oh, no, she said again in a voice he'd never heard from her before, a frightened child's voice. Even when she was a little bit and her granddaddy was dying, he hadn't heard her sound timid like that, so hollow, so small. It frightened him and he did everything he could to build her hopes up, reminding her how strong Bokay was and how Daddy said everything would be alright. You've got to believe me, don't panic now, dear, please don't. He concentrated more on soothing her than he did on the road, and he didn't notice that green Ford Maverick around anywhere. He could not tell if it followed them or when it was exactly those two inside hatched their plan. He could only swear that when he pulled up to the doctor's office and got Katherine Marie out of the car, he saw from the corner of his eye that green Ford Maverick racing off just as a bottle of Jim Beam with a flaming trail of cotton sticking out of it smashed through the front window of his daddy's examining room.

Now, sometimes blind luck is as much a servant to evil as to good, and the room where Daddy was stitchin' up Bokay's wounds housed all manner of flammable materials, oxygen tanks and the like, so the whole thing went boom! and exploded into a fireball before they could even register what happened except that Katherine Marie and Jackson were blown backward with the force of the explosion. They rocked back and forth in the street on their knees, drop-jawed, watching the fire. Katherine Marie screamed and tried to run into the building, but he held her back. Then Bokay crawled out of the wreckage, his hair smokin', his clothes in tatters. He dragged the doctor from underneath his armpits into the street and Jackson saw his father was on fire. On fire up by his hairline on the right and on fire on the same side by his sleeve. Both of them were bathed in blood. Jackson ran over, ripped off his shirt, and tried like hell to put the fire eating his daddy's eye and arm out.

The fire department came. The police. Daddy was out of his mind with pain and kept cursing the name of L'il Bokay Cooper. The next morning, when he was interviewed at the hospital, Daddy had no memory of anything at all, which caused the police to decide the first words he'd uttered after the event amounted to evidence. They drew up papers charging Bokay with arson and attempted murder. His supposed motive was revenge for the firing of Katherine Marie from Daddy's household and medical practice the previous year. Jackson's mama was in complete turmoil over Daddy's condition and did not contradict their theory.

That afternoon, the police arrested Bokay for setting fire to the doctor's office, convinced they had reason and not thinking any further no matter what Jackson or Katherine Marie told them. They roared into the village in four police cars, lights and sirens blazing at two in the afternoon. They ripped Bokay from the bed where he lay moaning while Katherine Marie applied ice packs to his burns. She tried to stop them, grabbing on to the backs of their belts with two hands. They pushed her into the dirt. Bokay howled like an animal but he was all trussed up by then and he couldn't help her.

That left Jackson to set things right. He tried to tell them no one had fired Katherine Marie, she'd quit. Nobody listened to him. He was that yankified jewboy niggerlover to them all. Not only that, he was concussed. His testimony was considered untrustworthy. The day after that, the Hicks and Turner boys had the nerve to step up and give witness. They said they saw Bokay drunk and driving his truck off the road earlier in the evening, which bolstered the police claim. With no precedent, no rationale other than meanness, the police sent Bokay to Parchman to await completion of their investigation and probable trial.

Parchman Farm, a hell hole if there ever was one, as the Freedom Riders who spent some memorable time there earlier that same summer found out. Those lucky boys got out for the most part in one piece. Bokay broke out, sure enough, not two weeks later, in the company of some militants he'd chanced to share his prison dormitory with. By the time he was reapprehended, he was living in a safe house in Natchez run by the Nation of Islam. The ACLU took up his defense and after many a high-profile battle, succeeded in freeing him on the grounds of false imprisonment that was further cruel and unusual. Only by the end of all that, he wasn't Bokay anymore. He was Mombasa, founder of the Black Warriors of the African Jesus, the party he created to give black Christians a militant home. He had respect for the Nation, it wasn't that, he felt gratitude for all their help in setting him free. And certainly he was done with going along, with yessum and nossir. He'd learned to stand up. He saw that his people needed leaders like those in the Nation. But he was a Jesus man through and through, no getting around it. After he was cleared, he came back to Guilford to collect Katherine Marie. He came with a busload of his Black Warriors of the African Jesus to cow the Hicks and Turner types into leaving his people alone. These were some of the biggest, meanest black men the town of Guilford had ever seen, and there were a lot of them. The kluckers left the village alone, alright. As long as the Warriors stayed in town.

When Jackson finished telling Stella the story of his Freedom Summer, he slumped in his chair, as finished with his story as he intended to be. He was exhausted. He'd taken his time and told her what he had to say leisurely because, betrayal or not, it felt good to tell and he'd savored the telling like a fine meal. Stella came around the table and stood in front of him to nestle his head between her breasts. Oh yes, she said. The devil's in the details, isn't it? Don't you worry. I'll be more circumspect with Bubba Ray if it helps. Now, we don't have to talk about him ever again. I understand better how you feel, I truly do. I'll never tell a soul, too. You can depend on that.

They separated and went to sleep. In the early morning, Jackson's dream, a particularly pleasant one featuring Stella and an airy swing made of feathers, was interrupted by a terrible racket followed by a host of ornate curses. Startled, he opened his eyes to the sight of Daddy dressed in a seersucker suit with a white shirt and open collar, no tie. A straw hat with a snap brim sat high atop his head. The very second Jackson awoke, his father let out a new curse, leaving his son to wonder who on earth the man was so angry with.

By the Lord God of Jacob, may you slide sideways down a rocky slope to hell in a flat-tired wheelbarrow!

Daddy dry spit twice in the air as punctuation, then rifled through the side drawers of his rolltop desk with his damaged hand, the gloved fingers strumming like spider legs over the tips of color-coded files.

And after that, he continued, may the spiteful wife of Samael crawl under the fiery gates like the cockroach she is to torment you with tiny bites of her sharpened teeth on your nekkid backside just before you set on a splintery bench to await recitation of your sins!

He chuckled in a particularly nasty way, tickled by his own wit, then fell to muttering while he slammed and opened drawers one after the other. At last, he found what he sought.

Aha! Here it is. Alright. Alright. You can suck a little ice on your way into the pit, then.

Daddy. Daddy. What are you doing? asked Jackson. Unaccustomed to his father's rants, the display before him alarmed. His father looked up, squinting his good eye. He noted his son's presence with an expression that was likely a kind of surprise from which all shame or self-consciousness was absent. He smacked his lips the way men twenty years older than him did before speaking and spoke.

Son. Jackson. I have an important meeting today. I am settin' down with the board of the White Citizens' Council to see about address of my grievances. I intend to pressure the chairman with this if I have to.

He waved a manila file with a bright blue tab around. A handful of lab reports escaped and fluttered to the ground, but Daddy ignored them.

As you are a lawyer in larvae, perhaps you'd like to accompany me.

Yes, Daddy. I would. Just let me get dressed and all.

Daddy studied his pocket watch. He sat at his desk, opened the file, and held X-rays up to the light. Without looking away from them, he said: You got half of an hour, son. Then I'm going with or without you.

His nerves charged, Jackson duly washed up and put on the best clothes he'd brought with him: the blazer, chino pants, and an oxford shirt. It seemed to him his daddy was setting out on a rash and temperamental adventure. Mama'd told him that Daddy'd been expunged from the Council rolls in the spring of '62, an event that amounted to a bitter pill for the old man. It did not matter, she'd said, that they'd dropped all Jewish members at the time in reaction to that gaggle of Yankee Jews who, the previous summer, bussed their commie hides into quiet, peaceful neighborhoods and stirred up trouble unprecedented since the War of Northern Aggression. Daddy took it personal. He figured he'd been dropped because of his infirmity and him a martyr to the violent notions of Mobissimus Cooper or whatever it was L'il Bokay called himself these days.

Knowing all this, Jackson was distressed. No doubt Daddy needed protection from both the Council and his own distemper. Accordingly, the good son wrote Stella a note on his whereabouts in case she wasn't yet up and about. Daddy seems quite upset today, it said, and I think it not wise to let him go out alone. I will be back as soon as possible. He was tempted to tell Stella more concerning the whys and wherefores but decided against it, thinking if she knew what was going on, she might insist on tagging along, thus ensuring disaster in a situation loaded with enough intimations of catastrophe without her participation. He stuck the note in an envelope, sealed it against prying eyes, and ran upstairs to stick it under Stella's door. It was not until he'd gone into the kitchen for coffee and a piece of bread that Eula, who'd arrived to put up breakfast for them all, told him, no, it was Saturday, it was nine fifteen in the morning, the doctor had no appointments. He just liked to get dressed up and take a stroll with his paperwork most times in the morning of a Saturday.

He sure do talk up a storm while he's at it, too, she said. Don't mean nothin'. Nobody pays mind to his Saturday morning conversations, Mr. Jackson. If you don't mind my sayin' so, I believe he goes on like that because he misses being busy. It's hard on a man like him to have so little to do.

You best be ready, son! Time to go. Time to go.

Daddy had arrived at the kitchen door. He now clutched two files, the blue-tabbed one and another tabbed in red, clutched them tightly under his arm between the sling and his jacket. He followed Jackson's eyes to the folders, tapped them one after another with his free hand.

The chairman, he said. His wife.

He cackled.

I've got 'em good, son. Eula! Tell Miss Missy we'll be back before lunch. I have not forgotten the party over to Mickey Moe's this afternoon. Not at all.

Father and son walked half the morning away, strolling through every part of Guilford familiar to them with the exception of the village and the street that housed the offices of the White Citizens' Council above Uncle Izzy Joe's hardware store. Until the last moment, Jackson held out the curious hope that Eula was mistaken, that Daddy was scheduled for a confrontation with those in whose service he had been fiercely faithful but who had rejected him. While the fulfillment of his hope would represent a perilous enterprise, it was preferable to its alternative. After their third circumvention of the White Citizens' Council offices, he accepted the truth. They were not walking anywhere but in circles. Daddy was engaged, not in a battle royal, but in a futile fantasy, the product of a broken mind.

Yet they marched on. Several times, bits of paper from Daddy's files fell out. Jackson chased them down, Daddy stuffed them back into place, but no further mention or use was made of them. Everyone they passed, black and white alike, greeted Daddy with the utmost respect. Good Morning, Doctor, the men said, tipping their hats, and Good to see you looking so hearty, Doctor, the women said with gracious smiles. Although they bid Jackson a fine day as well, no one, not a single soul, asked him how he'd been since last he'd visited home.

It was strange because it felt so unnatural, so anti-home. This was not the way Mississippi treated even its most prodigal sons. On the other hand, he realized he should have expected the cold shoulder from all and sundry because, of course, no one, especially the black people, wanted to be linked publicly with his recent history, with his defense of L'il Bokay, now the infamous Mombasa, or his insistence that the true authors of his daddy's adversity were the drivers of a certain green Ford Maverick, two young men who yet walked the streets of Guilford while their accuser slept sound and certain in New Haven. It wasn't right, but it was the way humans behaved, he knew that. Still, it was one thing to understand such treatment, it was quite another to experience it.

TEN

Spring, 1964

IT TOOK SOME FANCY FOOTWORK, but Jackson maneuvered the family into taking two cars over to Mickey Moe's, the venue of Stella Godwin's introduction to the extended Sassaport clan. The idea that either of them might be squished against Bubba Ray in the backseat of Mama's Eldorado was more than he could bear. It did not escape him that his resolution to show Stella the South he loved, the one he'd missed every day of his long exile up north, had devolved into keeping her as far away from Bubba Ray as possible. He didn't like the way his brother sidled up to her during breakfast or hovered over her when she took a little swing on the back porch. Every moment she spent in proximity to him fueled Jackson's animus. He began to wonder if they would get through their trip without an ugly episode.

He chose a route to Mickey Moe's that took them through the village, as Jackson wanted to point out to Stella the places where he and Mombasa Cooper scampered about as children, the house in which

Katherine Marie grew up, and also the site of the Little Children of Jesus Baptist Church. Things had changed. Many of the old tar-paper shacks he remembered, ones that served him as signposts in the deep wood, no longer existed. In their place were charred or otherwise broken-up mounds of rubble, left all in a heap like war memorials, and next to them a variety of replacement mobile homes—used ones, dented, rusted, with sheets of tin peaked over the roofs to run off the rain, the occasional expando porch at the rear, and in front vegetable gardens, green with spring growth under a cover of chicken wire as protection against night critters. Before he left home, Jackson thought life in the village the meanest possible. Once he went up north and saw the ghettos there, experience bathed his memories of the village in a sentimental wash of bucolic charm. Countless times he'd remarked in a bout of the exile's bombastic pride that at least the poor back home had something beautiful to look at from their windows every morning: flowers and trees and birds and the river, the kind of beauty that gives a man hope and faith in God's mercy. Now, confronted with a glaring vista of battered metal under the noonday sun, he was hard pressed to see a distinction between urban blight and its country cousin. Poverty's poverty, he thought with a young man's startled sense of enlightenment, whether countenanced in cement or magnolia.

It's not the way you described it, Stella said.

No, it's not. A tornado must've come through here.

It's like a ghost town, Jackson. Where are all the people? A bright warm day like this and not a single child playing outside. There's no one working in the yard, no one strolling the babies, not a soul looking out a window. Look. Everyone's got their curtains drawn, if they got 'em at all. And where are the dogs? Every other place we've driven through down here is loaded with dogs. What do you think that means?

Jackson thought about it. I do not know, darlin'. Maybe somebody died.

At least the Little Children of Jesus Baptist Church looked almost as he recalled, although the yard out front was wildly overgrown with weeds and tall grass. One of the windows was boarded over. There could have been any number of ways the glass had broken, but the possibility of tornado damage seemed to Jackson the more probable, the most reasonable. Some of the headstones in the graveyard must be hidden by all this vagrant vegetation, he determined, as it didn't look to him as if there were half the graves there used to be, and those that remained were curiously spare in floral tribute, a neglect unheard of in Mississippi. Whoever died, Stella observed as they passed, the funeral isn't taking place here, is it?

Jackson's daddy always said that Negroes switched houses of worship like a woman changes her dress on a hot afternoon. Maybe, he told Stella, the pastor of the Little Children of Jesus Baptist Church went out of favor.

Mickey Moe was now a married man. He'd done well working as a salesman for Uncle Tom-Tom's insurance agency, well enough to buy Great-Aunt Lucille's farm when she passed. He moved his wife and Aunt Beadie into the big house, kept a horse and two goats in the barn, leased out most of the fields, and scaled back his hours at the agency because, as Mama told Stella, he's just a good old boy at heart who likes nothing more than tinkering with tractor engines and strolling up and down rows of cotton.

When they drove up the long road to the big house, Jackson saw with pleasure that Mickey Moe had arranged a feast fit for the celebration of kings. Near the riverbank under a row of shade trees were picnic tables draped in red checkered tablecloths on which Sassaport women laid out huge platters of greens, biscuits, coleslaw, and deviled eggs while Sassaport men elbowed one another around the barbecue pit preparing the meat. The scent of spice-rubbed chicken, brisket, and ribs wafted through the air along with clouds of hickory smoke. Small children stood on benches and folding chairs at strategic positions around the tables wielding fans to keep flies off the food. Larger ones gathered sassafras leaves to use as napkins for greasy fingers later on. The eldest Sassaports sat in a long row of wicker chairs on the verandah of the big house. And next to, under the grandest shade tree of them all, Mickey Moe himself manned a bar with sweating pitchers of ice tea and lemonade for the women and children, plus bottles of beer set in tubs of ice and quarts of hard liquor lined up for the men.

The two cousins greeted each other like Esau and Jacob. Stern, solemn, they stood apart and extended hands, gripped hard, then burst into smiles wide as the river at its widest and hugged, Mickey Moe lifting Jackson off his feet. The men watching them hooted and hollered, made rude jokes about their manhood, and then each hugged Jackson in his turn.

At the same time, the women descended upon Stella like a cloud of birds, wings outspread, gathering an errant chick. She disappeared into the vortex of their number and was swept away to be initiated into the feminine mysteries of the Sassaport clan, which consisted of a series of rules such as (a) let the men see to themselves, (b) let them feel guilty about that, and (c) wield the power of said guilt on truly important occasions only, no squandering of such precious currency allowed. There were other rules of blood regarding issues of loyalty and the raising of children of which the affianced had no need yet, so the Sassaport women were silent on those matters even though they were more intrinsic to the survival of family and thus far more serious. Stella was overwhelmed as it was. She did not notice nor consider that more in the name of family allegiance might be required of her in the future. As she reported to Jackson afterward, half of what she absorbed that afternoon had to do with recipes and home décor, two areas of domestic life she rarely pondered. It's likely she missed the point of much wisdom dispensed to her by metaphor that afternoon, a fact that might explain a lot about how her clan relations went later on.

While she was busy misapprehending a large portion of what was so generously revealed to her, Jackson was busy catching up with Mickey Moe. He apologized for not attending the latter's wedding, feigning an obligation to take an oral examination before his provosts in order to complete a course in constitutional law that winter. Mickey Moe looked at him askance. I thought it was the influenza you'd come down with, that's what your mama told me, he said. While a flustered Jackson flapped his jaws, trying to come up with an explanation, his cousin stared stonily at him then broke into another wide, disarming smile. Son, he said, clapping him on the shoulder and putting a beer in his hand, you still can't set on a mountaintop and see a bald joke comin' from half a mile on a clear day. It don't matter to me you didn't come to the weddin'. I know you had your reasons. Jackson don't come home no more, I told my gal. Why do you think we're havin' this party? All of us down here notice you ain't been home a very long time, a very long time. Makes your visit quite an occasion. We know you have your reasons. Jackson wasn't quite sure what Mickey Moe meant, what he might know, even less how he knew it. He thought it best to dissemble. You all noticed? he said, veiling his fears in a quizzical demeanor. Mickey Moe had moved on. Never knew two brothers so dis-alike, he said, gesturing with a mason jar half-full of bourbon poured over shaved ice in the direction of Bubba Ray, who stood underneath a bald cypress with his hands clasped behind his back and his head tilted upward as if he were a tree inspector studying the cypress for rot or infestation.

Neither man spoke for a bit. Each regarded the creature that was Bubba Ray with grim detachment. Mickey Moe broke first: Let's take a little walk together. There're a few matters transpired hereabouts I feel you should know. But the rest of the family doesn't have to bear witness.

They strolled along the riverbank in silence until they were well out of earshot of the others.

You'd be surprised what confidences people tell their insurance agent, Mickey Moe said, both before and after tsouris strikes. I don't want to sound proud, but your family would be in very dire straits if I hadn't convinced your daddy to take out that disability policy not six month before he got hurt. He didn't want to, you know. He didn't think he could afford it. He was concerned about your college tuition and ol' Bubba Ray. Why, he's never spent a day of that boy's life he wasn't worried about his future. And I confess, those premiums were high. But I told him he couldn't afford not to make sure you all were covered if disaster came 'round. And come 'round it did, didn't it, Jackson?

Yes.

Yes, indeed it did. Your mama was very, very grateful to me after the fact. She confided in me. Oh, the talks we'd have sittin' outside your daddy's room over to the burn unit. She said she wasn't sure where it came from, but you and Bubba Ray were sworn enemies, couldn't hardly bear to be in the same room. She felt it had somethin' to do with your bein' complete opposites at first, but it grew so strong over the last few years she thought there might be some dark secret at bottom, jealousies as dark as Cain felt toward Abel. She tried to see if I knew what the secret was but hell if I know, I said, every time she asked, hell if I know. Anyway, she feels caught in a trap between you. She knows it's the Sassaport way to treat your children equally, no matter what, but she feels you can take care of yourself and she'll need to watch over Bubba Ray the rest of her natural life. To tell the truth, that's my feelin' as to why she spoiled the decency out of that boy and left him, well, what he is. And that's why her life insurance policy has his name on it, not yours.

Mickey Moe halted, stood back, and looked his cousin in the eye, waiting for a reaction. All he got was a shrug. This is the way Jackson looked at it: Bubba Ray was the son who stayed home after Daddy got hurt and he the son who went back to college. No matter that it was Mama herself who insisted on her elder son's swift return to Yale in those difficult and complicated days, principally because he was annoying the authorities with his version of events, or that Bubba Ray was just a kid with no place to go. She hadn't had to push that hard. He was eager to flee. For that reason, Jackson considered his departure a filial betrayal, one that hung over his head like the sword of Damocles. He'd spent not a few restless nights wondering what future price he'd have to pay. If the only price were his birthright, a mother's devotion to her firstborn, he'd got off easy. He'd paid it already, the very day Bubba Ray came into the world. News of the policy's beneficiary didn't hurt him, didn't faze him in the least. Mama was right. He could support himself. Who knew about his brother? If character was fate, that child looked destined for the gutter.

I don't care, Mickey Moe. It's alright.

Well, there's more, son.

Tell me.

She puts cash money aside for Bubba Ray's future, too. You won't need it, she says. He will. But I'm here to tell you, that boy can take care of himself.

Can and will are two different things, Mickey Moe. He's a block of sheer laziness. I'm not sure there's a cure.

Your mama thinks he stopped goin' to school because it tires him out, frail as he is, takin' care of your daddy and otherwise helpin' her out to home. Mind you, every doctor ever examined that boy for his health insurance claims he's strong as an ox. That seizure he had back when? A whaddayacallit. An anomaly. That's what the doctors work for Sassaport Insurance say. No. He dropped out of school so's he could spend most of his time in the village. People say he has a sweetheart there, but I have it on the best authority that's not it at all. He deals stolen goods. Young as he is—near sixteen, seventeen I believe?—he got a whole gang workin' for him. Did you know that, Jackson? That car he drives your daddy around in has a trunk stuffed with other people's stereos and fur jackets and watches and whatnot. That's what I heard. Yessir. His boys steal in Jackson what he sells in Hattiesburg. That's what I heard. Lord knows what your mama thinks he does when he's not to home. My guess is she turns a blind eye. The thing of it is, you need to take care of this situation. Before it blows up on all of them.

Jackson was at a loss how he could manage that. He opened his palms to heaven, lifted his gaze, his shoulders. What can I do? his posture asked. What exactly can I do?

You can take Bubba Ray aside and reason with him. Point out the danger he's puttin' your mama and daddy in.

I don't believe he'd listen to me. He couldn't care less what I have to say.

He needs whuppin', is what he needs.

Though unsure whether Mickey Moe was sincere or simply employing a common expression, Jackson considered then rejected the idea of corporeal correction. For a very long time now, he'd struggled against a powerful urge to do just that. If he ever came to blows with his brother, he wasn't sure he could stop before the boy was dead.

Maybe I should drop a dime on him, Jackson said.

Mickey Moe pursed his lips and looked away, embarrassed for his cousin that he'd clearly forgotten a core proscription of the family coda, one dating back to the days when the Savannah branch was fresh off the boat, when the law of the land was applied willy-nilly by the redcoats in command and rarely in the favor of ladino-speaking immigrants.

Sassaports don't turn in Sassaports, he reminded.

Then I am in a quandary.

The two men walked a dozen or more paces without a word between them until Mickey Moe had an idea: Why don't we collect a dozen or so of the boys and have us a little midnight cousins' party out in the backwoods with Bubba Ray the guest of honor, he said. Perhaps he'd find the weight of our number more intimidatin' than singular argument.

What do you mean "intimidating"?

The look in Jackson's eyes was read by Mickey Moe for what it was.

Come on, you know, bear down upon him. I'm not advocatin' actual bloodshed. Although Bubba Ray doesn't have to know that. Now, if he starts somethin', that's another story and shoot, I could use the practice. . . .

Mickey Moe drained his drink and for emphasis heaved the heavy jar against a rock a few feet away from the riverbank where it shattered in a fine spray of glass.

Never one to miss a subtext, Jackson asked: What are you talking about? and Mickey Moe told him the news he'd got last week, the news he was getting used to little by little, the news he'd still not had the courage to tell his bride, Laura Anne: he'd been drafted. Three more months to go before his twenty-seventh birthday and he'd been drafted.

I don't know what all's goin' on with the draft board, Mickey Moe said. I thought I was free and clear. There's been some pressure over to the State House from those Yankee lawyers, I do know that, pressure to start drafting a few more white boys and a few less Negroes. I guess the Citizens Council decided alright then, we'll start in with them agitators' brother Jews. As I am a Sassaport, a family currently in disrepute, I imagine I was chosen as vanguard for the rest of you all. . . .

Jackson did not know what to say. Mickey Moe did what he called his Elvis. He threw his head back and with it the long forelock that normally graced his brow, pulled out the cigarette stored behind his ear, lit it, and smiled.

I do not mind serving my country. I truly don't. It's an honor, a privilege. I'm proud to follow in my daddy's footsteps. And I'm not concerned about a little police action in Vietnam. There's hardly three Americans in a row over there, and that's how things'll stay, no matter what you read in the newspapers. Maybe I'll wind up someplace interesting. Like Italy or Japan. It's just the leavin' of the farm and Laura Anne. I haven't had 'em long enough to get tired of either one.

He gave Jackson a crooked smile.

I wish I could ask you to look after them while I'm off to trainin' and whatnot. You're my favorite, you know, of all the cousins. But you'll be up north a while longer, I suppose, so I guess I'll have to stick it on Tom-Tom's boy, Rodney. He's alright.

Yes, he is, Jackson said and, rendered speechless by all the news his cousin had dropped on his head like an iron skillet from three stories, he clapped Mickey Moe to his chest for a long manly hug. Mickey Moe disentangled himself when it went on a little longer than either of them knew how to handle, blushing scarlet. Lord, but we wandered pretty far from the homestead, didn't we? he said. We better get back before the others send a search party. When they were halfway there, he added: I'll take some of the boys aside and tell them about tonight. Jackson had no idea what he was talking about.

Tonight?

Yessir. Tonight. Midnight? Bubba Ray? We did settle on that, didn't we?

I suppose we did.

The rest of the afternoon went pretty well. Stella looked to be having a grand old time and an impressive number of his relations came forward to congratulate Jackson on finding her. Over and over, Sassaport men and women came up to him and pronounced: Why, she's not like a Yankee at all, in some ways. . . . This was high praise any day of the week in the spring of 1964 in Guilford, Mississippi. From across an expanse of picnic tables, he watched his daddy and mama proudly hold forth to the elders of the verandah on the subject of the beauty and qualities of character of their future daughter-in-law. This was made obvious to him by their gestures, doting smiles, and happy, bobbing heads after they sent her into the throng of blood to fetch them this dainty or that drink and she bounded away willingly, gracefully to do their bidding. On her account anyway, Jackson relaxed.

Evening came and the older generation, including Dr. and Missy Fine Sassaport along with Bubba Ray, went home, leaving the young people to their own peculiar amusements. Then the women with children to put to bed left while their men, in Sassaport fashion, saw to themselves. By this time, Jackson'd had more to drink than he'd had in his entire college life put together, or at least he felt like it. When Mickey Moe came over to him and said: You know, son, you need to get the fair lady here home so we can be about our business, Jackson had no memory of what that business was, or perhaps he was reluctant to acknowledge he'd a job to do—an ugly job at that, a job that if he'd been home the last number of years instead of hiding out up north, he might have done a whole lot earlier and saved himself and his band of cousins a pot full of trouble. It dawned on him slowly what Mickey Moe was about and when it did, when he stood in the full light of revelation, he had a request that came to him either out of second sight or from the bottom of a bottle, there was no telling which, he only knew it was a brainstorm of sorts. He said: You mind if Stella stays here, tonight, Mickey Moe? Then I won't have to explain to Mama or Daddy why I'm droppin' her off and headin' out again quick. In case they're up. Mickey Moe agreed and got Stella and Laura Anne together fast so that the men could be off to their midnight rendezvous in the backwoods a good half hour ahead of time to rehearse their methods and objectives.

Sitting next to Mickey Moe in his pickup, Jackson asked: What kind of reason did you give Bubba Ray for meeting him out here in the middle of the night?

I told him I had a load of goods I needed to offload. He was shocked, don't you know. First, that I knew his sideline. Second, that I might require his services. There was suspicion in his eyes, but I am a salesman. I know people, son. Greed is what makes that boy tick. I gave him what he needed to override suspicion on account of greed.

Jackson twisted around in his seat to see how the cousins in the bed of the truck were doing. All eight of them were down-home drunk, passing a bottle and shrieking like women when they bounced over the deep ruts and fallen branches of the dirt roads Mickey Moe plowed along as if his haul were tied-down bricks rather than flesh and blood.

And how do you know he'll come alone? What if he brings his own boys?

Aha! Great minds think alike. I told him I ripped them offa some Negro folks. He won't bring that gang of his if there's even a hair of a chance they might recognize some of the goods.

They came to a certain hollow known in the town as a lovers' lane for teenagers, but it was close to midnight and the place usually cleared out by eleven Saturday nights since kids were universally expected to get up early for church on Sunday in those days. That Saturday was no different. They pulled into a deserted clearing. Mickey Moe stopped the truck and everyone got out. Right away, Cousin Floyd yelped. Stepped in a damn pile of condoms, he said. He lifted his foot and maybe five of the things dangled from his sole. Dang, that's nasty, he said, wagging his foot around, but they wouldn't drop. Dang, he said after one of the others suggested he scrape it against a rock and he did so, muttering his disgust into the night. The others elbowed one another and laughed and staggered about on tippy-toes in case similar mounds lay around, casting shadows under the full moon and Mickey Moe's headlights in the shape of dancing bears or rearing deer according to their individual height and heft. How'd they get all in a pile like that? Floyd asked his brethren. What kinda horse makes a pile like that? Mickey Moe reached through his truck window to blast the horn. That put a stop to it all. The cousins gathered into a cluster at solemn, weaving attention.

I think you all should lay low by the treeline until Bubba Ray gets here. You too, Jackson. Let him think he's meetin' me all alone, or he might turn and run when he sees what's up. Now, when he gets here, let him get out of his vehicle and approach me. Let him get good and close. Then you all can step out and make a circle around us. Let's say five feet away. And while I'm talkin' to him, I want Jackson to come forward and join me at the center and the rest of you all, all you all can keep comin' in until Bubba Ray breaks a sweat. How's that?

The men faded into the shadows of brush and tree, Jackson making himself scarce at the position nearest Mickey Moe's truck so he could pop out easy when the time came. It'd been a long day on top of a longer one the day before. Two days in a row, he'd drunk more, ate more than he was used to. Whenever he let images from the morning come to him, anxieties about his father's mental state bothered him the way a swarm of gnats bother the nostrils, in a tickling wave of crushing annoyance. So he shut his eyes, held his breath, blew out, and when that failed, he behaved much as the rest of the Sassaport men hiding in the woods—that is, he gave up trying to make sense of anything swirling about his consciousness. After about three minutes, he fell asleep.

Headlights and the slow crunch of gravel and dirt underneath tires woke him. He blinked, wiped the drool from his mouth and chin. His daddy's car appeared out of the darkness, rolling slowly past him, high beams alight. It stopped in front of Mickey Moe's vehicle. Bubba Ray got out and stood so close to Jackson that when he hitched up his pants and spat, the spittle landed not six inches from his feet. His heart pounding, Jackson jumped out of the bush ahead of his cousin's signal, startling his brother into making a rapid half-turn back to his car but by then the other cousins had followed suit and he was surrounded.

What the hell is this, Bubba Ray wanted to know, and Mickey Moe as eldest took the lead in explaining reality to him. You, Bubba Ray, he said, are a criminal, endangering the life and liberty of your disabled daddy and dependant mama. We all are here to let you know we're wise to you, son, and you'd better change your ways or else.

While he spoke, the Sassaport men edged in close 'til Bubba Ray could feel their breath on his neck.

He looked a little afraid, but not much. He swallowed hard, curled his lip, looked Mickey Moe in the eye, and said: Or else what? You all going to finish the job my brother here started a few years back when I was just a big overgrown baby and he cracked my head open? Gave me the seizures and ruined my health? You all gonna kill me?

About to further lay down the law to Bubba Ray, Mickey Moe opened his mouth but no sound came out as it took a second or two to process what he'd just heard. It didn't make sense. When had Jackson ever been violent? What was the kid talking about? And then Bubba Ray smiled, thinking he'd won whatever battle it was he'd walked into unawares, which just about infuriated Jackson, who'd been twice as stunned as Mickey Moe by his little speech and just as immobile only in his case with fear that Katherine Marie's secret was going to drop out of that vile mouth next. When Bubba Ray's smirk crept out, that last straw of a nasty smile, Jackson lurched forward with his hands stretched out as if to strangle him.

A heartbeat after his fingers gripped his brother's pulsing flesh— and Lord, it felt good, that fleeting grasp of pulpy, beating, warm, soft neck—the cousins pounced on both of them and pulled them apart. Mickey Moe got in the middle and spread out his arms.

Look here. Everybody just calm down. And no, Bubba Ray, nobody's going to kill you. You're not worth the jail time, is he, Jackson? No, he's not. But what we are going to do is take aside your boys, that gang of thieves of yours, and give 'em reason to sever all ties with you.

Bubba Ray didn't think such a maneuver remotely possible.

Fuck you, he said to Mickey Moe, Jackson, and the rest, wresting away from them. Once free, he sprinted to the doctor's car, hopped in, gunned it, and drove off in a cloud of dust.

Hell, it's not over yet, Mickey Moe said to a dejected Jackson on the way back to his farm. The boys and I'll straighten things out, don't you worry about it.

Alright.

Jackson.

Yes.

What did he mean about you crackin' his head?

Just what he said.

You tried to kill him?

I wouldn't say tried.

What for?

I don't want to say. But he deserved it.

Mickey Moe hit his steering wheel in a gesture smacking of compliment, a gesture that reminded Jackson eerily of Bokay on that fateful night long ago.

Well, damn, Mickey Moe said. Damn. Who knew you had the balls, son? Who knew?

They drove past the southwest corner of the village. Jackson could see its lights through the woods.

Mickey Moe. What happened over there? It looks like a tornado struck. I took Stella past here on the way to your place and it looked like nobody's living there at all anymore. It's like a ghost town of mobile homes.

Shoot. They all's just hidin' 'cause they didn't recognize your vehicle. These days none can be too careful. But I want you to know: No act of nature put the hurt on or the scare in 'em. A tornado of kluckers, more like. When L'il Bokay came back home to collect his family, he brought with him a gang of his Jesus warriors or whatever it is his people call themselves. Biggest, meanest Negroes anybody ever saw around here. Scared the bejesus outta those Hicks and Turner types. Shoot. They scared the bejesus outta me. Once he left with them all, the kluckers had their revenge. Burnt down half the village and tossed Molotovs into L'il Bokay's church. That place would be an honest-to-God ghost town by now except the Committee of Concern raised funds to resettle them all.

Committee of Concern?

Gang of churchmen. Led by our very own Perry Nussbaum. More the fool, him.

I always liked Rabbi Nussbaum. I'd never call him a fool.

I just mean he's always stickin' his neck out. Makin' Jews look disloyal around here. Believe me, there's a lot in his own congregation not too happy with him. They're afraid for their lives on account of him. Mind my words. I don't know how long it'll take, but them kluckers'll have their way with him, too. Sooner or later.

I hope not.

Soon they were winding down the access road to Mickey Moe's farm and because he couldn't stand pondering it anymore, Jackson put aside any thought of his family's trouble and the community's misery, the better to enjoy the unanticipated pleasures of spending the night in Stella's bed, courtesy of Mickey Moe and Laura Anne's guest room up in a corner of the third floor of the big house far away from Aunt Beadie's eyes and ears.

But he was not to find peace there, either. He crept into the room, got out of his pants and shirt in the dark, and slid into the sheets of the bed in which she lay, still, silent, a real sleeping beauty, he thought, straight out of a fairy tale. He was busy leaning up on one elbow, the better to decide how to wake her while marveling at his blessed good luck when she suddenly shivered, startling him. When she spoke, her voice was alert if ragged.

Jackson, I'm sorry. I don't want to trouble you in the middle of the night and I do want to know what happened with Bubba Ray, but I'm trying to let go of something here and it's, it's hard. Your mother said . . .

Then she broke into a round of sweet, high-pitched little sighs. What the hell? he muttered, switching on the end-table lamp the better to study the uncommon sight of his bold, forthright fiancée struggling to stifle her thoughts. What is it, baby? What is it? My mama said what?

Stella cleared her throat, rubbed her eyes with the heel of her palm, and spilled her guts: Your mother informed me that the family could not travel north for our wedding. She said it would be too much of a hardship on your father's mind. But guessing from what you've told me about the veiled way she speaks, I'm guessing it's a financial issue. And I just don't know what to do about that. I really don't. My family would certainly be willing to sponsor yours in a trip up north for such an occasion. I'm sure they'd volunteer to do so without any kind of fuss. But much as I really do want to be married at home, I just don't want to ask. It would make us beholden to them. Can you understand that?

Jackson was taken by surprise by her revelations and had no considered response available for her so, yes I do, he said, yes, I believe I do.

Well, that's good. I understand that your mother is being as honest with me as she can be without compromising her dignity, and I don't want to start off with her on a wrong foot. To make a long story short, I agreed. The wedding will take place down south. Here. In Guilford.

She turned a big, soulful look on him then: eyes wide, brows raised, adorable mouth screwed into a posture of determination. Jackson pulled her in to his side. He was terrifically moved, unsure what to say beyond you are so sweet, you are so good. He was a Southern gentleman. He knew what weddings meant to a girl, even a Yankee one. The stunning realization that she would forsake whatever matrimonial daydreams she'd nurtured and embellished in her deepest heart from the age of ten, abandon them not so much for him but for his peculiar family's sake, filled him with the warmest, most pervasive glow imaginable. He could have broken her in two, he wanted to hug her that hard. He kissed the top of her head and had another brainstorm, an idea that he was sure would do much to ease her disappointments and reward her selflessness.

He was right. As soon as he told her he'd get Rabbi Nussbaum to perform the ceremony, her mood improved dramatically. An honest-to-God civil rights hero, he told her. Wouldn't she like that, he asked, and her family, too? It amazed him how her flesh went from heavy and slack to alive and electric at the sound of Nussbaum's name. He capitalized by reciting some of the man's achievements just for the joy of feeling her blood quicken, her muscles flex with excitement while he held her. In slow, honeyed tones he told her how Perry Nussbaum volunteered for the chaplain job at Parchman after the Freedom Riders were put there. It wasn't like he already had the job or even that it existed. There weren't exactly a lot of Jews on any prison farm in Mississippi before. He saw a need and pushed against the tide to fill it. The conditions there were always wretched, but they were worse for the Freedom Riders. They had cramped, hot-as-an-oven quarters, wormy food, filth and bugs everywhere. When the riders took to singing hymns to bolster one another's spirits as well as annoy the guards, the screens were removed from their windows, allowing an army of mosquitoes to feast on them day and night. These were the same conditions that were constant in the Negro section. No one but Perry Nussbaum was allowed to communicate with the riders, not even family or lawyers. Stella knew the last part, one of her father's accountants had a son who spent time incarcerated at Parchman, and if it hadn't been for Nussbaum's letters the old man would have expired from worry over him. She hadn't known that the job did not exist until Nussbaum lobbied for it. Wow, she said. Wait'll Seth and Aaron hear about this.

Stella covered his neck then with kisses. Jackson's chest expanded. His grin was so broad his cheeks hurt, he was that pleased with himself. Despite his uncertainty that earlier events of the evening had any affect whatsoever on Bubba Ray, he'd solved at least one family problem that night. Or so he thought at the time.

In the weeks before he left for basic training, Mickey Moe assembled a crowd of cousins, sober this time and in broad daylight, led them in an impressive caravan of pickups and Cadillacs over to the village. In such company, it did not take long to determine the identities of Bubba Ray's gang. Employing a combination of threats of exposure, cash bribes, and job offers from a variety of Sassaport businesses, they convinced the crew to cut Bubba Ray off. They weren't bad boys, he wrote Jackson from boot camp, just hungry from hard times is all. Rest easy, son. We have the situation under control.

Jackson believed him.

ELEVEN

Spring, 1964

AT LUNCH THE DAY AFTER Mickey Moe's barbecue, Mama and Stella hashed out a suitable date for the wedding, that is, the first Sunday in October, which fell just after the high holidays. Six months wasn't half enough time to plan a big wedding by Mama's lights, but Stella argued that a prompt affair would do much to ameliorate Mrs. Godwin's disappointment in the venue, since long betrothals were seen as morally suspect back home. Mama pointed out that Jackson would not be finished with law school yet. Stella countered that she would be employed in the fall. They would not starve or go without a roof over their heads.

My oh my, Mama said. Things surely have changed since I was a girl. We had names for young men who allowed ladies to support them in those days. Wish I could remember what they were. Daddy? she asked her husband, who was pretending to read the Sunday paper nearby while Stella chewed her lip and fumed, do you recall what they were?

Unfortunately, Daddy was having one of his more lucid moments.

Hmm. Let me think, Mama. Layabouts? Gigolos? Fancy boys? No, I do believe we called homosexuals fancy boys. Useless? Yes, useless is what we called them. That would be it.

Well, I imagine if I'm supporting him, I can call him whatever I wish, replied Stella, and I'll just call him my brilliant husband with the fabulous future, if you don't mind.

Mama acquiesced. There followed a flurry of phone calls to Rabbi Nussbaum in Jackson and to the Godwins up north. Back and forth they went, confirming this, changing that, while a symphony of excited feminine squeals in a variety of octaves burnt up the telephone wires. Afterward, Mama and Stella faced Jackson with their arms around each other's shoulders. Their lips glistened, their chests heaved. We have achieved agreement by all parties, they announced, and broke into ear-to-ear grins, both of them. It was pretty much the first and last time he noticed them in harmony, although it was too early for him to recognize the seeds of the power struggle that would emerge between them over time. During the next six months, he put their near-constant little conflicts of opinion down to the universal phenomenon amongst mamas and brides known as wedding jitters.

As the date grew close, he found he was not without a few jitters of his own. The thing that made Jackson most anxious about the wedding was not how Mama and Daddy would get along with the Godwins, though that was a mighty concern. He'd figured out that Daddy was prone to saying out loud whatever cracked impressions flitted through his damaged cortex, while Mama took pains to flip whatever it was he said on its ear to make it sound alright. This was the way they managed life these days. In the family and in the town, there wasn't a soul who did not understand, but the Godwins were neither family nor from a town anything like Guilford, Mississippi. He worried some, then decided they'd either like one another or not. If they did, swell, and if they didn't, there was no reason for their parents to associate with each other after the nuptials, so it hardly mattered. Nor did he worry whether or not the Godwins would offend just about everyone at the wedding party with their Yankee ways and superior attitude. He knew the folks back home would be startled into sheer disappointment if they didn't behave rudely. He didn't worry at all about the things that obsessed Mama and Stella—that is, the food, the flowers, or whether the guests would all fit under the tent should it rain. He didn't even worry about losing the rings. He worried about Bubba Ray.

Bubba Ray hadn't spoken to him since that night in the woods months before, which under normal circumstances was a very good thing, something for which the Lord should be highly praised. With the wedding preparations and all, Jackson was obligated to travel home a number of weekends with Stella so that she and Mama could hash out the thorny details of ceremony and reception. Every trip was a trial, as both women had their very particular ideas of what was required. He had more than enough to do smoothing the ruffled feathers of each without taking into account Bubba Ray, but like an inconvenient truth, there his brother was anyway, a hulking presence glowering from doorways, out of dark corners, and at table when they ate in—silent, oppressive, exuding odium as naturally as a flower does scent. Oddly, he gave them a very nice wedding present, a silver nut bowl engraved with the initials "HL." It's an antique I found, he explained when Stella opened it. She later said to her fiancé: Bubba Ray may hate you, but this is a beautiful bowl. I think he likes me. Jackson could not help feeling the kid's generosity was a ruse. He was plotting something, Jackson felt sure. Lord alone knew what, but something.

Stella worried about everything. It was only by enlisting the influence of Rabbi Nussbaum that she'd got Missy Fine Sassaport to agree to a kosher wedding supper, for example, and she'd not yet tackled telling her parents to expect the genders to mix together during the ser-

vice. To tell the truth, it fascinated Jackson to witness the manifesta-
tion of his virago's frailties. The girl who lived to challenge her family,
her professors, statesmen in their chambers, bureaucrats behind their
paper-laden desks, crumbled around planning a Southern Jewish wedding. She asked his opinion when problems arose, which gave him the
uncommon elation of feeling needed, since she nearly always followed
his advice. Watching her fret one night, Jackson suggested that when
her parents arrived for the festivities everyone sit down with Rabbi
Nussbaum, and he could explain the facts of Mississippi life to the
Godwins and the sensitivities of the Godwins to his. This struck Stella
as an excellent, positively event-saving idea. It helped that she and
Perry Nussbaum had grown close during successive visits. She loved his
bravery, his politics, his caustic sense of humor, and she was quick to
point out to whomever would listen that he was no Torah slouch either.
She knew her parents already respected him by virtue of his civil rights
reputation. So let it be Perry who told them there would be no best
man or maid of honor, that Jackson and Stella would accompany each
other down the aisle. They might arch eyebrows, and Mrs. Godwin
might dart a disapproving look Stella's way, but then they'd both nod
pleasantly without comment. Let Perry tell them the ceremony would
not be at the temple but under the tent pitched on the Sassaport front
lawn. She could well imagine her father's frozen smile when Perry said:
Under halachic law all there needs to be is a promise from the groom,
acceptance by the bride, and a bridal ring. The presence of a rabbi, even
a chupah, is customary only. He would say these things in the stento-
rian tone he used from the pulpit, a tone that brooked no disagreement.
Leonard Godwin would not dare to argue with such a rabbi. No, he
was all unctuous concord when it came to confident rabbis.

When the invitations went out, most of the Boston ones were
returned promptly with regrets. Nineteen sixty-four was not exactly
a good summer for public relations in Mississippi, what with church

burnings and murders and all. It was obvious that Stella's people were afraid to come. To the Sassaports' credit, they did not rub it in. Well, you know, just after the holidays is a hard time for people to travel, was all Mama said, adding: If only your people married during the month of repentance, we could have had the wedding before the holidays in August, but then, of course, it would have been very hot in the tent. She forgot to mention it would be dang hot in the tent in October, too.

Perry Nussbaum was more forthright.

Stella, he said when she complained, I don't know if you know this, but I was born in Canada. I studied and worked all over before I settled here. I worked in the Philippines in the Army during the war and Texas just after, but I worked in Massachusetts and New York and New Jersey also. I know Yankees. Yankees are very good at telling other people how to live, especially us backward folk down here. But they don't seem to care that they stir up a lot of bad feeling and then skedaddle back home where they feel safe and cozy in their de facto lily-white neighborhoods and schools, issuing speeches and edicts about a thousand miles behind the front lines. Which leaves us on our own to take the blows and put out the fires. I'm not saying we don't need to change down here, no, not at all, but no one knows as well as I do that we who chose to stand up, stand alone.

Stella blushed, shamed on account of the entire region north of the Mason-Dixon line.

You'll never stand alone as long as I'm around, Rabbi.

He chuckled, and his eyes with their great bushy brows crinkled. Nussbaum was a man of average height. His hair was salt-and-pepper, short, wiry, his belly round and hard. Chuckling like that, he resembled nothing so much as a bemused gnome.

That's a real firecracker you're bringing us, Jackson.

Yes, she is, sir, she is indeed.

Long about August, time sprouted jet wings, flew by, and suddenly it was the week of the wedding. The bridal couple arrived in Guilford the Monday before. Everything was whirlwind. Presents arrived every day in the post. The lawn was manicured, the tables and chairs delivered. By Wednesday, the scaffolding for the tent was erected. A generator arrived for the fans that would be plugged inside the tent to keep them all cool. Stella had the final fitting for her dress, a gown inspired by a photo in *Vogue* magazine, hand sewn by Annie Althea over in the village, although her mother wanted to see her in one by Priscilla of Boston. She explained to her mother that eventually she and Jackson would like to live in his hometown. I want to have good relations with everybody from the ground up, she told her. Plus, it's good for the local economy to throw some money over that way. You have no idea how hard life can be for those people, Mom, you really don't. She'd lost some weight from nerves, so the fitting was more than a pro forma event. The dress was made from an ivory satin chosen for the creamy way it set off her flame-red hair, which she intended to wear down and studded with flowers underneath a half veil fastened to an ivory ribbon beaded with pearls. The veil was a marvel of delicacy, although Stella planned to ditch it the second the ceremony was over. The neckline of the gown was lower than her mother was going to like, she knew that and didn't care. It had long sleeves that buttoned from the inside of her elbows down to her wrists, and from her breasts to past her hips it fit tight as a wet leather glove dried in the noonday sun. It came to a deep V below her waist front and back then flounced out in a wide skirt that stopped, scandalously her mother was sure to think, above her ankles. Stella liked it because it made her feel half ballerina, half lady of Camelot. Jackson would dress in a black suit with a Nehru collar rather than a tux, and for underneath, Annie Althea had sewn him a collarless shirt of fine cotton the same shade of ivory as Stella's dress. There were no groomsmen or bridesmaids, which Jackson and Stella insisted upon over the objections of both mothers. Their unspoken reasoning went that with no bridal party, there was no need to come up with an excuse to exclude Bubba Ray.

The Godwins arrived on Wednesday, the same day as the tent scaffolding. They flew to Jackson, which in those days represented a two-stop, seven-hour trip. Guilford boasted a single bed-and-breakfast inn that, while perfectly charming, happened to be far below the Godwin standards. Stella didn't want to spend the few days before the wedding listening to them whine about sharing a phone line, about their lack of a television or, should they require it, air conditioning, not to mention the annoyance of hearing the conversations of other guests in the hallways or through the paper-thin walls. So she booked them a suite at the best hotel in Jackson, to which they taxied directly from the airport to rest and freshen up before the young couple collected them for a drive to the Sassaport residence, where a getting-to-know-you-all supper with Rabbi Nussbaum was planned.

The evening started out better than any of them had a right to expect. The Godwins were pleased with the hotel. They greeted Jackson with affection and hugged Stella long and hard as every bride might expect her mama and daddy to do at such a time. They apologized that Seth and Aaron were not able to arrive until just before shabbos, as someone had to mind the factory during the busy season, family wedding or not. The high holidays had caused enough disruption to the management of the assembly line and the shipping office. On the drive to Guilford, they kept their eyes peeled for trouble, staring into the dark night of country roads and twice asked Jackson if he was sure he knew where he was going.

Mo-ther! Stella said, exasperated. What makes you think Jackson doesn't know his way home?

Well, it looks like the very ends of the earth around here, doesn't it?

I assure you, it is not. She was about to instruct her mother on her ignorance and provincial judgments when Jackson, fearing the storm about to break out inside the confines of his vehicle, interrupted.

We're almost there, Mrs. Godwin. In just a few minutes, we'll be in the center of town.

You know, I think you should start calling my husband and me by more familiar names. I've never liked it when people call their in-laws Mother and Father as if they didn't have any of their own. So how about Mildred and Leonard?

Alright, Mildred, will do. Thank you very much.

From the back seat, Leonard Godwin put his hand on top of the front seat cushion and pulled himself forward to speak more intimately to his daughter.

And what do you call Jackson's parents, Stella? he asked.

Mama and Daddy.

He fell back against his own seat, sighed. Of course.

When they arrived at the house, Perry Nussbaum's car was parked in the driveway. Stella breathed a sigh of relief, which no one but Jackson noticed. He put his hand on her knee and squeezed.

Well, here we are, he said.

Jackson's parents peered out the doorway, then stood on the front porch, beaming welcome. Rabbi Nussbaum joined them. Between a lot of so-happy-to-meet-you-at-last and can-I-get-you-a-drink, everyone introduced himself, the rabbi included, and the whole lot of them were ushered into the living room, where Eula had laid out crackers and cheese and a bowl of fruit along with a pitcher of sweet tea, as the night was particularly warm. Do you have anything a bit stronger? Mrs. Godwin asked straightaway. It was an awfully long trip. . . . Well, we do have wine, but that's for dinner, Mama said in a flustered tone, so Daddy went into his office and clattered about noisily until he popped back out with a bottle of peach schnapps under his bad arm. Locking the bottle under his armpit, he screwed off the top then poured for Mrs. Godwin, who grimaced at the first sip but drank it down anyway. Daddy narrowed his eyes at her, chuckled, then without being asked, exchanged her cordial glass for a larger one and poured again. Mama was busy showing Mr. Godwin her array of family photographs set in their silver frames all over the mantel of the fireplace and noticed nothing.

We're picking up the liquor for the wedding tomorrow, Daddy said. Guess you came a day early, darlin'. Mama, there used to be some bourbon in my desk, I know that it's true. It's gone now. Who drank it, do you think? My money's on that rascal Bubba Ray. Where is that boy, anyway? Wasn't he told to be front and center tonight?

Oh, I'm sure he's upstairs, dear. He'll be down a bit later. She popped a cracker into her mouth to signal to the assembled that they should begin enjoying what was sitting there before them when, at that exact moment, just as if she sat in her own living room instead of being a guest in another's, Mrs. Godwin said:

Rabbi, before we partake, would you care to make a blessing over the . . .

Her gaze took in the cheese platter, the purple grapes, and sliced Granny Smiths. Her bemused disdain was not so much in her eyes but in her pause, in the angle of the hand she waved over the food before she continued.

. . . the fruits of the earth prepared for this wonderful occasion?

Mama spit her mouthful out into a cocktail napkin as surreptitiously as circumstances allowed and shook her head in Nussbaum's direction with a close lipped smile, encouraging the suggestion. Jackson and Stella looked at each other and both saw all hope for a strife-free few days sprout legs and run under the floorboards. Rabbi Nussbaum stood, spread his arms. *Baruch a-tah Adonai,* he sang, and then everything went directly to hell.

First, there was the sound of sirens blaring, then columns of red and yellow light flashed across the living room wall from the street. A police car and paddy wagon had pulled up front. Chief Duncan got out of the car with three of his officers to approach the house, walking rapidly with his head down. He held paperwork in one hand and banged on the door with the other.

What on earth? Mama muttered, signaling to Eula to answer the door.

The Godwins stood and clung to each other, shrinking back into a corner of the room. Their eyes were wide, panicked. Stella went over to them to say that surely this was not the kind of problem they feared, and for them to please just calm down, no one was going to hurt them, but there were tears in her eyes when she said it. Jackson, the almost-lawyer, opened his mouth to say he'd go see what it was about when the rabbi interrupted him.

They've come for me, he said. I'm very sorry, but I'm sure they've come for me. I met Chief Duncan on the street in the capital last week and he told me he thinks my last speech at the Rotary Club was seditious. I have no idea what he meant. It was about a joint faith conference I attended in Mobile. Perhaps he's found a way to charge me with something. . . .

Eula came into the living room with the chief and his men behind her. She stepped aside. Chief Duncan handed Daddy his paperwork.

I'm sorry to have to do this, Doc. Especially as I see you've got company. But I have a search warrant here, instructing me to go through your house top to bottom and look for certain stolen goods. Bubba Ray here?

Mama fell back into the quiet comfort of a well-cushioned chair, buried her head in her hands, and breathed from between white-knuckled fingers: Upstairs, she croaked out, upstairs.

Chaos erupted. The three policemen charged up to the second floor to locate Bubba Ray, dragged him downstairs, handcuffed and shirtless. Mama shrieked. Daddy got in the chief's face and wagged a finger at him, shouting about his history with the Citizens Council and his many political connections who would subsequently ruin the man's career. Rabbi Nussbaum got angry and flustered and charged the chief with taking out their personal disagreements on the Sassaports while Stella began to weep in earnest when the chief's men rifled through the wedding presents piled up in the foyer. Jackson obtained the search warrant papers and sat down to try to read them carefully amidst all the wailing and shouts.

He didn't need to get very far before he could assume with confidence that Bubba Ray had assembled a new crew in the months since Mickey Moe and the others hired off his old one. When he studied the list of objects the police sought, his blood heated up in a hurry. He cursed and left the house, marched over to the police car where Bubba Ray sat cuffed to the inside door handle, brooding. You bastard, he said, waving the list through the open window. A silver nut bowl engraved "H.L."? For our wedding?

Bubba Ray smirked. You accepted it, didn't you? What did you think? I'm an unemployed high school dropout, you stupid fuck. Where was I going to get the wherewithal for a silver nut bowl?

If it hadn't been for a police officer holding him back, Jackson might have punched him out through the window.

Rabbi Nussbaum drove the shell-shocked Godwins back to their hotel. Stella wept most of the night away, sitting on the couch with Jackson's arms around her while Mama and Daddy cussed and moaned and helped Eula work until three a.m. trying to put the mess the police made back in order. Lordy, Lordy, Eula muttered more than once, this is just plain mean. They didn't have to throw everything around like that. Not at all.

By morning, the Sassaports had got hold of themselves. Mama announced at breakfast that they all needed to drive over to the jailhouse and get Bubba Ray sprung. I will not have that child incarcerated. I am afraid I have to assume he has sinned, yes, but he would not survive in an institution, juvenile or otherwise, she said. I need him home with me to help take care of you, Daddy. We would not survive without him.

I can take care of myself, the doctor said, caressing the sling on his arm, adjusting his eye patch. You grossly exaggerate my disability.

You cannot drive. I called the jail just now before you all were up. He's being transferred this morning to the courthouse in the city for arraignment. Bail will be set and we need to be there to post it. Jackson? Why don't we drop off Miss Stella at her parents' hotel and then we all can go over to wherever we need to go and pick up Bubba Ray.

Jackson didn't respond. He was contemplating the fact that neither Mama nor Daddy seemed to think he'd take care of them in Bubba Ray's absence. She asked again if he'd drop Stella off and help them collect his brother.

Now, Mama, you have to prepare yourself, he said slowly. I don't know if it's going to be all that easy.

It shouldn't have been, but in the end it was.

On entering the courtroom, Mama nearly fainted catching sight of Bubba Ray parked on the defendants' bench and dressed in a jailhouse jumpsuit. When the list of charges against him was read out loud by the bailiff, the list was so long Daddy couldn't take it all in. He retreated within his mind to a hospital ward and began asking court officers if they knew where the requisitions were, growing increasingly agitated when such did not materialize so that his wife was forced to come to herself and seize control. She ordered Jackson to take his father out for some fresh air, which usually helped clear his head. But Mama, Jackson protested, you need my help here. I can explain the procedure.

No. I know what to do. You just get him out of here. Can't you see how he's irritating everybody? I don't need two men locked away.

For the next two hours, Jackson walked his daddy up and down in front of the courthouse with the occasional breather of sitting on the steps until Mama appeared at their head with Bubba Ray, now attired in the fresh shirt and pants she'd brought along in a brown paper bag. Her eyes glinted like one mad.

It's all over, she said. The charges are dropped.

Mama, you must not have understood. Didn't you post bail? Isn't that what's going on?

No. The charges were dropped. Here, read the paperwork you don't believe me.

To his great astonishment, Jackson discovered his mother was right. How did you do that, Mama? How?

It was simple. I requested an audience with the judge and the sheriff in the judge's chambers. You all think I don't know what goes on in the world, but I do, I do. You know there's been trouble around here with the draft board drafting too many coloreds and not enough whites. Even the toughest of these old men are deep-down terrified of the federal government nowadays, so I made them an offer to put them in the clear. I told them that in exchange for my boy's freedom, Daddy would sign deferments for anyone they wanted. That they could draft white boys all day long but Daddy would make sure they had asthma or flat feet. He still has his license. He'll sign whatever dotted line they want. Well, Lord, didn't they get on the phone fast after that. The judge called this one, the sheriff called that one, and all of a sudden Bubba Ray was free. I even got him a job out of it. He'll be the courier. They'll pay him to go over to the draft board and pick up the forms and the names and then Daddy will fill them out and sign them and Bubba Ray will bring them back. Keep it all in the family.

Jackson was appalled, his sensibilities deeply offended. He tried to point out to Mama that rather than let Bubba Ray pay for his mistakes, she was spoiling him worse than ever she did before, and his behavior would get more and more wicked down the line. Plus, she put herself and Daddy in great danger under this arrangement, she was committing federal offenses up, down, and sideways. Mama was having none of it. Why are you so afraid? she asked him. That judge and sheriff and the draft board aren't going to tell anyone. Neither are the boys who weasel out of the Army. That leaves you. You're not telling anybody are you, son? Of course not. Now, you just focus on getting married this weekend. We're going to put all this behind us, tell the Godwins it was a colossal mistake, and have us a party. Isn't that right?

No, thought Jackson. It wasn't right at all.

But it was what happened. Aaron and Seth arrived the following day. The canvass was hung over the tent scaffolding. The fans were hooked up. The liquor was bought. The catering trucks came at precisely the scheduled hour. The flowers were perfect, Stella was a vision in her dress, Rabbi Nussbaum officiated with panache, and the only snafu—when Aunt Sofie tried to lay her platter of baked oysters with bacon stuffing on the hors d'oeuvres table, claiming it just wasn't a Sassaport wedding without them—was hushed up in a flash before any of the pitifully few Yankee guests were the wiser.

TWELVE

Spring, 1995

FROM THE DAY THEY WERE married, kitchen maintenance was Jackson's job. In thirty years, he'd never come to trust Stella with the glassware or crockery. Her idea of a spotless countertop was one that looked tidy when squinted at with the overhead light off. Sometimes, he felt she'd tricked him during the honeymoon, that she'd feigned ignorance of what a properly hygienic kitchen was in order to weasel out of a chore she had no use for. So when Hinds County's Unsung Civic Hero of 1995 told the others after Katherine Marie's brunch to go set themselves in the front parlor where she'd join them after washing up, Jackson protested.

I'll do that, he said, you must be tired from your big night.

No, no, no, Stella insisted. It was a big night for everybody. The two of you did all the work so far. Let me do my share.

Jackson and Katherine Marie settled down on the parlor couch together, photo albums balanced on their knees. They went through old pictures that made them laugh: Jackson with hair to his shoulder blades and muttonchop sideburns the years he worked in Washington for the Civil Rights Commission; Stella standing on a ghetto street corner dressed in a pantsuit, holding her black-bound social worker's case book aloft the way a preacher does his Bible; Katherine Marie in an Afro that blocked out half the face of whomever she stood beside. There was one of Mombasa that made them both tear up. Although neither could remember the year or the occasion, he stood impressive and impassioned behind an outdoor lectern studded with microphones. A sea of young black students surrounded him. He wore a jellaba, a giant wooden cross was slung around his neck, and his fist was raised, clenched.

The sound of glass smashing followed by the clatter of tin hitting the floor interrupted them. Stella! What broke? Jackson yelled out. Not much, came her weak response. He made an apology to their guest and rose to see what disaster Stella had wrought. When he got to the kitchen, he found his wife on her knees picking up shards of glass while dishes were so precariously balanced in the dish drainer it was only by the grace of God that a few more plates and pots had not hit the floor. He kicked Stella out to finish the cleanup himself. Because he was thorough, this took a while.

By the time he returned to the front parlor, Stella and Katherine Marie nestled together on the couch like sisters. Joined at the shoulder, their feet side-by-side on the coffee table, they held hands and spoke in hushed tones on intimate matters the nature of which he could only guess at from his position just outside the room. Something about Katherine Marie's children, he gathered from a syllable caught here and there, or Stella's miscarriages. He heard Mombasa's name, he thought, and Dr. Carnegie, Stella's doctor in the old days when they'd lived in Washington those terrible years. Then in the midst of reminiscing, one of them, he wasn't sure which, sighed in a most sorrowful way. He poked his head around the corner to watch the two women face each other and embrace, at which point Jackson felt it most politic to back off and leave them to their feminine comforts unobserved. When he heard the shift of couch springs, a murmured joke, and small, wry laughter, he guessed they'd moved on from their special moment and coughed to let them know he was about to enter. They pushed apart to make room for him on the couch, both patting the central cushion in welcome.

Jackson, Katherine Marie said. Stella just had an idea I think might help Mombasa at his hearing.

He put his arm around his wife and bussed her cheek. Well, we know how brilliant she is. Whatever advice she gives, I'd say follow it.

I'm glad you feel that way. Well. Here it is, then.

Immediately on hearing Stella's idea, Jackson regretted his largesse. It seemed the women, lost perhaps in some remarkable haze of forgetfulness, thought it would help Mombasa if Jackson appeared before the parole board to testify on his behalf. Or it might have been they wanted him to represent him. They weren't that clear. Oh, I don't know what good I'd do, Jackson started to say when the two of them interrupted to dissuade him. Stella: You'd do worlds of good. You're the missing link. Katherine Marie: We've tried everything else. What's left to lose?

Only my sanity, thought Jackson, but then he looked at the women looking at him. Their eyes were bright as full moons, their lips open and damp. They looked prepared to thwart any argument he might propose, even the most reasonable one, which was that, although a member of the bar, Jackson had no experience in parole matters. He was just a country lawyer with a civil practice. He drafted wills and wrote commercial contracts. He rarely litigated. After they'd all moved back south and lawyers were hired to petition that Mombasa be moved from the federal penitentiary in Virginia to the one in Yazoo City for his family's sake, he'd not even been called upon to draft a letter. How

MARY GLICKMAN

could he prevail where some of the best minds of the ACLU had failed? What had he to add to the case beyond a few personal anecdotes that might lend context to Mombasa's crimes but could hardly effect anything else? What were these women thinking? He looked into their eyes again, sighed. Under the fierce light of such determination, he was forced to acquiesce.

Alright, I'll try. But Mombasa has to agree. I have to see him beforehand and he has to agree. What do you think, Katherine Marie? Can you get me an audience with himself, then? Will he see me?

I'll make certain of it, don't you worry about that.

Alright. If you do, I'll try.

The women fell on him then, fondling and kissing him in the most pleasant way imaginable. He found it entirely impossible that he was in the middle of them once again after all these years. The wonder of it all had an odd effect on his reasoning, inspiring a surge of hope that maybe he could get Mombasa sprung from federal prison after all. How strange life is, he thought, entirely euphoric, how strange these two women met in the first place, how much stranger the friendship that sprang up between them, how even stranger than that, the fact that they'd reconciled after more than a decade of estrangement preceded by the worst argument he'd heard of in his life between two mature women, absolutely the worst.

Not even the most desiccated skeptic would deny that from the beginning Katherine Marie and Stella's bond was a fateful one. It originated at a time and place no one expected, during an era when Jackson had decided his childhood friends were lost to him forever. Stella considered their storied selves two more of those ghostly attachments Southerners revel in, stuck in the past as they always were, her husband no exception.

Stella and Katherine Marie met independently of Jackson, which was the fateful part, on the maternity ward of Hamilton Hospital, an understaffed, poorly endowed health-care establishment that was more clinic than hospital, located in one of DC's poorest neighborhoods. Stella was taken to Hamilton in an ambulance after passing out four months into her pregnancy in the home of an illiterate single mother of five whom she was helping fill out the new forms for food stamps. Katherine Marie was there to hand out Black Warriors of the African Jesus pamphlets on child-raising to the new mothers on the ward. At first, she only glanced at Stella, her brows knit with dark surprise that some white woman was taking up space a sister needed, a white woman who didn't look half poor enough to belong there. As it happened, Stella Godwin Sassaport looked over in her direction at the same moment.

Jackson's wife had already bled out the child he'd given her after three years of ardent, fruitless trying. She lay on a gurney in the hallway waiting for him to arrive and take her home. In those days, communication was neither swift nor certain. It was unclear whether Jackson knew yet where she was or why. She'd already waited three hours for him. If she'd been strong enough, she would have walked out and taken the subway home. She tried to get up on her own steam every twenty minutes or so, but her head swam each time. It was too much, the best she could do was half sit up. She was stuck there waiting, bleeding, stoic, dry-eyed, but she didn't have to like it.

And now this black woman dressed like an African missionary in a white robe and head wrap, a giant wooden cross around her neck, cast a look at her that was not at all pleasant, so Stella stared back at her as if to shout: Dammit, do I look like I want to be here? In that moment, their eyes locked with the suddenness of a thunderbolt's strike in an open field on a dry afternoon, each overwhelmed by an attraction, a comprehension neither could define, an intimation perhaps of the pairing between them that would take place in the days and months to come, although neither understood it at the time, neither could tell you what it meant even today. Still, there it was—undeniable, pulsing, hot as a living thing, pulling at each of them, striking then pulling them toward each other, and because they were women, they gave in to its force. Katherine Marie walked over to Stella, stood there at the side of the bed, and asked: Do you need something? Yes, thank God you're here, Stella said, resisting an urge to take up the stranger's hand and kiss it, her gratitude was that strong. You look like a kind woman. I lost my baby today. I want only to go home. They say my husband's been called, but I'm not sure. I've been waiting hours and hours. Can you find out for me if a Jackson Sassaport is on his way to collect me? Could you, please?

Katherine Marie's jaw dropped, her eyes bulged, she was that shocked by the sound of a name she'd not thought to hear again the rest of her natural life. She may have reeled, since a gang of burly black men in camouflage pants, black berets, and white T-shirts emblazoned with a clenched fist holding a crucifix stepped forward from out of nowhere to surround her. They were the bodyguards Mombasa assigned to protect her when she went around the city for her works of charity and consciousness-raising. Jackson? she said to Stella after waving them off, S-a-s-s-a-p-o-r-t? Not out of Guilford, Mississippi? Surely not that Jackson Sassaport?

Yes. That would be my Jackson. Do you know him?

I do believe I do. It's been a fair amount of time.

Are you from his part of the world, ma'am? Of course you are. I hear it in your voice.

Both women felt an odd sense of nausea next, the kind of nausea that affects sensitives just before an earthquake or visionaries before giving up their selfhood to an invasion of alien spirit. Katherine Marie introduced herself.

I am Malaika Cooper, only Jackson would know me as Katherine Marie.

And your husband is Mombasa, once known as L'il Bokay.

Oh my Lord.

Katherine Marie sank onto the foot of Stella's gurney, overcome by the queer coincidence of it all. It was not long afterward that Jackson arrived at last, rushed to Stella's side, unaware the woman sitting with her back to him was his unrequited love from back home. He rushed past her, embraced his wife, weeping into her neck, while he mumbled I'm sorry, I'm sorry, our poor little child, I'm sorry, I'm sorry over and over again. Now that he was with her, Stella allowed herself to sob in his arms. For a time, the rest of the world faded away. Out of respect, Katherine Marie removed herself to the opposite end of the ward. She tried to keep an eye on them while preoccupied with her proselytization, waiting for an opportunity to present herself to her old and dear friend. A swarm of accidents prevented this. First a listener of Mombasa's weekly radio address buttonholed her to pepper her with scriptural quotations. Next, a new mother all of fourteen years of age grabbed her skirts and begged for information on public assistance. By the time she fended off the first and helped the girl locate a social worker, the Sassaports were processed out of the ward. Katherine Marie consoled herself thinking she could easily find Jackson again through the hospital records. Meanwhile, Stella had recovered her equilibrium enough to tell her husband in ragged voice of the extraordinary resurrection of his past mere hours after the demise of his hope in the future, pointing with an unsteady finger in the direction of Katherine Marie's back, which disappeared at just that moment around a corner. He turned, saw nothing, did not believe her. Her story sounded exactly the kind of hallucinatory experience a person in extremis might achieve. Then he saw a Black Warrior of the African Jesus pamphlet in the lap of a woman with an infant at the teat and wondered.

Later on in the week, Katherine Marie determined where the couple was living in the town. She took the train over without her bodyguards or calling first and rang the doorbell. Jackson answered. He dashed down from the third floor of the building to the first and stuck his head through the entryway, as the buzzer was broken. When he saw her, he knew her instantly despite the passage of time and her African costume. He embraced her there on the front stoop, saying: So my wife is not insane! And the two of them beamed and rocked back and forth close as twin babies in their mama's arms until they became aware of the stares of passersby, at which point they released each other and Jackson ushered her into the apartment. How is your wife? Malaika Cooper née Katherine Marie asked right away. Jackson shrugged. Depends on the day. She tries to be strong, but her hormones are crashing. It makes her difficult, she's just not right most days. And you, Jackson? How are you doing? He smiled. Why, sad. Of course, I'm very sad, thank you for asking. I do think your arrival, though, will perk us both up quite a bit.

Which is exactly what happened. Despite everything else that came to pass, for a good number of years following that day, the Sassaports clung to Mombasa Cooper's family with a kind of relief borne out of the desperation caused by three more miscarriages before the issue of offspring was finally put to rest. In a way, Malaika and her children became for them a repository for all the emotions they'd had to squelch along with any hope for their own progeny. She needed them, too, after her own reversal of fortune during that same year as the first Sassaport miscarriage.

The day Katherine Marie ventured over to a pocket of white neighborhood near DC's Embassy Row to pay her first visit to Jackson and Stella, Mombasa happened to be in Chicago at the University of Illinois, participating in a three-day panel discussion with representatives from the organizations of Dr. King, Bobby Seale, and Stokely Carmichael on the various philosophies of black liberation current at the time. He felt lucky to be there, as he didn't enjoy the cachet the others did. The sun that shone on him the day the ACLU vindicated him and he announced the establishment of his party had long ago set. The Black Warriors of the African Jesus had devolved to a footnote in a movement overshadowed by the rising stars of newer constellations, that is, more recent victims and heroes engaged the public mind. Mombasa was entirely aware of his status as a minor satellite of civil rights activism. He hoped to reignite community interest in his ideas through the conference, although he had no allies there. None of the other participants lived on his side of the street. To a man, they considered him not enough this, too much that. Dr. King's people, the most honored by the white world, were never separatists although the spiritual countenance of his movement came closest to that of the Black Warriors of the African Jesus. The others, arrivistes when compared with the works of Dr. King or Mombasa, were suspicious of anything he had to say. Bobby Seale, at the dawn of his romance with Marxism, considered Christianity a slave religion, while Stokely Carmichael reckoned the Black Warriors too focused on negative imagery. Their founder's awareness of all this had an effect on his performance that day. After hours of timid discussion and deference to opinions contrary to his own, he became confused, dissatisfied with himself, and he needed to consult his wife. Why did I take a backseat? he wanted to ask her whom he trusted above all others. Why did I beg pardon so many times? How would his subservient demeanor appear to his followers? Would they be as disappointed in him as he was in himself?

As soon as he could get to a phone, he called his wife at the apartment that served as both their home and party headquarters in DC. Her mama answered the phone. She's gone out, he was told, I'm watchin' the kids. Where'd she go? he asked. Well, now, I don't really know. To see some friends. Mombasa arranged that he would call back later that night, but when he did Katherine Marie was still not home. He called the head of her bodyguard detail. He had no idea where she was either. Mombasa worried himself into a near fit. The bodyguard called the chief of Black Warrior security to let him know the wife of the leader was missing. This man, a man called Dume, was a small, suspicious man well suited to his work, a man disastrously married three times to three different roundheels, a man who considered all women untrustworthy, morally weak, generally inferior. He parked himself outside the Cooper apartment watching for Malaika's return to see if he could catch her up to anything untoward.

It was Jackson's fault she stayed out late that night. She tried to leave three or four times, and each time he dissuaded her, begging her to share their evening meal with them, promising to drive her home. How often is the lost found? he asked. Better yet, how often does my wife find a friend? And that made Katherine Marie laugh, even though she didn't know Stella well enough yet to get the joke. She was just guessing by the tone in Jackson's voice and by the way Stella hit him in the shoulder that there was some truth in his question, some exaggeration and wherever the meat of it lay, she could see he loved his wife anyway, purely, to distraction, the way she loved her husband. And that felt fitting and right and good in an extraordinarily satisfying way, which, if she analyzed it, had something to do with both Jackson's feelings about her and her own shadow feelings about him. Now that they were all securely married, she could admit to herself how much she'd always cared for him without seeing him as some kind of forbidden threat, and so she did.

He made dinner for them all, a down-home dinner with grits and spoon bread both, and he served wine, the best jug they could afford, Tavola Red. Everybody got a little drunk. Stella made sure Jackson drank half a pot of coffee before he drove Katherine Marie home. On the way, he said: Malaika, Malaika, you know it's real pretty, but I just cannot get used to it. You're always going to be Katherine Marie to me. How's your mama do it? How's she set into calling you a different name than she's called you her whole life? Now, I can easily call L'il Bokay Mombasa because, let's face it, look at him, he's a Mombasa. Just say it slow and deep: Mom-bas-a. Mom-bas-a. Yes, indeed. He's a Mombasa if there ever was one, although I don't know if there ever has been one before now, has there? It's a place not a person name, isn't it?

Katherine Marie was pleased with Jackson that he knew that, because there were maybe three white people in all of America at the time who knew that.

Yes. It's a port city in East Africa, a major trading post of slaves passing through the hands of Moslems and the Portuguese.

Why would Bokay want to do that? Name himself after a slave city?

Well. He feels it emphasizes that the shame of slavery does not belong to the enslaved. Plus, he feels it brings him closer to the African Jesus who was a slave to the empire of Rome which killed him.

Since he was elated for the first time since they'd lost the baby and in his cups no matter how much coffee he'd swilled, Jackson said: Well, indeed, darlin'. I do not know about that, but better you all blame the Romans instead of the Jews for killin' your Lord Jesus. My whole life, I got plenty neighbors blamin' the Jews. Don't need the ones I actually love doin' so.

Katherine Marie looked at him with a blank, startled look, and then she started to laugh. As they'd pulled up to her building, she kept laughing, making of her laughter a good-bye accompanied by a buss on the cheek, which was innocent, and Jackson, though terribly pleased, knew it was innocent. But Dume, on watch from the street corner, did not. Jackson yelled out the window: So, we'll see you a week from next Tuesday? as Stella had suggested a reunion dinner for the four of them, the children included if the Coopers wished. Dume wrote the phrase down along with Jackson's license plate number and cursed them both under his breath.

When Jackson returned after driving Katherine Marie home, Stella was awake and excited, pacing around the house taking dessert dishes and ashtrays into the kitchen, straightening magazines on the coffee table and the like all in a manic putter. Oh sweetheart, she said as soon as he walked in the door, I understand why you fell in love with that girl as a child. She's fantastic! So beautiful! And so smart! And what noble bearing, right down to the point of her chin! Have you noticed how it always points sort of up? Did you see how well she wears those robes of hers, which, let's face it, must be tremendously hot and uncomfortable? Stella pretended she wore them herself, miming the sweep and grace of Katherine Marie's perambulation through the living room. I saw at the hospital how everyone she talks to respects her. She treats everybody the same, young and old, male and female, ignorant and refined. When you were cooking, she told me about her pet projects with the Black Warriors. There's a preschool and food pantry in Anacostia, a drop-in clinic and youth counseling center in Marshall Heights. They're so well organized, and she created everything by herself without formal training. She's had to learn how to do it on her own, from working in the trenches. Oh, how I wish she were my protégée. I could make her into the head of Human Services in half a dozen years! I'm telling you, Jackson, she's the most inspiring woman of her race I've ever come across, maybe the most inspiring of any race, and I do believe I'm in love with her myself!

Jackson laughed and put his arms around her just to get her to stop moving. With a feverish head resting over his shoulder, she continued praising Katherine Marie nonstop. If it hadn't been for the miscarriage, he'd have thought she'd gone mad, but he suspected his wife's sudden, even bizarre passion had something to do with her acute swings of hormone and her need to transfer her attachment to their dead child to someone else. Having suffered dreadfully over the past week with both her grief and his own, he decided on this occasion if it made her feel good, let her do it.

The next morning, Stella went to the library and looked up everything she could find about the Black Warriors of the African Jesus. She discovered much that impressed her and became even more stimulated. Although she was on medical leave from work, she went to her office at DHHS afterward, gathered a sheaf of funding applications, stuffed them into a file, then headed home to call Katherine Marie at the phone number she'd left with them the night before, the number of the Black Warrior preschool where she parked her kids and worked four days a week.

Malaika! Stella said, full of her particular brand of enthusiasm that electrified everyone who heard it, you've got to come over here today. I've got the paperwork for some grants I know you can use, and since I'm on leave these days, I can work them up for you pronto if you give me the information I need. I'll get them expedited through the system, too.

Now, there's not a grassroots organization on the planet that doesn't need money. As soon as school was over for the day, Katherine Marie dropped her kids home for her mother to watch. She took the subway to the Sassaport apartment for the second time in as many days. Dume followed her, stationing himself outside the building to take notes. Once again, the spy scribbled down a description of the car and driver who took her home later on. He was nothing if not careful and thorough. He took down the eight names on the mailboxes of Jackson's residence to cross reference with the registrant of the car whose identity he still did not have, because the Black Warrior contact at the police department was a janitor whom everyone at the station liked, but those granting favors took their sweet time about it.

On Monday, Mombasa arrived home from Chicago. He'd spoken with his wife several times during the last few days and knew all about her surprise encounter with the Sassaports, the grant applications, the dinner planned for the following week. He looked forward to seeing

Jackson again. For a long time, he'd felt there was unfinished business between them. He'd never thanked him properly for his efforts back in the day, when the poor boy'd hung upside down and whistled Dixie trying to get the authorities to believe the truth about the night of his daddy's catastrophe. When he got home, his wife was at work at the preschool and their children, two toddler boys and a ten-month-old girl, were with her. He dropped off his bags, took a shower, and went to his office on the first floor of their apartment building. There he found Dume and a contingent of his men, all with grave looks on their faces. What's wrong? he asked, and Dume stepped forward while the others looked down at the floor unwilling to meet his gaze.

Read this, Dume said, handing him a file with an ominous black cover. Running crosswise around it as a seal was a thick band of red duct tape on which Dume had scrawled in magic marker: Top Secret.

What is this? Mombasa asked again. I ordered no reports of any kind. Read it.

True to his name, Dume was a small bull of a man: dun-colored, low to the ground, ropy with muscles. He stood in front of Mombasa with his feet planted square and his arms crossed. He looked like a minotaur or a shrunken genie. The other man sighed.

And the rest of you, he said with a bit of a growl as too much drama was irritating to him, you all know what this is about? You all in on this "top secret"?

The half dozen men behind Dume continued to study the floor and shuffled their feet. Like a pack of danged slaves, Mombasa thought, despairing of his movement and its foot soldiers. As he cut the report's seal with a pocketknife, he prayed that its contents were not as dire as their demeanor intimated. Please, Jesus, he prayed, don't let it be about the KKK planning a raid on us or, worse, the FBI. Then he opened the thing and saw the file contained a single page dense with words. Its first sentence read: "A report on the activities of Malaika Cooper during Mombasa Cooper's absence, especially those activities involving her intimate association with a white male, age undetermined, identity unknown." Why, it's Jackson, Mombasa thought immediately, and nearly laughed. He chewed his lip to maintain decorum in front of his men. Read the rest. "At one a.m., there came from the vehicle a frolicsome noise and Malaika Cooper and unidentified white male embraced and kissed and made reference to an assignation next Tuesday. A license plate number was taken down and is currently being tracked through our usual source at the police department." There followed more information about the return of Malaika to the Sassaport residence, the two nights she went to work on grant applications with Stella, all of which he knew about while he was yet in Chicago. But in the hands of the document's scribe, her activities looked to be those of a queen of whores, practiced in every art of deception and lust. Her lover—the eight last names taken from Jackson's building's mailboxes were supplied as a list of possible candidates—looked to be in bondage to her foul enticements.

Mombasa let the page fall from his grasp. It fluttered to the floor in eerie silence. He stood there, his arms sagging, holding the empty file as if it were a heavy book of ten thousand pages. He looked at Dume and the others with a great impenetrable sorrow, which they mistook for heartbreak on account of Malaika's treachery. They murmured, inched closer to him to be of comfort.

As they drew near, his eyes widened, his hands clenched, which stopped them in their tracks. He glared at them in fierce silence, cleared his throat of the bile that had gathered there, then delivered a speech none ever forgot. My friends, he began in a tempered, paternal tone. It was the reassuring, authoritative timbre of his weekly radio address. There is nothing here that is a mystery to me. My wife has been in contact with an old and dear friend of ours from childhood. Our families worked for his family, we are intimately intertwined. His wife is a social worker. She's been helping my wife with grants for assistance for our community programs. This is why you have seen her with this man and this is why she has been going to his address.

He paused to look the men in their eyes, each one in his turn, then continued.

I am gravely disappointed in you. You, whom I have loved. You, whom I have nurtured, worried about, sacrificed for as if you were blood of my blood. How can you slander my wife so? How could you rush to judgment about the mother of our movement?

As he spoke on, his volume gradually increased until his voice became loud, almost booming, and there was a graveled quality to it that bespoke an enormous effort at self-control, as did his tight, bloodless fists that raised to just above his waist then stopped as if an invisible bar kept them low, restrained, unable to pound the daylights out of the assembled, each of whom surely deserved it.

What has she ever done but school and heal your children? Have you no respect for her? For her work? Have you no respect for me or for my work? How you have angered me! I cannot stand the sight of any of you. Get out. Get out. You have angered and disappointed me to my core. If I attempt to deal with you now, I might do something I regret.

All of them, to a man, trembled in their boots.

What? You are still here? Get out, I said. Get out. You, whom I loved, have broken my heart. I warn you. My rage cannot be far behind.

Their heads low, they shambled out.

And close the door on your sorry asses!

To a man, Dume and his cohorts were stunned, shamed, frightened, and yes, even more hateful toward Malaika Cooper than before, because she was not like them, warriors deserving of Mombasa's understanding and support even when they were wrong. She was nothing but a woman in the year 1967, therefore, a nonentity, but a nonentity who had somehow tricked them, somehow shown them up.

That she had tricked them in collusion with a white family, a white family whose head had been, so to speak, her massa back home, well, this was, considering their separatist beliefs not to mention the times, traitorous, inflammatory in the worst possible way. A campaign began among certain members of the Black Warriors of the African Jesus, one of whisperings and malicious conjecture worthy of a tribe of Iagos: a campaign to dishonor, to destroy the marriage of Mombasa Cooper, a campaign that only redoubled its efforts when their objective looked more and more difficult to achieve given their leader's weakness— which is how they saw it—his weakness for the wiles and falsehoods of his wife, Malaika Cooper, the treacherous whore.

Dume struck upon the brilliant idea that one of them should go to Guilford, Mississippi, and investigate the history between the Sassaports and Coopers. He sent a man known as Matata, who traveled south under his slave name, Michael Borden, so as not to arouse suspicion or hostility among the locals.

Born in New Jersey and raised, if you can call it that, by a heroin-addicted jazzman and his songbird wife, Michael Borden was a born con man. A creature of the streets, he was sleek and handsome, a silver-tongued charmer, expert at determining within the first five minutes of a stranger's acquaintance what it was exactly that a person expected him or, really, wanted him to be and then, like a shape-shifter, he became it instantly, which had a hypnotic effect on those he met. They opened up to him without hesitation, gave him whatever he asked for, whether money, information, or love. Against such talents, the simple folk of Guilford didn't have a prayer. They gave Michael Borden everything they had in a weekend. Only, many of them didn't know what they were talking about, and the rest had forgotten exactly the details of what they did know. The story he brought back to Dume was incomplete where it wasn't inaccurate. At the same time, it was all Dume needed to stick a knife in the back of Malaika Cooper.

He went to Mombasa with his tidbits of half-truth and stale gossip, arranged them in the most damaging manner possible, and whispered their venom into his ear so that they dripped like acid from an eyedropper directly into the most tender part of his brain. Bubba Ray, he hissed. Unnatural lusts between them, he murmured, or it's thought by some he gave her money. The boy ruined, obsessed and always in the village, he hissed some more, ending with: Jackson knew, Jackson always knew. And Mombasa remembered the year Katherine Marie seemed to turn on him. How he'd reached out to Jackson for help that night everything changed forever. It was as if Dume put together for him the pieces of a puzzle he'd long ago given up trying to solve. He could not believe any of it for a Yankee minute, but it fit so well he could believe all of it. Confusion and heartbreak and anger came over him in a rush. His finer impulses were crushed in that tidal wave of emotion until all that was left was the rage of his speeches, of his philosophy—an epic, transcendent rage, a primeval rage borne of his blood.

He did the only thing he could with it. He let it explode in a verbal barrage of disgust and condemnation. At the top of his lungs, he cursed all Sassaports. He cursed his wife. He wondered aloud if his eldest child was a shade too light. He fled his office with the starburst of a preacher's fire trailing behind him to find his wife or Jackson or both and settle these matters once and for all.

Ignorant of the danger awaiting her, Katherine Marie chanced to stop by her husband's office an hour later. When she closed the door behind her, she found Dume there, sitting behind Mombasa's desk with his feet up and a half-empty bottle of Jack Daniel's at his elbow. He was celebrating his victory over her, his most-hated enemy, icon of all the women who had betrayed him. She greeted him with her mouth pursed in disapproval but, as she was afraid of no man, she went to the desk to find a file she needed for Stella's forms. Suddenly, Dume stood, grabbed her by the wrist, and swung his other arm to strike her, openhanded, so that she fell to the floor. Pervert! he shouted. Whore! And with a cracker child! He laughed at her lying there stupefied by his accusations and, pulling her up by a handful of hair, began to beat her in earnest. Your husband has cursed you, he shouted, and I am his instrument! His hand came down and down and down until she could no longer see and the lights went out and then nothing. Nothing.

While Dume took it upon himself to discipline his wife, Mombasa went to Jackson's house to confront him. Matata drove him there. He stayed in the car but Mombasa leapt out, charged up the building's front steps. He gained entry, nearly broke down the door of the Sassaport apartment screaming: Jackson! Jackson! Do not think you can hide from me!

Jackson was at work. It was Stella who opened the door in an act of either bravery or foolishness. She took one look at the enraged giant before her, and coolly, calmly said: He's at work, Mombasa. He should be home soon, but until then will I do? It didn't make sense, but something about her stopped him cold. He couldn't tell what it was, she just did. He calmed just enough to tell her he needed to talk to Jackson about something important, very important. He shook. His words were accomplished with difficulty, torn from his gut between deep gasps of breath. A child could see he was near collapse under the weight of some wretched emotion. So she introduced herself, invited him in, offered him tea, employed every skill she had by nature, education, and experience to soothe him, to draw him out. Once this was accomplished and she understood what had transpired, she got up, walked over to the back of the chair in which he'd sat, and put her hand on the back of his neck. She couldn't face him anymore. She felt she knew him already from all that Malaika and Jackson had told her, and her heart broke to see a proud, strong man, a leader of his people, leveled by misery. She wanted to help him. Whatever Malaika and Jackson were like, they were not like her. She didn't believe in secrets.

She thought one of the healthiest things Jackson had ever done was tell her the truth about the long-ago. He couldn't have gone on holding all that in. Look at the tragedies those stupid secrets had spawned! Look at this ruined man, for example! So she stood behind Mombasa rather than be further tempted to tell him everything.

Yes, I agree. You really need to talk to Jackson. He could answer so much.

He does know things, then! He knows? He always knew?

She hesitated.

Well, he knows things. But not what you think he knows.

Mombasa jumped up, turned around, and seized on her shoulders.

It seems you know, too, girl! You know!

She turned her head. She couldn't lie to that huge, suffering black face so close to her own. Not when her lips itched to tell him everything anyway because, in her mind, it was the right thing to do.

Tell me!

Oh, God, she thought, if Jackson doesn't walk in here in the next thirty seconds, I'm telling him, I am. It's up to you, God. Get Jackson in here in thirty seconds or it's done.

Tell me! It's my right to know!

Twenty-eight, twenty-nine . . . Stella felt a stab in her heart, a quickening of her pulse. She imagined this was the way heroes felt just before the great act that defined them was committed. She said: Yes, yes, I'll tell you. I'll tell you.

Stella then corrected all the inaccuracies of Dume's report by telling him everything Jackson ever told her about the past, including his vow to keep Bubba Ray's attack of Katherine Marie secret all those years ago. That secret tortured him back in the day, tortured him mightily, she said. It destroyed his relations with his own family. She emphasized how he'd kept his vow out of loyalty, out of respect for Malaika, known to him as Katherine Marie.

But he told you, Mombasa said. His voice was a pale echo of the one that an hour before had barked at her front door, demanding her husband present himself. It was as if the truth had scooped out his muscles and nerves and left him in a raw, green shell, the kind a serrated spoon leaves after digging around the pulp of a ripe melon.

She shrugged. Yes, he told me.

They say that truth can set you free, but sometimes too much truth can bury a man. You might say Mombasa was laid in the grave that afternoon, sipping tea in the Sassaports' living room, each word out of Stella's mouth another shovel of dirt filling that shell, covering him up, and this was before he returned home, his anger dulled by shock, chastened, to find his wife battered by a psychopath who'd thought to do his leader's dirty work for him.

Katherine Marie came to in her bed with her eyes failing to open more than a slit, yet through that slit she could see him, Mombasa, weeping at her bedside, begging forgiveness and behind him, Stella Sassaport, holding a stainless-steel bowl of ice chips wrapped in a terry-cloth towel.

Miss Stella told me, Mombasa said through his tears in a voice and manner that sounded very like Li'l Bokay in the old days, she told me the truth about Bubba Ray and I am so very, very sorry, my angel, my queen, so very, very sorry. If you don't forgive me for failing to protect you, I will kill myself. I will take a rifle and stick it in my mouth, I swear.

Her head hurt. She could not think clearly. She asked him where the children were, and he told her they were ok, they were with her mother. Curiously, she did not ask next where Dume was. Instead, she said: What do you mean about Bubba Ray? Stella told you what about Bubba Ray?

He let the truth spill. He told her about Dume's accusations, how they'd thrown him for a huge, disastrous loop. But he now knew everything, he told her, from the adolescent Bubba Ray's rapine episode to his stalking of her, and she could only ask: But how did you know, Stella? How did you know all these things?

Jackson Sassaport's wife raised her brows, grimaced, and shook her head. There was only one possible answer to that question, which she opened her mouth to deliver, only Mombasa interrupted, begging forgiveness again, promising the arrest and punishment of Dume once he found him, grasping her hand and covering it with kisses. Katherine Marie feebly drew her hand back, finding that her husband frightened her now, repulsed her as if he had been the agent of assault himself, while at the same time her heart broke at the sight of him destroyed by his own lack of faith in her.

Their marriage was never the same again. It took some time, but Katherine Marie decided to hang on with him mostly for the sake of the children, and because her life was devoted to the Black Warriors preschool and the Black Warriors walk-in clinic. She chose to continue to work tirelessly at his side in the world, but at night in their bed she was stiff and cold. She was hurt, disappointed in him that he had succumbed to the machinations of Dume and Matata. No matter what else happened in their lives, she'd always believed in Mombasa, believed in his character as much as his causes. Ever since that day in front of the village whorehouse, when he'd made his first vows to her, she believed that he'd take care of her, protect her. When Bubba Ray did what he did, it wasn't her husband's fault he wasn't there to pound him into the ground and save her. But this time, this time she couldn't help herself. She blamed him. Some part of it was his fault in her mind. Mombasa's lack of trust, his anger, Dume's violence: it got all mixed up together in her mind and she could not break away from any of it no matter how often they knelt together and prayed to Jesus.

In the greater community, she was in control. Once she had her strength back, she held a powwow with Dume's men, demanding

apologies and loyalty oaths, which they offered. But because her innocence and Dume's guilt made them co-perpetrators of the worst crimes,
they hated her more than when they'd thought her guilty. Since Dume
had disappeared off the face of the earth, one or the other of them
daily suggested to Mombasa in either a veiled or direct manner that
what they all needed more than anything was to even the score, to take
revenge upon the man and town who had come between him and his
wife, him and his warriors, to take revenge upon Bubba Ray Sassaport
and Guilford, Mississippi. On a dark and pitiless day fresh on the heels
of a long, dry night when his wife had turned from him in their bed
once again, he agreed and asked his men to create for him an opportunity. They came up with a plot to blow up the draft board while Bubba
Ray was there running paperwork in and out. The timer on the bomb
failed. The plot was uncovered.

The day the federal agents came to arrest him, Mombasa was home
helping his wife bathe the children. When the SWAT team knocked
down his door, they were dressed in full battle gear with vests, helmets,
shields, the finest rapid-fire weapons the year had to offer. The two
boys screamed. The baby wailed. Mombasa stood up in his running
suit, all soapy from the splashing of the kids, and without resistance
offered himself up to the police as quietly as a lamb, saying: Please,
please put down those weapons. My babies are here. They shackled
his hands. They shackled his feet. Just before he was led out through
the broken door, he turned to look at Katherine Marie. She was holding their youngest, Njeri. Her eyes were full of tears that did not flow.
What have you done now, she asked. What have you done? I'm sorry,
was all he said. I'm sorry.

He certainly was. Sorry enough to plead guilty. Every day before
his trial and every day after, that look of cold tears refusing to fall
burned into his soul. That and the eyes of his children, largest to small-
est, rounded by fear. He sought redemption. He sought punishment,

without which he knew redemption could not come. And punishment the federal court was happy to provide. When the time came for him to say his piece, he spoke openly.

A madness overtook me, he told the judge. An anger and a madness. I saw that all my teachings were for naught. For there was a country I'd envisioned, a country of black men and women proud and strong, steeped in their African heritage, living apart but equal from their white neighbors, living apart but with Christian love the river between them. I saw them black and white fording that river that its currents might guide them in all their relations, I saw that river feeding the crops of righteousness on the banks of both sides. For then the black man would no longer be the thorn of infamy in the white man's foot preventing him from walking blameless into the future nor the white man the sword of intimidation and dependence over the black man's head. Each would become what the Lord Jesus intended: perfect men, loving each other without sin, without anger. Oh, the day came when I saw that all this was a shibboleth, a sham, the ridiculous dream of a ridiculous man. I was betrayed by my loved ones and made blind by a world that fostered their betrayal. And all the thoughts I had thereafter were thoughts of revenge.

While the story he told was only half the story, the judge believed the half he heard. He also believed every piece of evidentiary propaganda the feds put before him about Mombasa Cooper. He read transcripts of the famous speeches and radio interviews, whose centerpiece was the rage of the black man, Mombasa's oratory métier, so to speak. From the birth of his movement, in the days after he fled from Parchman then rose up from the underground transformed, he preached loudly and on all occasions that rage was a phenomenon that came to the Negro as naturally as lilies came to the field, for the black man had neither to toil nor spin to experience it. From the moment he drew his first breath, he carried the seed of rage in his blood as the birthright of oppression. Only as a Black Warrior of the African Jesus could he find the balm of divine love to transform it, he further taught, but that part of his theology was redacted by the prosecutor.

Considering him an imminent danger to the community at large, the judge sentenced him to life in federal prison, where the Black Warriors of the African Jesus survived in chains as a prison cult. Out in the free world where it mattered, the Panthers and others absorbed those Mombasa left behind. Soon enough, Malaika Cooper went back to being Katherine Marie, returning to Guilford with her children in the company of Jackson and Stella Sassaport, who returned for their own reasons, an event that did nothing at all to mitigate Mombasa's anger and no doubt enflamed it further, reviving in the man a constant fire of discontent, which he battled against every waking hour of his imprisonment. Many days, he was victorious and offered thanks in prayer and sacrifice. Other days, he failed, exploding into acts of brutality large and small to his great remorse despite the fact that the objects of his outbursts nearly always deserved a beat-down or worse, no matter what god sat in judgment.

Katherine Marie's world was in shambles. She had her own set of unchristian responses to all that happened. She was furious with Mombasa for ruining his life, their children's, and her own—angry enough to abandon the Black Warriors to their imprisoned founder, refusing to take on the role of surrogate for the movement, which hastened its demise. She was angry with the government that sentenced her husband so harshly after all the injustice he'd experienced in the past. She was plain angry in general, angry with a whole pack of people. She couldn't work up anger toward Stella, though. Stella was an outsider. A wrongheaded, willful, but well-intentioned outsider. When she contemplated the catastrophe that was her life, she made diagrams of cause in her mind drawn crisscross with betrayal. Stella was off the page. Jackson was not.

One night during Mombasa's trial when Jackson brought a gift of groceries and children's toys over to her house after work, she lit into him for telling Stella what he had promised to keep secret forever. He had to bear some guilt, she told him, for everything that went out of control after that, including Dume's beating and Mombasa's bomb plot. If only he'd kept his vow forever, everything would have been alright. Nothing so irrevocably awful as what had happened would have happened. The vow, she said, had been sacred. The sacral power of the vow had protected both Mombasa and her. But once it was broken, bad juju had flooded them. Oh, why did he do it? Why did he betray her confidence? Why did he tell Stella? Why did he not see that his vow to her took precedence over what he felt for his wife? Oh, never mind, she said, don't even try. She knew why.

You've been corrupted! Katherine Marie charged, stabbing a bony finger into his chest. It's insane you can't see what she's done to you! Changed you into a lowlife weasel! My dear white Southern gentleman manqué. You are a fraud! No true gentleman would do what you've done! For what? For her!

Jackson begged her forgiveness until she granted it, groveled without understanding at all how she came to these conclusions, especially the one that made him the scapegoat, the bad guy of the whole debacle. He'd never forget the way he'd at last dropped to his knees in front of the couch on which she sat, her sweet chin pointed up, her arms folded across her chest, her mouth wrinkled up in disdain. Her right hand suddenly shot forward to just under his nose and he kissed it as if she were a queen or a pope, begging pardon one last time before she said: Alright. I'll forgive you. Now, get up. You look ridiculous.

When he reported their conversation to his wife, expecting her to defend him, to wonder with him at the remarkable inconsistencies of Katherine Marie's thoughts, Stella only laughed. Good! Good! She's angry and fighting back! At first I thought she was headed down that

sad road of victimhood when she chose to stay home with a man so easily convinced to betray her trust, but now I see: She is back to herself!
She has the fire again! Oh, Jackson, can't you see how wonderful this
is? Well, yes and no, was his response, he could and he couldn't.

Not that either woman cared. They had bonded and their bond was
fresh, tight, it innervated them. Like all women who feel finished with
seeking the love of a man, whether because they are supremely secure
in their attachment or supremely disenchanted, this bond took center
stage in both their lives while Jackson and Mombasa became ancillary,
taken for granted.

After Mombasa went to prison, Katherine Marie needed the Sassaports as much as they needed her. As the man left standing, Jackson
was doted on by each of the women, his attentions fought over on
occasion, but in a way that threatened no one. Although he remained
in the carnal sense absolutely faithful to his wife, he could not help
but sometimes feel as if he had two wives, one of whom he lived with
and another for whom he ran errands, dispensed professional advice,
and whose children he chauffeured from school to sports to dance
lessons and sometimes, when it could not be helped as their mother
was busy, to the prison to visit their daddy. Until the women argued,
Stella was content. She had her work, her friend, her friend's children
to foster and lobby for. Under her wing, Katherine Marie got the
education she'd always longed for and started her nursing career in
earnest. Everybody's lives were busy, productive. Stella led the local
fund-raising drive for the new temple Rabbi Nussbaum built over in
Jackson, but the building was bombed not six months after its dedi-
cation. Two months later the front of his home was blown off too.
Nussbaum wanted to leave Jackson after that but couldn't find another
job. He remained depressed, despite Stella's best efforts at cajoling him,
until 1973 when he finally retired to San Diego. Six months after Beth
Israel was bombed, Dr. King was assassinated. Bobby Kennedy joined

him in the afterlife shortly thereafter. Stella, Jackson, and Katherine Marie might have fallen into a deep depression themselves over all this death and mayhem, but a war was declared on poverty and there was too much to do to mourn for long. They moved back home where the South was slowly changing while essentially they did not, a fact that made them all delirious with a sense of purpose, achievement, and happiness—all of them, that is, except Mombasa, who moldered in prison, stewing in his anger and regret.

THIRTEEN

Summer, 1995

JACKSON SAT IN A GRIMY wooden chair trying to keep his elbows off a grimier wooden table in the attorney's consultation room at the penitentiary in Yazoo City. He felt conspicuous, like a child stuck alone in a classroom while all the other kids were outside playing, a child spied upon by a teacher who had eyes on the back of her head, eyes that could see through doors and walls. Katherine Marie told him that in conflict with the law on the matter, she was positive that everything he said to Mombasa would be observed and recorded, so he got up and looked around, studying the vents and the lighting fixtures for microphones and tiny cameras. He found nothing suspicious.

He sat down again. His nose itched from the musty, sweaty smell of the place. With great effort, he stifled a sneeze, since the only thing he had to blow his nose was the handkerchief he'd used to wipe down the chair's seat when he got there. The door opened. He whipped around in his seat. An officer ushered Mombasa into the room. Jackson stood, wanting to reach out, embrace him, but Mombasa saw that, shook his head infinitesimally in warning, and stretched out a hand for him to shake instead. They gave each other a strong, heartfelt shake of two hands each and sat down on opposite sides of the table. The officer left. They were alone.

Each man murmured greetings and grinned. No matter the circumstances, they were happy to see each other again. Aged just a little bit, didn't you, son, Mombasa said first. You've got your daddy's hair and jawline I see, and just a hint of your mama's belly. Then he laughed his great booming laugh of long ago, and Jackson laughed too, saying: Well, look at yourself. Looks like the snow has fallen on the mountaintop. He meant of course that Mombasa's hair had gone completely white. To be honest, it was the only sign of age he could find in the man, which struck him as odd in one who'd been incarcerated for near thirty years. Mombasa's muscles bulged like a young man's through his prison shirt, and there were no wrinkles or sags on his face.

Their laughter faded into sighs, and there was silence. Jackson dropped his head and shuffled his paperwork about. Forgetting about the table grime, he put his arms on its top and leaned forward.

I want to help you at your hearing, Mombasa, he said. I want to bring you home to Katherine Marie.

The other man blinked.

That would be something, Jackson. But I don't see how you can do that. I don't mean to be critical. Unless things have changed more than I know, you're not a criminal lawyer now, are you?

No, but I can tell them the truth. I can tell them the story that's not been told. About what happened all those years ago. How your anger was about Bubba Ray, not the draft board. You've paid for your crime and you are no longer a threat to society. I can explain what life was like back then. How you saved my daddy's life. You've had all the legal argument and manipulation a boatload of lawyers can think of, but no one's ever told the human side of the story. Katherine Marie and Stella think that's the one piece of the puzzle that's been missing, the one piece that'll find you mercy and release. I believe I agree. Or at least that it's worth a shot.

When did those two get thick as thieves again?

Excuse me?

Our wives. When did that happen? I asked mine and she told me something about an awards dinner she went to. I don't know, it all sounded like a supper party in Shangri-la to an old boy stuck behind bars half his life.

Jackson told him as many of the details as he knew.

Then they came out of the kitchen hand in hand, he said. I don't know quite what went on between them in there. You know how they are. Got their little secrets.

It was Mombasa's turn to lean forward across the table: You know, son, I never did hear the story of what separated them in the first place. If you don't mind, I'd like you to tell me what it was now. I know you know. Think of all the trouble being quiet got us into in the past. I've asked my wife several times, and I've got every evasion from "I don't want to waste our time together talking about that" to "I'll just get depressed today if I tell you all that, let me tell you another day."

When Mombasa quoted Katherine Marie, he imitated her sweet, dusky voice in a way that made Jackson smile.

Well, I guess it doesn't matter.

No, it don't. And I do believe I'm making your telling me a condition of allowing you to appear before the parole board. How do you like that?

Alright, alright. I'll spill.

Stella was over Katherine Marie's house helping her set up a sweet-sixteen party for their daughter, Njeri. They'd blown up about a hundred and twenty balloons, strung up streamers announcing the happy

229

event, laid out the paper plates and cups in bold African colors, and made her a crown in the same scheme out of crepe paper and wire and tropical flowers. They were particularly pleased with that crown: It was a real work of art. It came time to prepare the food. They cleared off the kitchen table, which was full of papers: bills, application forms for the eldest Cooper boy's assistance with college tuition, checking-account statements. Stella scooped up a bunch and asked Katherine Marie where to stash them for the afternoon and she said, in the break-front, top drawer, and it was there amongst a whole mess of other paperwork that Stella saw something that near stopped her heart.

It was an envelope with bank deposit slips falling out, it was so stuffed up with them. There were also two checks that had not yet been deposited. These were from a checkbook she recognized. They were welfare checks, and they were made out to Malaika Cooper. She examined the dates of deposit slips and checks alike. They were all recent. She grabbed up the envelope and marched back into the kitchen to wave it in Katherine Marie's face.

What is this? You have not been eligible for welfare for nine years, Katherine Marie. I know that for a fact. Nor have you used the name Malaika for about that time. So what is this? You been cheating the government, girl? Have you?

Katherine Marie grabbed at the envelope and a fight ensued. A ter-rible, terrible fight with those two thrashing around the kitchen, bang-ing into things since neither one was willing to let go of the evidence. They shouted at each other the whole time. Stella shouted: Thief! Is this where you wind up after all these years! Stealing from out of the mouths of those that need it! Thief! Katherine Marie shouted back: What do you know! How can you possibly know how I've needed that money, how my children have needed that money! What do you, Miss Silver Spoon in the Mouth, know! What do you, Miss Whitebread of Boston with the Husband in Perpetual Residence, know! You know nothing of what my life is like! What it's been like! What the goddamn white world owes me! Stella shouted louder: Can't do enough for you, can we? Wasn't helping you through school and setting you up in a decent career enough? Is there a time we can all sit back and applaud while you stand on your own two feet? Katherine Marie gasped then shouted in a scornful patois: Oh, well, Missy Stella, youse sounds like youse thinks me ungrateful. So then why don't you bend over so I can kiss your white ass!

Jackson was near out of breath, as the only way he'd been able to get the story out was to tell it fast. He gulped for air, choked by the coarseness of the tale he'd been compelled to tell.

He went quiet, deciding he had not the courage to tell Mombasa about the threats Katherine Marie made if Stella exposed her. How her husband could dispatch men from the prison to hurt her if she told the authorities about the checks. The threats were all temper and desperation born of the moment anyway, Jackson was more than sure, so why bother exposing them now. Stella had kept her mouth shut anyway, out of pride and at his encouragement. The Sassaports owe that family greatly, he told her and she'd listened. And Katherine Marie had restrained herself.

The silence in the room stretched, became brittle, 'til the room felt full of noise: the noise of breath, of clothes rustled against furniture, of bodies shifting weight.

I'm very sorry, Mombasa said at last. I'm very sorry that things came to that.

That's alright. It took more than a decade of stubbornness, but they both got over it and made up. If you want to know the truth, I think Stella thought in the end that Katherine Marie had a point. She couldn't know the pressures Katherine Marie was under from the very moment of her birth by virtue of a simple thing like skin color and the place she was born and the date. She might be able to guess what it was like to raise children with a husband in prison, but she couldn't know that. It embarrassed her that she'd given her life to civil rights and social services and she still couldn't know the half about that.

Mombasa had his head down but he smiled: But you know don't you, Jackson? You know a little bit about it.

I should say I do know a little bit, just a little bit. I grew up in the goddamn middle, didn't I?

Yes, you did, son. I was there. I recall. I recall everything.

They spent another hour together that afternoon and they shared three more appointments together before the parole hearing. After the final one, Jackson drove from Yazoo City to Guilford, where he met up with Stella over to Katherine Marie's, as it was her turn to feed them supper. Against all reason, he was feeling optimistic about the hearing. His step was light up the walk to the Cooper home, one of those postwar ranch-style homes on the edge of town. It was situated in a nowadays-integrated neighborhood with damn decent property values, he thought to himself, proud of his town and its growth. He knocked on the unlocked door, let himself in, dropped his briefcase on the floor of the living room where the two women sat on the couch waiting for him, worry and consternation writ fierce upon their brows. He opened up his arms, smiled wide, and said: Well, we talked. He's agreed to let me try. The women rose with features suddenly alight with hope and he wrapped his arms around them.

Acknowledgments

Home in the Morning is my seventh novel and the first one published after more than thirty years of effort. I had resigned myself to perpetual obscurity when the bold, bright energy of Peter Riva burst into my life and agented me into the light with remarkable speed. He was a godsend. So was my editor, Diane Reverand, a most wise, generous woman who made the editing experience a complete pleasure for me. I hope we work together again and soon. I must also thank my long-time agent Mary Yost, who was my lifeline during decades of rejection, keeping me honest, keeping me working no matter what.

During those years in the cold dark, there were the faithful who sustained me: my long-suffering husband, Stephen, of course; my beloved and most refined parents, Frank and Freda Kowalski; my siblings who encouraged me against all odds, Carl, Robert, and Debra Kowalski, Kathleen Baber, Patricia Romanello, Margaret Cerilli, and the inestimable Jeanne Kowalski; my loyal friends Karen Oakes, Sam Boyd, Linda Pochesci, Adele Lurie, Wally Kelly, Susan K. Howards, and Felicity Carter, all of whom kept me going by saying: This is the one, Mary! This one will make it!

How happy I am that they were finally right. And how grateful I am that all stood by me.